THE RECLUSE OF WOLFETON HOUSE

The
RECLUSE
of
WOLFETON
HOUSE

LADIES *of* DEVON 4

KASEY STOCKTON

For Audrey, my little Hattie. She has your love for animals, artistic talent, and spunk. Thanks for helping me plot this story.

PROLOGUE

a cold, stiff breeze swept over Hattie, rustling her mousy brown hair and sending a volley of shivers over her skin. Or perhaps that was due to the apprehension swirling in her stomach. Her gaze swept over the moonlit church, an eerie blue glow cast over the stone building, and she took comfort in the stillness the night provided. Gripping her horse's reins, she swallowed hard, sliding from the saddle. She had one chance, and she wasn't going to blow it.

Noises from the inn at the end of the street punctuated the quietness of the night, reminding Hattie that she and her friends were not the only ones who had chosen to remain awake this late in the evening on Midsummer's Eve.

"Are you absolutely certain no one will catch us?" Amelia whispered loudly from atop her horse.

Hattie released a soft, irritated groan. Not this again. Amelia needed to recall that they weren't doing anything nefarious. If they were caught, the very worst they would receive would be a scolding from their half-blind vicar. Certainly nothing to worry over so greatly. "No. But I am *nearly* positive."

A muffled cheer rose up, floating through the open windows

1

of the inn's taproom. Amelia got down from her horse and guided him closer to Hattie. She took the reins and tied them to a branch on the hawthorn tree in front of the church. Hoping to calm her friend, Hattie said, "The only people awake are either completely foxed or they work in the inn and thus have no reason to leave it. Especially not to come to a churchyard at midnight."

"Very well," Amelia said, radiating unease. "Let us get this over with. Do you have the hempseed?"

Hattie grinned, feeling for the corded handle of the reticule around her wrist. "Indeed, I do."

"Then let's get on with it."

Excited energy pulsed through Hattie. Mrs. Fowler had promised that if Hattie completed the incantation *exactly* as the Cunning Woman prescribed, she would see the face of the man she was meant to marry—and Hattie was desperate for any clue which indicated the man was out there. At five-and-twenty with no prospects, she was beginning to lose hope that her true love even existed.

No, enough of that negative thinking. She was about to receive answers.

Hattie pulled a small, woven bag from her reticule, tugging at the drawstrings to widen the opening. She clicked open the watch that hung on a chain around her neck, angling it toward the moon. Twelve o'clock sharp. It was time.

With a decided snap, she tucked the watch into her bodice and glanced up. "Wish me luck."

"You don't need luck," Amelia said dryly. "You have magic."

Hattie nodded, resolute. Amelia was correct. Hattie didn't know whether there was anything to this magic notion or not, but she had a very strong feeling she was about to find out. Facing the church, she pulled out a handful of hempseed, the small seeds rough on her palm, and began to walk around the building.

"No, Hattie!" Amelia called softly behind her. "Clockwise!"

Hattie jumped. She had not even been paying attention to the direction. How foolish she would be to waste this opportunity by not following Mrs. Fowler's directions to the letter.

"Oh, right." Pivoting, she turned the other way and skirted the perimeter of the church, reciting the poem in a soft murmur. "Hempseed I sow, hempseed I grow. Let him who is my true love show."

She repeated the poem, tossing small handfuls of hempseed as she walked. Not much, of course, but Mrs. Fowler had mentioned that she didn't need much. It was more of a symbol than anything else, an ingredient in the ritual. Rounding the church again, Hattie shot Amelia an excited smile as she continued with her process. According to Mrs. Fowler, Hattie needed to circle the church three times before she could look over her shoulder and see the face of her true love. Only two rounds to go.

She hardly felt the cold evening air as she circled the church again, cautiously tossing seeds about the ground and reciting the poem over and over again. The closer she grew to completing the second round, the more her anticipation mounted. She hoped it worked. It was not easy being her age with nary a man in all of Devon with whom she could imagine herself falling in love. She was only grateful she'd had the weakness to complain about her plight to her maid, for the woman had immediately suggested paying a visit to the local Cunning Woman.

Mrs. Fowler had not disappointed. She'd seemed to understand Hattie perfectly. Far better than Hattie's friends had, at least—even though they had all found *their* true loves. Of course, Amelia had lost hers to a wretched carriage accident, but she'd still had him for a time.

Her friends clearly believed Hattie to be delusional, but she wasn't. She knew magic was not real...not in the way that casting a spell would bring about a husband out of thin air. No, what Hattie desired was a clue. Insight. Anything that might direct her toward her true love.

For she *hoped* he was somewhere out there, waiting to meet her, but she was growing restless waiting, and she longed for a confirmation that her waiting would not be in vain.

Turning the corner of the church for the final time, Hattie's heart hammered in her chest, pulsing like the erratic thrum of choppy waves on a stormy shore. She reached the place that signified three full circles of the building, stepped around the corner, and stopped. Drawing in a deep breath, Hattie glanced over her right shoulder—careful not to make the same mistake she'd made when going the wrong direction—and looked directly into the dark, gleaming eyes of a fox.

A scream ripped from her throat, tearing into the quiet night, and the fox jumped, turning about and fleeing with swift agility into the trees behind him.

Hattie stepped back, her shoulder blades bumping into the rough wall of the church as her mind flashed with the image of the fox. Perched just yards from her on the edge of a small copse of trees, he had stood still, one paw raised fractionally as though he'd been caught sneaking the final biscuit from the tea tray. But the most entrancing aspect had been his eyes, shining in the moonlight and fixed on her.

It was a sign of something greater, she just knew it. She could feel it deep in her soul.

Hattie pushed off from the wall, her mind racing with the possibilities of what this could mean, when Amelia barreled around the corner, nearly crashing into her.

"Oof!" Hattie stepped back, leaning against the church again, chest still heaving.

Amelia gripped her shoulders, her slender fingers digging into Hattie's arms as her wild eyes raked over her. "Are you well? What happened?"

Hattie nodded. "It worked. I saw a face."

"Whose face?"

How would she explain this to someone possessed of such a logical mind? "Well, it wasn't *human*—"

Charles Fremont rushed around the corner of the church, and Amelia swiveled, grabbing his sleeve and putting up her other hand to stall him. "She is well, Charles. She isn't hurt."

"Mr. Fremont?" Hattie said, panic lacing through her stomach. When had he arrived? "We—I, that is—well, this is not as it appears."

"I'm not sure I know how it appears," he said, stumbling forward a step before righting himself. His gaze shifted between the women as he tugged down his waistcoat. "So perhaps you may tell me what is going on here. Are you in danger?"

"No, no danger," Hattie said, shaking her head.

That did not appease her friend. "Then why did you scream?" Amelia asked.

Hesitation nipped at her. She had a hard enough time determining how to tell Amelia what she saw. She was absolutely not telling Mr. Fremont. "Perhaps later," she said through her teeth.

Amelia slipped her gloved hand around Hattie's shoulder. "If you are safe, then let's find Giulia. She is undoubtedly worried."

They fled the shadows behind the church for the moonlit churchyard, but Hattie could not slow her mind. She'd hoped for a sign, for something to indicate that she was correct in holding on to hope. A fox could mean a host of things.

Amelia leaned in, lowering her voice. "Why did you scream?"

"I saw a fox," Hattie whispered, holding her breath against her friend's undoubted scrutiny. "I'm not certain what it means, but surely it carries some significance."

"A fox?"

"Indeed. Isn't it delightful?"

A light scoff lifted from Amelia's throat. "If it was so wonderful, then why the scream?"

Hattie squeezed her friend's arm, drawing closer. "I did not actually expect to turn and find *eyes* staring back at me, Amelia. I may be more of a believer than you are, but I am not wholly mad."

She had wondered if it was foolhardy to hold onto hope, but now her beliefs were confirmed. There was a man, her true love, out there in the world somewhere. Now, she need only to find him.

It appeared as though Hattie was about to embark on a fox hunt.

CHAPTER 1

Five Months Later

The brim on Hattie's bonnet was not nearly wide enough; not if she could train her face toward the ground and *still* be recognizable from a distance. Hattie shifted her body toward the storefront on Graton's High Street, pulling her cream spencer tighter at the neck to ward off the chilly wind, and pretended not to hear her sister-in-law call her name from the passing carriage. If only Hattie had known to slip around the edge of the building two minutes earlier, she could have avoided this very situation.

But that was the trouble. One never did know when trouble was afoot and undesirable acquaintances were about to pounce. Hattie was sure to face her brother's wrath when she returned home later that day, for he certainly would not believe that she had not heard his wife calling her name at so close a distance—despite the sound of carriage wheels and hoofbeats on the cobblestone road. Best to stretch her shopping excursion as long as she was able.

"Hattie! Can you not hear me, my dear?" Lucy called again from the open window, her voice fading as the carriage slowly continued down the street. Jeffrey was undoubtedly inside with her. Why was he not quieting his wife?

Drat! Would the blasted woman not take a hint? Hattie needed to disappear before Lucy got the notion to stop her carriage and beg to transport Hattie home or commit some other horrible act of generosity. Not *real* generosity, of course. Lucy Green had a motive for everything.

Peeking to her left, Hattie noticed another carriage coming their direction. If she planned it just right...

Wheels of a deep green landau rolled down the dusty lane behind her, and she slipped around her maid and into the millinery shop while the carriage sheltered her from her sister-in-law's view. The bell jingled above the door as she closed it sharply, and she spun to lean against it, her chest heaving.

Hattie tugged on her watch chain and checked the time. It was just her luck that her brother and his wife had arrived an hour earlier than their letter had warned. Hattie should have known better and made an effort to escape her house to a far more secluded place than High Street, but she'd thought she had plenty of time before there was a chance of running into them. Closing the watch with a snap, she tucked it down her bodice and looked around Mrs. Dawson's millinery shop.

A man stood to her left looking at a table of gloves, and Mrs. Dawson was busy behind the long counter arranging an assortment of lace.

Hattie shot the older woman a smile and glanced about the rest of the shop. She may as well make use of being in the store. At least until it was safe to return outside.

Wood polish and floral perfume warred for superiority in the cramped room, and Hattie fought the inclination to slip her handkerchief from her sleeve and use it to cover her nose. Ah, speaking of handkerchiefs, the new shipment Mrs. Dawson had ordered was likely in by now, and Papa had properly soiled the last two Hattie had embroidered for him. She really should purchase a few more and prepare them before it was time for him to leave for his sister's estate next week. Or maybe she was better off buying two for Papa and two for his dogs. Then he wouldn't keep ruining his nicely personalized squares of linen wiping mud from the hounds' blasted noses.

Or perhaps her money was best spent obtaining a wider-brimmed bonnet for future excursions. She'd briefly noticed a fine chip straw bonnet when she was peering through the window. She really should have another look at it. If she took it home and did it over with that pink ribbon Papa brought her from—

"Oof!" Hattie tripped over the leg of a tall, brass mirror and pitched forward, her arms flailing for purchase as she searched for something to hold on to.

A sturdy arm slid around her waist and pulled her up before she could crash directly into the mirror and send it shattering on the floor. She clutched her savior's arm on impulse.

"Careful," a deep voice said just behind her ear, standing the hair on the back of her neck on end. The man's grip around her waist seared into her with a warmth that surprised her, and she extricated herself from her rescuer's arms quickly, eager to be rid of the unwelcome feeling.

Stepping back, she shook out her limbs, chuckling. "That was a near miss."

The man was not as amused. Mouth pressed into a firm line, he swept his gray eyes over her, his thick, dark eyebrows pulling together in consternation. His scowl reminded Hattie of the tutor her father had engaged on her behalf almost a decade ago, and she wondered briefly if this stranger had the same innately censorious disposition.

Though her middle-aged tutor certainly wasn't this handsome.

If it wasn't for the two days of stubble that shadowed the sharp curve of this man's jaw and bled clear up to his unkempt side-whiskers, Hattie would fully believe this stranger was a tutor or school teacher himself. He had the bearing and the expression of a man used to telling others what to do.

She dipped in a grateful curtsy. "I thank you, sir. I would not have liked to damage Mrs. Dawson's mirror."

"Perhaps watching where you step would have saved it in a much simpler manner," he said smoothly, without hesitation.

Well, *that* was uncalled for. She must be correct. Unshaven face aside, he was most certainly some form of teacher. Or perhaps he dabbled in pugilism, given his knack for verbal sparring.

Hattie dropped her chin, affecting her most innocent expression. "I certainly would have if my mind had not been preoccupied with the pretty bonnets on display in the window. How can anyone expect me to focus on anything at all when surrounded by all this beauty? What with such lovely ribbons over here, and dainty fans over there vying for my attention, it is a preposterous notion! I'm certain you couldn't have meant it." She considered stomping her foot for added measure but decided to hold on to that gem for later. It would be more appropriate if he pressed the matter further.

The stranger looked down his straight nose at her with mild curiosity. Perhaps he was wondering if she was simple-minded. She felt inclined not to change that particular opinion of his. There was something very satisfying about intentionally giving the wrong impression—it failed to allow anyone the chance to *truly* know what she thought.

"In that case," he said, watching her closely, "may I help you retrieve a particular bonnet from the window?"

His offer caught her off guard, but she quickly tried to cover her shock. Disapproving school teachers were not usually so chivalrous, at least not in her experience. They were far too concerned with books and maps and things to hand down items from tall shelves. Or perhaps that was simply Hattie's tutor and his suppressed frustration over being in the position to school a girl. He'd always preferred her brother, Jeffrey, and lamented the fact that Hattie was the one interested in learning.

This man looked intent on further helping her, and Hattie did not intend to take her game of playing insipid and helpless so far as that. "I think I can manage but thank you again." She trilled a grating giggle for good measure. "You must desire to rid yourself of this nuisance, so I give you leave to do so."

"I would not have phrased it so plainly," he argued, but then he did not further disagree. How unkind of him to consider her a nuisance. It was irritating that his voice was smooth and deep, like a cup of warm chocolate on a crisp morning, and she found it unfair that such a disagreeable man would possess such a soothing tone.

Well, that was quite enough of that. Hattie looked once more into his handsome gray eyes and decided that she could not tell if she liked the man's quick wit and blatant honesty or despised him for it.

"Good day." Dipping her head in a curtsy, she turned toward the bureau against the wall where Mrs. Dawson typically displayed new handkerchiefs. The bonnet would have to wait for another day. She could likely not reach it on her own, and she had the strongest desire *not* to ask for any help with the stranger nearby.

Hattie selected two clean, white squares of linen, putting away her idea of purchasing extras for the dogs—they could have Papa's old ones—and checked her reticule to ensure that she'd brought enough coins to cover the cost. Well, she hadn't. She'd have to put it on Papa's account.

"Mrs. Dawson, good day," she said, sending the older woman a bright smile as she laid her things on the counter.

"Are these for you or your father, dear? Because I did happen to get a set of delicate, silk gloves in my recent shipment, and I know you mentioned that one of your pair got a nasty stain on the elbow." Mrs. Dawson pushed her spectacles up on her nose, her curly gray hair falling low in its knot at her nape.

"Oh, they did. I forgot I mentioned that. It hasn't been on my mind with no assemblies in the near future. But I suppose it would be good to be prepared." She glanced over her shoulder to the rack of gloves and caught the dark strangers' eye before dropping her gaze to the glove table again.

Why was he watching her? Apparently, he was inquisitive as well. Could he not mind his own business? Another point against him.

Crossing the shop, she selected an ivory set of satin gloves and ran them over her fingers. She wasn't sure when she'd next wear them, and in truth, Agnes had done a remarkable job of getting the chocolate stain from her last pair. But she knew Mrs. Dawson's store had struggled since the new millinery shop had opened in Melbury a few months ago, taking the Melbury portion of her clientele.

What good was pin money if it wasn't going to help her neighbors? Hattie hardly had need of it otherwise.

"Will you add these to Papa's account?" she asked, laying the gloves over her handkerchiefs on the counter. "I am certain he will settle it with you before the end of the week."

Mrs. Dawson beamed. "Certainly, dear."

Or perhaps she could settle it herself if her sister-in-law Lucy wished to shop in Graton while she was visiting. She was certain to want to do *something* alone with just Hattie, for she always made an attempt to do so when she and Jeffrey came to visit. Hattie may as well help Lucy to spend some of their money in Mrs. Dawson's shop while she was here. Followed by a visit to Madame Chastain for new gowns, of course.

Lucy had a terrible habit of complaining about Graton's shops and their lack of elegance but always found something she simply couldn't live without. It was a game of Hattie's to guess just how many things from Graton's countrified stores Lucy would simply *need*.

Mrs. Dawson wrapped her bundle in brown paper and tied it with string before pushing it across the counter. "I will send a note round to your father, dear. Did I see Agnes just outside? Give her my love."

"Of course. Oh, Agnes!" Hattie looked to the window and found her maid standing where she'd left her just on the other side. The poor thing was likely wondering what had gotten into Hattie. She took the bundle and hurried toward the door, careful to give the dark stranger and his curious eyes a very wide berth. Whatever was he doing in the millinery anyway? All he'd done so far was browse gloves and watch her as he did now, his heavy gaze following her as she let herself outside.

Whatever she'd done to bother him, she hadn't the faintest idea. She'd never seen him before in her life, and she was glad she never would again.

"Agnes!" she said, clutching her maid's arm and entreating her to forgiveness with her eyes. "I do apologize for leaving you out here. I only wanted to escape Lucy and Jeffrey. You should have joined me inside."

"I know that, miss." Agnes's green eyes twinkled, and she tucked a strand of blonde hair behind her ear. "I stayed out here to make certain your brother's carriage continued straight down the road. I thought you'd like the warning if they were to circle back around."

Hattie squeezed her maid's forearm. "You brilliant creature. Whatever did I do to deserve a friend such as you?"

"You left this inside," a male voice said behind her, and

Hattie startled. The stranger held up her pale yellow reticule; it hung from his gloved finger by its corded drawstrings and looking entirely out of place beside his clean, black coat sleeve. She had not realized how bright his gray eyes were, nor how fine a coat he wore in the store, but the sunlight highlighted just how well-made his clothing was. His bronze waistcoat was tasteful under a snowy white cravat, and he certainly did not dress like any school teacher Hattie had had the pleasure of knowing.

Hmm. Perhaps he was a headmaster instead.

"Thank you again, sir." She took the reticule and slipped it over her wrist. "You saved us the trouble of needing to return to town after I got home and found it missing."

He gave her a measured look before nodding once. Opening his mouth to speak, he seemed to think better of it and dipped in a quick bow before spinning on his heel. Even his walk was refined, and Hattie was struck by his contradicting behavior.

"Goodness, who was that?" Agnes asked, pulling Hattie's attention.

Hattie shook her head, drawing her arm through her maid's and beginning down the walkway toward their waiting horses in the innyard. "I haven't a clue. He didn't say one word to your aunt while I was in her store—she gives her love, by the way—so we must hope he was merely passing through town on his way to anywhere else."

"You didn't like him much, then?"

Shrugging, Hattie cast a glance over her shoulder and spotted him walking away. "That's the trouble. He was rather enigmatic, and I can't tell if I like him or not. It's dreadfully uncomfortable. I'd much rather know I hate the man than be left feeling so uncertain about his character."

Agnes took their horses from Tim Tucker in the stableyard of the inn and held their heads while Hattie stored her purchases in her saddle bag. "If it's any consolation," Agnes said, "I do think he's handsome enough to like."

It wasn't. Hattie didn't much care if he was handsome or not. She couldn't make out his character, and that was what bothered her. Climbing up the mounting block, she pulled herself onto her saddle and adjusted her position in the seat until she was comfortable. "I've always had the ability to tell right away if a person possesses a goodly soul or not, wouldn't you agree?"

Agnes looked as though she was giving the question some thought as she mounted her horse. "Yes, I would say I agree."

"Then why can I not do so now?"

Agnes shrugged. "Perhaps he has no soul."

Hattie laughed. "Perhaps. I suppose I'll never know."

CHAPTER 2

The Duke of Bentley was about to pass his thirtieth birthday and thus was far too old for games. He eyed the letter on his desk with misgiving, the familiar scrawl peeking from the bent paper and mocking him. He'd read it over and over again, doing his best to ascertain the jest, but it seemed his mother was entirely serious. She truly wished for him to travel all the way to her estate in Kent to visit her and her husband.

Bentley scoffed, running a hand over his stubbled jaw. *Surely* she could not be in earnest, contacting him after all these years to beg him to reconsider. He had no interest in her husband, as she should well understand, and the man's declining health bore little hardship on Bentley.

Mother had mentioned her husband's various illnesses over the previous few years, and never once had Bentley felt the least concern or desire to go to them. He had a feeling this latest letter was nothing but a ploy to force him to travel to Kent. But even if it was the truth, the last sickbed he'd attended had been that of his father seven years ago, and he had no further reason to duplicate the experience. He'd since sequestered himself in the wilds of Devonshire to safeguard himself from this very thing.

Egerton, his butler, came into the room and placed a polished, silver tray on the edge of his sturdy, oak desk. "Your tea, Your Grace."

"Thank you, Egerton." Bentley stared at the missive, ignoring the tea. It would take much more than this measly letter for him to reconsider. His lodge was secluded, quiet, and peaceful, and he was content where he was. He did not plan to change that now, not even for the man who was married to his estranged mother.

"The *Times* has come." The tall, slender butler took the folded newspaper from under his arm and set it beside the tray, casually awaiting more instruction.

Bentley should tell the man he was permitted to leave now, but he needed a distraction. Besides, curiosity had taken root on the edges of his consciousness since leaving the milliner's earlier that day, and he was terribly desperate to set his mind to anything besides his mother's letter.

Shoving the folded paper to the side, he set his gaze on his butler. "Do you know much of the woman who runs the millinery shop in Graton? I believe she is called Mrs. Dawson."

Egerton's hands came to rest behind his aged, stooped back. The dying fire flickered just beyond him though it had long since ceased giving off any real heat. "Yes, Your Grace. Mrs. Notley and I have had occasion to speak to her after services on Sundays."

"What do you make of her?"

A flicker of uncertainty passed over Egerton's face. "She is a good, God-fearing woman. I believe she was widowed some five or six years ago, but she has not remarried."

What relevance her marital status held was beyond Bentley. He nodded. So the woman was alone, reliant on her shop patrons for income—and companionship if he had his guess—

18

and completely willing to persuade young women to spend more than they ought.

Bentley had nearly inserted himself earlier at the shop and mentioned to the young woman that she needn't buy the expensive gloves if she had no use for them. He'd noticed her indecision but had held back, curious to see what she would do.

He hadn't been surprised by the young woman's actions. So easy it was to be swindled. Bentley would know.

But he *was* disappointed. He'd wanted this woman to be different. When she'd tripped over the mirror stand and he'd reached for her impulsively, he hadn't expected to feel such a strong response—he'd merely reacted to her fall. It had been years...*years* since he'd held a woman in his arms, and warmth had ripped through him with swift ferocity, spiking his intrigue at once. But she had hastened to remove herself from his hold, as if she couldn't get away fast enough, and her somewhat insipid speech had put him off her right away.

If only Bentley could determine why the small, inconsequential meeting had left him so unable to focus on anything else for the last hour.

He hadn't even meant to stop in Graton. He usually avoided it at all costs. But he'd been sorely in need of a new pair of gloves and that wasn't the sort of thing one could send a servant for. Not when the milliner had to measure Bentley's hands. Today he'd chosen to save some time and order the gloves in Graton—he could send someone to retrieve them when they were ready.

He hadn't realized the quick trip was going to become so lively, or that he would be so troubled by a strange woman's behavior.

"Is there anything further I can do for you, Your Grace?"

Flattening his lips together, Bentley gave a shake of his head. He ought to push the woman from his mind and drink his tea before it went cold.

Egerton, as stoic and calm as ever, continued as though the odd line of questioning had never been pursued. "I took the liberty of having Edwin set up the blue room, Your Grace."

"Very good, Egerton. I shall be in shortly."

His butler gave a stiff bow and let himself quietly from the room. When Bentley had chosen this estate from all his father's holdings to escape to years ago, he'd done so largely because of its distance from his mother, and secondarily because of the sheer seclusion it provided. The small woods which encircled the house were a barrier between his estate and the neighboring ones.

He prepared his tea precisely how he liked it, with one small lump of sugar and a dash of milk, then he brought the cup to his lips and tentatively sipped the steaming beverage.

Bentley had once met his neighbor to the east when he'd fished in the lake they shared, but the man was too jovial and friendly, too *interested*, and Bentley hadn't bothered to pursue the acquaintance.

People, he'd found, were far too curious by nature to allow a man to live in peace unless he took particular measures. Bentley had accomplished this easily by refusing to form relationships with anyone. He did not smile at those he passed in the road, nor did he bother with frivolous greetings to strangers. He merely built and cultivated a simple existence in his small estate with his servants and himself for company. He had nearly everything he needed here.

The one thing he missed in his chosen life of seclusion was attending church. But doing so would be dangerous. It led to building relationships with the townspeople, to caring. He risked enough by his monthly jaunts to Melbury's apothecary for the ingredients he needed to make his paints—but that was not a task he wished to relegate to the servants. And anyway, the visit he'd received from the vicar, Mr. Conway, had gone a long way in ensuring that he'd not regret missing that particular man's services. He was too pushy by half.

Lifting his teacup, Bentley tucked the newspaper under his arm and crossed toward the low-burning fire. His eyes scanned the familiar handwriting on the back of the letter, depicting his name and direction, before he tossed it onto the grate. The paper glowed over the flames as they licked its edges, curling them up and into ash. He waited for remorse or guilt to permeate his chest, but neither arrived.

Walking away, Bentley sipped his tea and shook out his newspaper. After seven years, Mother should know her pleas would fall on deaf ears. He was better off alone.

<hr />

Hattie strode into the dining room, careful to look pleasantly surprised when her eyes fell upon her brother and his wife.

"Sorry I'm late, Papa—oh! Jeffrey, Lucy, you've arrived! How wonderful. Did you have a smooth journey?"

"Yes," Jeffrey said, standing upon her entrance. His observing eye did not waver from her. "So smooth, in fact, that we happened to arrive earlier than planned."

She smiled and took her seat across from her brother and his wife, holding Jeffrey's gaze. She would not allow her brother to trick her into any sort of confession about her poor manners from earlier in the day. Indeed, it was *his* fault she had been forced to act so shabbily. His and Lucy's presence on High Street had caught her unawares. What else was she to do but pretend she had not seen their carriage nor heard Lucy's calls when they had so rudely appeared without any sort of notice? She'd been under the impression that she had another hour free of their company.

But she also had a feeling that were she to voice these observations aloud, no one else would see her logic.

"We thought we saw you earlier today, in fact," Lucy said, her blue eyes wide. "But it must have been someone else."

"I've spent a good deal of time riding this afternoon and came away so frozen it took nearly an hour to thaw by the fire," she said. A change of conversation was exactly what they needed. "These Novembers are growing colder every year, I believe."

"Perhaps," Papa said from the head of the table. He flicked his wrist forward. The footmen stepped toward the table and began serving roasted fowl and asparagus onto the plates.

Lucy watched her with interest, and it was all Hattie could do to keep her eyes on her plate and feign interest in the browned meat. Did Papa have a larger fowl than her? It was only fair, she supposed.

"Hattie," Jeffrey said from across the table. "Do you have any intention of attending the assemblies in Melbury next week? Papa told me that you haven't gone to the last few."

Maintaining her focus on the bird as she cut her dinner, she replied, "No."

"Why not?"

"Because they are in *Melbury*," she said. Was that not explanation enough?

Jeffrey scoffed lightly, chewing around a bite of meat. "Do not tell me you *still* hold a prejudice against Melbury."

"They cheated at cricket just this summer," Hattie said in defense. "I believe it is perfectly justified."

Jeffrey scoffed again.

"And they stole two of my horses," Papa added.

"Oh, bother. That was *one* man," Jeffrey said. "Surely you cannot hold an entire town accountable for his actions."

"I can, and I will." Papa cut a bite of meat and shoved it into his mouth, unrepentant. "I told you before, and I shall say it again: I will never force Hattie to attend a Melbury assembly."

Hattie turned her attention to her asparagus, gratified by

Papa's support.

"Dash it, Jeffrey, do you realize what could happen?" Papa said, his thick eyebrows pulling together as though he was considering the implications of such an event. His chin tucked in, his lips turning down at the ends. "Hattie could meet a Melbury man and find him to her liking."

He stated this with such distaste that Hattie had to make a concerted effort not to spit her wine across the table. She swallowed, coughing discreetly to the side.

"Would that be such a terrible thing?" Lucy asked.

Papa glanced at her sharply. "Indeed, it would. Did you not hear us earlier? They cheated at cricket this last summer and stole my horses."

Lucy blinked. "Did Jeffrey not just say that it was only one man responsible, not the entire town?"

"Oh, bah," Papa said, shoving a bite of meat into his mouth. He shot Hattie a long-suffering look, and she felt her cheeks warm.

She might not like Lucy's pushy nature, but the woman was family. One ought to be more circumspect in their dislike. It was time to turn the tide of the conversation.

"How long do you intend to stay in Graton?" she asked, directing a pleasant smile toward Jeffrey and Lucy. "Your letter mentioned something about a fortnight?"

Lucy smiled back, though she was not skilled at hiding her irritation, and it was plainly obvious that they were trying her patience. The thought crossed Hattie's mind to press her advantage here. If she could anger her sister-in-law enough, would Lucy then force Jeffrey to return to London earlier than expected?

No, that was unkind. Suppressing her desire to drive them out of the house, Hattie turned interested eyes on Lucy. It was time to be kind and engaging. "I heard that green silk is all the fashion now. Do tell me what you've seen in London."

CHAPTER 3

*H*attie tucked her ankles underneath her and shifted on the sofa as her cat climbed into her lap and settled in. She was halfway through reading *Othello*, a feat of which she was quite proud. She had made a personal goal to work her way through the Shakespeare plays she hadn't read with her tutor, and this one was proving to be more heart-wrenching than she'd anticipated.

Lucy swept into the drawing room, bringing with her a cloud of rose scent that would send the poor hounds out of the room if they'd been nearby. It nearly sent *Hattie* out of the room, but she had better manners than the dogs. If only just, sometimes. "Oh Hattie, dear, put down that wretched book and come for a walk with me in the gardens."

"We went for a walk this morning," Hattie reminded her, absently rubbing a hand over her cat. The feline hopped down and darted from the room. Well, Hattie didn't blame him. She wanted to do the very same thing. She lifted her book. "And I should like to continue reading."

Lucy's golden eyebrows pulled together. "But what would a gentleman think if he were to see you now?"

Hattie blinked. "That I enjoy reading?"

Shaking her head, Lucy delicately lowered herself onto the sofa beside Hattie, her eyes wide. "That you are a bluestocking," she whispered nervously.

"But...that would be true."

Lucy leaned back. "You do not wish for them to know that before marrying you, dear, or they might change their mind."

Hattie refrained from looking over her shoulder to emphasize the empty room. There were no gentlemen nearby to catch her reading, and if there were, she certainly would not care. She had never understood why learning was so very terrible for women; besides, Papa hadn't ever attempted to restrict her growth.

"When I find myself courting a gentleman, I will concern myself with how I appear to that man, you need not fear."

"Ah, but how will you obtain the honor of that gentleman's courtship without first making yourself appear to advantage in every way?" Lucy sat back, smug. Her blue gown brightened her eyes, and her blonde coiffure was styled flawlessly, not a hair out of place. It gave Hattie the desire to ruffle her sister-in-law in some way.

Swallowing that impulse, Hattie bit her tongue. She knew she could never get Lucy to fully understand her feelings. But she had confidence her future husband was out there somewhere, that she would meet him when the time was right. Fate was not to be forced. It would happen on its own time.

"There are more important things to worry about than a husband, Lucy. I have Papa to consider, and I do not believe love can be contrived. It will come about at the right time."

"Of course love cannot be forced," she said. "But lying about in your drawing room in the middle of the day will not find you a husband, either. You are much better off listening to me, Hattie. I have been in your shoes, and I must say I was successful, was I not? I managed to find a husband any woman would be proud to have on her arm."

Any woman except Hattie, of course, since the man in question was her older *brother*.

Lucy might be married to Jeffrey, but if the woman thought she had a right to step in as some sort of mother figure in Hattie's life, she was sorely mistaken. Time to put an end to that.

Shutting the book with a snap, Hattie stood abruptly. "If any handsome, eligible gentlemen come calling, do let me know. I shall be painting."

She crossed the floor before Lucy could beg an invitation to join her. Lucy had proven herself to have a major dislike of painting during their last visit by refusing to participate and instead choosing to sit behind and *watch*, which had been complete torture for Hattie. She would not allow a repeat of that situation.

"But Hattie, you *must* prepare yourself. I can help you."

Cold, icy dread dragged its unwelcome claw down her spine. She paused at the door and pivoted to face her sister-in-law. The woman's voice was too pointed to not mean something specific. "To what do you refer?"

Lucy blinked, her round, blue eyes fixed steadily on Hattie. "I only mean to help you, of course."

She could not possibly mean what Hattie believed she implied. "You have come with the express purpose to help me find a husband?"

"Surely you did not think we would leave London in November for anything less important." Her petite nose wrinkled. "If the snow comes early, we will be forced to remain here for months."

Good heavens, that *would* be dreadful.

"Then allow me to put you at ease," Hattie said. "You

27

mustn't stay longer than the fortnight you intended in the first place."

"I believe it is best if you allow those of us with experience to guide you, Hattie."

Hattie wanted to scream. This condescension from a woman nearly Hattie's own age was infuriating. She settled for leaving the room in a dignified huff and going in search of her father. Naturally, he was nowhere to be found.

"Out, miss," her butler told her. "He went for a ride with Master Jeffrey."

"Of course he has," she muttered.

Very well. If he and Jeffrey were allowed to escape the house in the middle of the day, then so was she. Hattie lifted her skirts and climbed the stairs to her bedchamber where she located her satchel of supplies. She checked to make sure she had everything she needed before slipping from the room and quietly letting herself out of the house. Papa and Jeffrey had likely traveled the fields to the left where they could practice hedge jumps with reckless speed.

Hattie enjoyed hedge jumps as much as the next person. And she was absolutely *not* pouting about being left out of the fun. But if her painting made her stay out for the rest of the afternoon, then her brother could not complain. It was *his* spouse he had left to fend for herself.

Hattie went to the west, where she hoped to find a secluded spot in the wooded area. Maybe even a starling would make herself known and sit for a portrait. Hattie wished she had the ability to paint from memory, but it was not a skill given to her. She had to paint what was before her very eyes in that moment, or the image would fly from her mind.

It was very boring and not the least bit romantic.

But sneaking into the wooded area owned by the neighboring estate wasn't boring in the least. The woods held a magic in them, a quiet and peace Hattie had grown to appreciate. And as far as she was aware, the reclusive duke never left his house, so he would likely never know she was in his woods. She often stayed near the perimeter of her own land anyway, so she was unlikely to be caught.

It was all perfectly above board in Hattie's mind. If a gardener or land agent would happen upon her, she could easily slip into the persona of an insipid young miss and fool them into thinking she believed the land was her own.

Any silly young girl couldn't be expected to know the precise boundaries of her property. It hardly mattered that Hattie was five-and-twenty. She was petite and could certainly pass for much younger if she made her voice high enough.

Slipping between the trees, Hattie walked slowly, heedless of her blue gown snagging on the brush that lined the forest floor. She'd seen the perfect location during a walk just a few weeks prior where the trees opened up to reveal a portion of Hattie's house in the distance. She'd thought then of painting it, of creating an image of forest in the foreground and a minor focus on her house in the back, through the curtain of trees. She was close. Now if only she could locate the exact spot…

Ah, perfect. She found it. Standing in the small clearing, the painting formed in her mind as she looked for the right angle from which she should capture the image. Stumbling upon the precise location was the easy part. Finding a decent place to set her things was not going to be quite as simple.

It was just as well that she'd thought to bring her painting smock, as it looked as though she'd be kneeling on the ground. Lowering herself to the cool dirt, she began pulling brushes and paints from her bag and setting up her mixing implements. Rolling her shoulders, she raised her face, gathering all the irritation she'd felt at Lucy and pushing it from her mind.

It was time to focus on more pleasant things.

Bentley sat in his study, the half-read newspaper he'd received the day before spread over his lap while he swirled the brandy in his glass. The fire in the grate glowed in his peripheral vision, stealing his attention each time he'd managed to make it to the end of a paragraph. Folding up his paper in a frustrated huff, he tossed it onto the table beside him and crossed the room in agitated steps. He could no longer read the words of the burned letter, as it had now turned to a pile of ash, and yet, he couldn't stop thinking about it. He'd burned plenty of his mother's letters, but this had never happened before.

He found himself wondering *how* his mother had phrased her request for him to visit. It was irrelevant—he would not go, regardless of how it was said. But he was curious, and he wanted to know. Had she written that her husband's health was *declining* or that it was *failing*?

Not that he cared, of course. The distinction only mattered if Bentley cared at all for the man. Maybe he just needed to be away from his study so he would cease staring into the fire.

He paused at the sideboard and swallowed the rest of his drink, squinting as the sunlight slipped through the window and pierced him in the eye. A soft crying came from somewhere near the window, and Bentley paused. It couldn't possibly be a baby, but it certainly sounded like one. Perhaps his imagination was running wild again.

Well, if that was the case, he either needed to stretch it further or go outside and allow the fresh air to cleanse him. The woods outside his window were a beautiful array of reds and golds, like an artist had dipped his brush in multiple colors and dashed them every which way across the trees, blending them into a rich tapestry of leaves. Outside it was. He might as well go for a walk while the afternoon sun was high enough to keep him warm in the autumn chill.

Egerton helped him into his greatcoat and gloves at the door, and Bentley slipped his hat over his overgrown hair as he stepped from the house. He was due for a haircut, and his valet was perfectly capable, but as the days grew shorter and slipped closer to winter, he was more inclined to allow the hair to grow. It wasn't as though he would see anyone outside of his own household anytime soon. After his visit to Graton's shops yesterday, he was determined to steer clear for some time, to allow the shop owner ample time to forget him.

In the meantime, he would be much warmer with his hair grown out and his beard growing thicker over his jaw.

Bentley walked the perimeter of the woods, skirting the edge of the vibrantly colored trees. When he heard the same mewling sound again, he halted. Cocking his head to the side, he quieted and listened, but silence met him. Sweeping his gaze over the edge of the woods and the lawn which led to the overgrown hedges butted up against his house, he did not see any disturbance besides the minor breeze ruffling the leaves. A chicken clucked behind the house, its head bobbing as it walked across the packed-dirt earth, and he turned away.

Bentley stepped slowly, picking his way across the forest floor as he kept an eye out for animals. He'd seen a fox just a few weeks ago and wouldn't mind finding it again.

The woods felt oddly still today, nearly reverent. Inhaling the rich smell of earth and bark, Bentley continued to pick his way through the trees and leaf-strewn earth when a flash of color caught his eye. It couldn't be the fox—not unless the creature had rolled through burgundy paint.

No, this was a woman in a dark gown, a smock tied about her waist as she knelt on the forest floor. On *Bentley's* forest floor. His personal property. Was she mad? Trespassing was illegal.

But something about her bearing rang familiar, and he froze, his stomach constricting. Either this was the woman from the shop, or Bentley wished for it to be, and neither of those possibilities weighed positively on his conscience. She turned her face to the side slightly as she dipped her brush in paint, and he noted her freckled cheeks. It was absolutely the same woman.

He stood just behind her, close enough to peer over her shoulder at the work of art before her. She was certainly talented, he would grant her that. And judging by the way she had not flinched at his approaching steps, he assumed she was rather consumed by her work. He understood that sentiment completely.

Only, if she had mixed the darker green with just a smidge of blue, the color would have been *perfect* for the shadowed foliage beneath the house.

Bentley didn't blame her for missing it. It was so close to perfection as it was. He loved it. The dark curtain of trees with their bursts of autumn colors was breathtaking, and the way they opened at just the right place to show the estate was striking. Not only did this poor, innocent miss have a talent for painting, but she clearly had an eye for what constituted a good image. And he would know. He was something of a connoisseur himself.

But the color. The depth needed in that green truly could have made the shadows better. Perhaps if he told her of the trick, she could try it next time, see if it was to her liking.

Taking another step, his foot snapped a twig underneath, and he paused, but still, she did not seem to notice. Hesitation filtered through him briefly, but he pushed it aside. He hadn't spoken to an artist in years, and the thrill of talking about painting with someone who was adept was too tempting to resist.

Clearing his throat, Bentley said, "The color is wrong."

CHAPTER 4

*H*attie stiffened, her hand pausing just before the freshly dipped yellow brush could meet the thick paper. A man had just spoken behind her, and if she was correct, it sounded *exactly* like the man who'd stopped her from crashing into Mrs. Dawson's mirror the day before. The same smooth, low voice that reminded her of a hot cup of chocolate. But it couldn't be. What in heaven's name would he be doing *here*?

Lowering the brush, Hattie rested it on her messy palette. Her shoulders were tense as she turned to face her critic, and she did her best not to flinch when she met his piercing, gray eyes.

Though their color was stormy, it was their depth and steadiness that made Hattie feel as though the man was looking straight through her. Though if he was, then he would likely take a step back, for he would know precisely how much she disliked him in that moment.

"Pardon me?" she asked. "I do not think I heard you correctly."

Shifting to lean on his other leg, he indicated her painting. "I believe the color for the foliage underneath the house could have been made richer had you added a touch of blue."

Gazing up at him from her location on the forest floor was not ideal. Moving to stand, she fell onto her rear, unaware that her legs had gone wholly numb. Well, this was entirely the opposite of how she wanted to appear before this regal, well put together headmaster.

"More blue, you say?" She pulled her legs out before her, shooting a dazzling smile at the man to cover her frustration and waiting for the pin pricks to subside as the blood returned to her limbs.

"Well, yes," he said, as though he'd made a perfectly reasonable suggestion. "Your color is well-chosen, but the tone is not quite right. There are varying degrees within each color, you see, and sometimes the most minimal addition can make all the difference."

Clenching her teeth, Hattie decided that Agnes was correct in her earlier assumption: this gentleman clearly had no soul. She got to her feet on wobbly legs, straightening her skirt as pin pricks surged up her calves. There. Now she could meet him on more equal footing. Though he still towered unfairly above her.

"And are you an expert on matters of painting and color?"

He held her gaze. "I have studied the masters."

"Ah, well. It is rather ridiculous to critique others when you haven't tried to accomplish the thing yourself, do you not agree?"

He paused, shifting back to the other leg. "Yes, I would agree with that."

So he had *some* sense, at least. "Good. Then perhaps we shall postpone this discussion. I can see how late it's gotten, and I should be returning home. My father will wonder where I am."

"Of course."

She waited for him to leave, but he didn't comply. Watching her, he merely clasped his gloved hands behind his back. His throat, she noticed, was bare underneath his coat. Had the man truly ventured outside without a cravat?

She tore her gaze away from his exposed sliver of skin, and a shiver swept over her. How long *had* she been out here? And when had it grown so cold? Pulling at the chain of the watch she always wore around her neck, Hattie checked the time. Drat. It had been hours. She knelt, not daring to put her back to a stranger, and began to gather her things together. She would need to carry her brushes, palette, and painting back to the house somehow, but she hadn't planned to juggle all her things before an audience.

"May I be of any assistance?" the man asked.

As though she would take him up on such an offer. Hattie recalled belatedly how scatter-brained she'd tried to appear in the shop—so much for that. She considered raising her voice an octave and pretending to not understand him, but she could see that he would not believe her. His eyes were too knowing, his expression too studious. "How kind of you to offer, but I wouldn't want to soil your fine coat with my poorly-mixed paints." Her voice held an edge to it, but she couldn't help it.

"I can see that I've offended you."

And she would likely be less so had he sounded any more penitent. "Think nothing of it. You are entitled to your opinion, however false it might be."

"I was only trying to be of some help. The rest of your painting is magnificent."

Her heart squeezed from the praise before she promptly squashed the warm feeling. "May I offer you some advice, then?"

"Please do."

Oh, it was *so* grating how cool and level he seemed. If only she could rile him up the way he did her. "The next time you wish to offer advice to a complete stranger—particularly when you lack any experience in the matter—you may want to lead with the compliment. Learning whether the person in question *welcomes* your advice may be helpful, too."

He nodded gravely. "Consider it noted. For what it's worth, I did not mean to offend."

"No one usually does, do they?"

A smile flickered over his lips, and Hattie thought it was something of an accomplishment that she had caused it. Oh, heavens, she needed to *not* feel that way.

Rising, she slung her satchel over her shoulder before bending to lift the wet painting and the palette, the brushes resting precariously atop it.

"You are certain I cannot help you with your things?"

"I am quite certain, thank you." In fact, his very presence was enough to cause her reason for concern. Who was this man, and why had he appeared so suddenly? Two days in a row, at that. She glanced at his well-made greatcoat and dismissed the headmaster concept immediately. If he was in these woods and dressed so well, he was either a guest of her father's—which was unlikely, since Papa would have told her—or a guest of the reclusive duke.

She rather assumed it to be the latter. Perhaps he was the duke's tutor. Though she'd heard it said that the duke was a handful of years older than Hattie was, so a tutor seemed odd. Dash it, if he was going to be visiting her neighbor, would she have to see him again?

"You mentioned postponing this conversation. May I ask when I shall see you next?" he said, stealing the question from her thoughts. Though he sounded as if he believed it was an inevitability, whereas she was afraid of the possibility.

"I'm not certain you ever shall. We are unacquainted, and I will certainly not be returning to this spot if that is what concerns you. In fact, I rather wonder if you have been following me."

His smile was wide and far more handsome than he

deserved. "I could ask the same thing. You are the one trespassing on my land."

Oh. On *his* land? Hattie swallowed, tightening her grip on her painting before it could slip from her fingers. If this was his land, that could only mean one thing. "You are the duke."

He didn't flinch but instead nodded gravely. Bending into a low bow, he raised his face, his eyes on her. "Most people simply call me Bentley."

"Your Grace," she said, dropping into as low a curtsy as she could manage while balancing the paints and brushes. At least she'd been right about one thing: the man was clearly authoritative.

He motioned for her to rise. "Please, I do not wish to be so formal."

As though she had any other option. Hattie had never knowingly stood in front of such a high-ranking person until today. She was a regular visitor at the Earl of Hart's home, as she was a friend of his niece, Giulia, but the earl never frightened her. This tall, dark, scruffy-faced man was quite the opposite. She did not know what to make of him, and that was altogether terrifying.

"May I have the pleasure of your name?" he asked.

She hardly had anyone else nearby to do the introductions, and neither could she refuse a duke. She dipped her head. "Miss Hattie Green."

His eyebrows lifted a fraction. "My neighbor?"

Drat, she should have given a fake surname. Now he knew where she lived. "I didn't realize you were aware of who your neighbors were, Your Grace. All we know of you is that you wear your hair long and refuse the vicar's calls." Hattie snapped her mouth shut.

A sparkle of amusement lit his eyes. "I should not be surprised that the townspeople speak of me. What is a community if not a source of gossip?"

"A source of kinship and support, I should rightfully think. Gossip comes second," she added flippantly.

Bentley seemed to be attempting to take her measure, his head tilting to the side while he raked his gaze over her face. "Shall I arm myself against a renewal of ducal gossip now? I fear that you'll send the vicar back to my door after learning how agreeable I am."

"Oh, you needn't fear on that front. I shan't say a word about you."

"Why not?"

"And have the whole town thinking I've gone and tried to catch myself a duke?" She scoffed lightly. "Goodness, how desperate do you believe me to be? Besides, I cannot tell the vicar you are agreeable."

His eyebrows hitched together. "Why is that?"

Widening her eyes in innocence, she said, "I can't very well lie to a clergyman, now, can I?"

Despite the slur this woman had just thrown his way, Bentley found himself disappointed with her sudden departure. He watched her pick her way through the trees, balancing the paint-covered palette and brushes while carefully holding her completed painting in the other hand. She reminded him of a barmaid with platters of food resting upon each outstretched palm, but somehow Miss Hattie Green managed to look much more confident. Given the barmaids he'd had the pleasure of interacting with, that was a feat.

Now that she was a safe distance away, Bentley allowed his shoulders to relax. He wasn't sure what had just occurred between himself and the woman. He usually fought such friendly, neighborly conversations. When her father had introduced himself all those years ago at the lake, Bentley had immediately written the place off as somewhere he should not visit again. Building relationships was dangerous. Particularly when the woman was so lovely and full of spark.

Though, she interested him, too. He'd never before seen a woman with such pale skin so utterly covered in freckles. She looked as though she'd been carefully painted herself, speckled with the end of a brown-tipped paint brush until her flawless, porcelain skin was completely covered.

And it was beautiful.

Scrubbing a hand over his face, he tore his gaze from the petite, retreating figure and headed back toward Wolfeton House. He quickened his steps, eager to be back in the safety of his home. He shouldn't have stopped and spoken with her, but he'd been taken with her painting and had gotten caught up in the tones of her colors.

Miss Green's honesty was amusing, and he'd had to make a great effort not to reveal his surprise at her words. Of course, he'd assumed that the people of Graton speculated about him, but to have it confirmed did not bother him as he might have believed it would.

As far as he could tell, none of them knew the truth of his situation.

The meddlesome townspeople could speculate as much as they wished, so long as it amounted to nothing more than how he spent his days. He was not eager for that particular piece of information to become widely known, but at least it would not harm his reputation or his father's name.

Breaking through the treeline, he crossed the small lawn toward his house. Ivy climbed the side of the pale gray stone building, encasing it in a layer of spindly green webbing.

A soft meow floated on the cool breeze and stopped Bentley in his tracks. It was no coincidence; he'd now heard that sound three times, and it was clearly a cat in distress.

Hesitating only a moment, he dismissed the idea of sending

out a servant in search of the creature. He'd heard the sound from his study, so it stood to reason the animal was somewhere in that general area. Bentley stepped quietly to his study window, raking his gaze over the ground in search of a disturbance.

A chicken squawked, its head bobbing in his peripheral vision as he narrowed his gaze. A portion of the hedges appeared darker just under the study window, as though a heap of dark clothes was puddled there. Squatting low, he searched through the dense bush.

A cat lay still, huddled in a circle, and Bentley reached in to pull it out. Slipping his hands around the soft, silky fur, he gently pulled the animal from its hiding place, surprised when it came easily. The only cat he'd ever known had been his mother's, and that creature was so taciturn it made the local innkeeper, Jolly, look like a sweet, old grandmother.

At least this one didn't seem interested in testing its claws on Bentley's coat. He looked the animal over as it climbed slowly onto his lap. Sucking in a breath, he avoided touching the angry red line which marred the cat's gray-striped back. It had clearly gotten in a fight with a sharp branch or another animal.

Seeming to notice him from the far end of the yard, the chicken pivoted, coming toward them with increasing speed. The cat reacted at once, climbing up and over Bentley's shoulder, its claws digging into his neck as it fought to stay on.

"Blasted—get *down*." But the cat had other ideas. It fought to stay put as the chicken neared them, and Bentley stood. "Is she the culprit, then? Did you get in a fight with a chicken?"

Moving away from the fowl, Bentley went toward his front door. He carefully pried the cat from his shoulder, its stubborn claws digging into the fabric of his coat.

"Let's take you inside and clean your wound, shall we?" he asked before stopping himself. He'd never had an impulse to carry on a conversation with an animal before. Hopefully, this wasn't an indication that his solitude was driving him to madness. He was rather comfortable with the way his life was now.

Egerton opened the front door for him, and Bentley stepped inside. "Please tell Mrs. Notley that I have a cat in need of some medical care. I need some warm water, cloths, and something to bandage it."

Egerton looked down his large nose at the feline. "Shall I take the cat to her, Your Grace?"

He shook his head. "Have her bring the things to my study. Or send Edwin. I do not care who assists me."

"Very good, Your Grace. I'll see to it at once." He hid any measure of uncertainty he felt, talented butler that he was, and left.

Bentley fought a smile and took the cat toward his study. There would be a decent fire built up by now, and the animal would need the warmth it provided. It was settled snugly against his chest, and he had felt the calming of its frantic heartbeat, grateful he'd managed to put it slightly at ease.

Kneeling before the fire, Bentley laid the cat on the floor. It turned and climbed back onto his lap, and he chuckled.

"Ah, you're a boy. Very well, sir, you may sit here. But first, allow me to remove my coat."

Bentley took his greatcoat off and somewhat awkwardly tossed it over the chair just behind him. He slipped his fingers between the cat's ears, stroking the silky fur. "I will clean and bandage you, but then you will be put back outside where you belong. Understood?"

He used his best ducal voice, but somehow the cat didn't seem to be paying him any mind.

Oh well, he'd just have to show it what he meant. Just after he brought it up to snuff, of course.

CHAPTER 5

*T*he painting Hattie had done from the duke's grove was sitting upstairs above the fireplace in her room, directly facing her bed. Tacked onto the board she'd painted it on, it appeared just as unfinished as it felt. Throughout the week since she'd accomplished it, it was the final thing she looked at before going to sleep every night and the first thing she looked at when she awoke in the mornings. Each day Hattie had analyzed the color of the wretched foliage beneath the house, considering the duke's advice. His unwarranted, unasked for, and—much to her dismay—potentially accurate advice.

The temptation to return to the place she had painted it and analyze the color of that foliage was very strong, but Hattie's fear of running into the Duke of Bentley was even stronger and had successfully kept her away thus far. She'd told the man she would never return to his woods. How vile would it be if he found her there?

Her sister-in-law's voice trickled from the parlor and reached Hattie in the corridor, and her resolve slipped more and more. The location where she'd painted was directly on the edge of

Bentley's woods. If she was to sneak in and out quickly, she would likely remain unseen.

Buttoning closed her cream-colored spencer jacket, Hattie debated the merits of slipping outside against entering the parlor where Lucy currently sat. Checking the colors of the shrubs from that distance was as good an excuse as any to leave the house before Lucy found her. Papa knew how seriously Hattie took her painting, and perhaps if she could perfect the piece enough, she could show it to Lucy and the woman would leave off trying so desperately to make an accomplished lady out of Hattie.

If Hattie had not yet earned the title of an accomplished lady at the age of five and twenty, she was quite set in the fact that it was never going to happen for her. And to Lucy's dismay, that was not a hardship to Hattie. Quite the reverse, in fact, for she rather liked flouting convention when she was reasonably able to do so.

Footsteps tapped on the marble floor behind her, and Hattie refrained from cursing under her breath, angry she had missed her window of escape. Instead, she turned a bright smile on her brother. Perhaps she could slip past him after a quick greeting.

His knowing, brown eyes rested on her. Drat. There would be no escaping to the woods today. She appraised his clean, orderly appearance, searching for a way to remove herself from the house, though her brother tended to see through her antics. While similar in some ways, the Green siblings' coiffures spoke volumes about their differences. They shared the same mousy brown coloring, but Jeffrey's hair was neatly combed and orderly, whereas Hattie's was usually thrown into a simple style, as she was too impatient to sit for anything more elaborate, with wisps falling out around her face and trailing over her neck.

"Jeffrey," she said, her tone dripping with added sugar. "Do tell me your target shooting was successful. I should like it if

Papa is in a happy mood when I ask him for another advancement of next quarter's pin money."

"So you may take my wife to Graton and spend more than you should on gowns and trinkets? I think not." He smiled despite his words, a deep crease etching into the side of his mouth. "No, I'd much rather tell you that Papa had a very unsuccessful day at shooting, he missed every single target, and you'd best hold off on the request and wait for a more favorable time."

She narrowed her gaze on his flawless skin. Why was it that her brother's face did not sport a single, solitary freckle when hers claimed hundreds? It was unfair. "Are you speaking the truth?"

"No." He stepped forward and opened the parlor door for her. "But I can clearly see what you are playing at. Does that not make you wish to come up with another scheme?"

"Hardly," Hattie said, preceding him into the drawing room. "If anything, it only makes me want to do it more."

She flounced toward the sofa and lowered herself across from Lucy just as their maid was removing a cold tea service. The sound of barking in the corridor warned them of the dogs' impending arrival before Papa's hounds ran into the room and shot directly toward Hattie. Daisy stopped before her, resting her wet, brown nose on Hattie's knee, her white tail wagging.

"I have nothing to give you." Hattie leaned forward and rubbed the hunting dog behind the ears as her sister, Rosie, pushed in beside her. Their brown and white spotted bodies rumbled with eagerness. "Be kind," she admonished. "You can share. I have two hands."

Lucy stared at Hattie so pointedly that she was forced to look up. She gave her sister-in-law a questioning glance. "Is something troubling you, Lucy?"

"You do realize the dog cannot understand you, yes?" she asked, her blue eyes wide.

"Why is that?"

There was only a beat of silence before Lucy delicately cleared her throat and spoke slowly, as though she were addressing a child. Did the woman not realize that such actions only put Hattie off her more? "Because they are animals."

"And therefore they cannot speak to us," Hattie agreed. "But who has proven that they cannot understand us?"

"Give it a rest, Hattie," Jeffrey said, sighing. He brought one ankle up to rest on the other knee and leaned back on the sofa cushion beside his wife.

Lucy tilted her head a little to the side. "I realize you say such ridiculous things because you take delight in goading me, but surely you know it is unbecoming of you to be so intentionally contrary. I take comfort in my faith that you will not stoop to such depths in company. It is the only thing that allows me peace." Giving Jeffrey a conspiratorial smile, Lucy settled into her cushion.

The woman was correct on all accounts but one. Fixing a smile on her lips to soften her words, Hattie's gaze did not waver. "Then you must not know me as well as you think, for I do not tailor my behavior to any person, I assure you. What you experience with me is exactly the same treatment the rest of England receives."

She stood quickly, forcing the dogs to retreat, and then pointedly looked at both of the animals vying for her attention. Their tails wagged furiously as they trained excited, dark eyes on Hattie. They knew what was coming, and Lucy clearly knew nothing if she believed animals could not read or understand humans. "Come, Daisy and Rosie, let us go outside."

They followed her at once, their slender brown and white bodies a blur as they crossed the room swiftly. She paused at the door and turned back. "Speaking of animals, have either of you seen my cat? He has been missing for a week now."

Lucy gave a subtle shake. Her pinched lips likely held in all the things she planned to say to Jeffrey the moment Hattie left the room.

"If you see him, please let me know," Hattie said. "I've searched everywhere, but he is nowhere to be seen."

Jeffrey gave an apologetic look. "I'm sorry, but I haven't seen him since the day we arrived. I shall keep my eye out for him, though."

Delivering a wide smile, Hattie pretended as though she did not take delight in the fact that her sister-in-law was slowly turning the shade of a cherry. "Thank you. Good day."

The afternoon sun provided no warmth against the cool wind and Hattie tugged her spencer tighter about her neck. The hounds ran ahead of her, circling back every so often as if to check that she was still with them. She'd much prefer to return to her painting location and check the color, but the part of her that did not wish to be proven wrong was happy to avoid it. She'd never been particularly skilled at selecting the exact right color, and the duke had criticized the very thing she found to be a weakness in herself, only causing her further frustration. No, she would not confirm his declaration by checking the foliage from the vantage point of the woods. A splash in the banks of the lake would be much better, anyway. The dogs could use a swim.

They skirted the edge of the woods, Daisy and Rosie dodging in and out of the trees, chasing a small bird and then returning. Sometimes Hattie wished she'd been born a dog, too, for they had nothing to concern themselves with besides their own happiness.

That would certainly be preferable to managing Society's expectations.

The dogs slipped ahead, barking rapidly. Their tone shifted from playful to something far more earnest, and the hair on the back of Hattie's neck stood on end in warning. This was not the joyful sound of cheeky dogs chasing a bird. This was dangerous.

Lifting the hem of her gown, Hattie broke into a run, slipping into the trees and chasing the sound of her dogs barking. "Rosie! Daisy!" Her calls went unheard against a volley of angry barking and she quickened her speed.

Oh, goodness. What had they found? Likely a poor, unsuspecting fox.

She couldn't hide a smile at the thought. She was on a fox hunt herself, but of a different nature. If only Lucy knew the truth of *that* situation, she would likely give Hattie more space. But given her desire for matchmaking schemes, Hattie didn't feel like her sister-in-law needed to know.

Trees blocked most of the sun, the spotted light around her highlighting a foreign part of the duke's woods. She'd never ventured so deep in them before. Now that she'd met the man —Bentley, as she thought of him in her mind—she felt uncomfortable being on his property. Not exactly the best feeling when it seemed as though her dogs' barking was retreating deeper into the woods, though now the sounds were growing louder.

She needed to find them before Wolfeton House and its inhabitants took notice.

A deep voice called out angrily, and one of her dogs whimpered, stopping Hattie in her tracks. She spun, gripping her skirts and trying to determine the direction the sounds had come from. She was surrounded, encircled with tall trees, covered overhead by branches and what few leaves remained this far into Autumn. But the dogs weren't anywhere in sight.

"Off that, you mongrel!" a man yelled.

Hattie took off in a run, nearly positive the sound came from her left, and weaved through the forest until she broke through the treeline. A short lawn spanned before her, leading up to a stone house covered in ivy. The house was something out of a fairytale, and she would have spent time admiring it if her attention wasn't stolen by a stout man in grungy trousers standing a few yards away, clutching a nervous chicken and glaring at two snarling hound dogs. *Her* hounds.

He lifted his leg as though he meant to kick Rosie, and Hattie leapt forward. "Stop at once!"

She frightened the man, and the chicken leapt from his arms, flapping its wings angrily as it charged the dogs. Rosie and Daisy jumped away before circling back. Their erratic motions and barking were similar to how they played with one another when they were restless. Only now they were attempting to play with an irritable fowl.

Hattie immediately took measure of the situation and knew the best way to put an end to it was to remove the chicken. The poor thing was looking for a fight and didn't realize how willing these dogs were to playfully oblige her.

"Retrieve your chicken!" she yelled to the man, for he remained dumbstruck, his rounded chin tucked against his neck. He glanced up at Hattie, eyebrows raised, and she wanted to groan.

Must she do everything herself?

"Down, Rosie," she said, gently shoving the dog aside. "Daisy, *no.*" She reached for the chicken as she'd learned to do when she was younger, with lightning-fast motions, tucking the talons beneath her and holding the bird tightly against her chest. Her dogs barked, jumping up against her legs, and she admonished them.

"Daisy, Rosie, *enough.* This behavior is not befitting young ladies."

"But catching chickens is?" a deep, familiar voice said just behind her.

Hattie spun, her hold on the chicken slipping in the face of Bentley's wit. A talon broke free, and the bird kicked, slicing through her sleeve and across the underside of her forearm, tearing the flesh. She gritted her teeth, sucking in a breath and tightened her hold on the fowl again.

Bentley stood in shirtsleeves and a waistcoat, his cravat and coat missing, and his house looming behind him. She forced her eyes up from the exposed portion of his neck and swallowed down the sudden attraction that rose within her.

Her arm stung, but she did her best to turn her grimace into a smug smile. "No, it is not. So I should be glad I am not a young lady, shan't I?"

He studied her for a moment before his gaze flicked over her shoulder. "Will you take the chicken from Miss Green and put it away, Devlin? And lock the thing up, would you? I've half a mind to order her for my dinner."

Hattie sucked in a breath, tightening her hold on the bird. Surely he could not be in earnest.

"Yes, Your Grace," Devlin said, approaching her.

Hattie refused to release the fowl. "You will not eat her simply because my dogs wished to play."

"She will not be punished for that alone, no," Bentley assured her, though his amusement was not comforting.

"She has done nothing wrong," Hattie pressed.

"That chicken is a menace," Bentley argued, resting a fist against his waist and throwing out his other arm in exasperation. "She's terrorized more animals than just your dogs this week, and I'm certain they won't be the last."

Hattie squared her shoulders. "My dogs take equal blame in this situation, yet I have not ordered them to be put on a platter."

"Well you wouldn't, would you? They're dogs." The ease in which he stated his logic was too much for Hattie, and she barked an unladylike laugh at the absurdity of their argument.

"Will you allow my man to take the chicken now, Miss Green?" he asked.

How could she argue? It wasn't her bird. She handed the fowl into Devlin's waiting arms and pulled back, but not before Bentley noticed the red line staining her cream spencer jacket.

He deftly took hold of her wrist as the servant walked away, twisting it to expose her forearm. Bentley's gentle grip seared through the fabric and heated her skin.

His voice was steady and deep. "That chicken did this, didn't she?"

"No."

Bentley looked up, his fingers still wrapped around her wrist, but his gaze fixed on her. "No? You mean you came by it before stepping onto my lawn and stopping the fight?"

He'd seen her do that? She swallowed, searching for an answer. She didn't want this bird's life on her conscience—but neither did she want to press her lie.

His gray eyes held hers. "If I promise not to eat the chicken, will you be honest with me?"

"Yes," she said. "But only because I expect a duke to keep his word."

A shadow of emotion passed over his face, and he dropped her wrist. Clearing his throat, he placed a hand over his heart. "I vow to not eat that particular chicken, despite how horribly she terrorizes the other animals."

Hattie bit back her curiosity and the temptation to ask why he'd been bothered by what she said. She had a feeling he would not welcome further questioning on the matter. "Thank you, Your Grace. Then yes, it cut me with its talon."

"Will you come inside and allow my housekeeper to look at your arm? She has a knack for cleaning wounds."

"That is an interesting skill. Did she gain it because of your knack for *obtaining* wounds?"

His lips did not so much as flicker. Had she been impertinent? Well, Hattie's cut wasn't too deep, but it continued to bleed over her cream-colored sleeve. She could certainly make it home and allow Agnes to tend to it, but she would likely never have another opportunity to see the interior of Wolfeton House. After the duke's reclusive behavior, hiding here for so many years, she couldn't deny how wildly curious she was about his house. She badly wanted to see it.

When he did not respond to her jest, she swallowed her pride. "That would be very kind of your housekeeper, Your Grace. Thank you."

He looked surprised. Had he expected that he would need to convince her further? He gestured toward the house. "This way, then."

Stepping alongside him, Hattie motioned to her dogs to follow. Daisy and Rosie calmly walked beside them as they made their way across the lawn. When they reached the door, she turned and put a hand on each of their heads. "You stay right here. Understand?"

Their dark eyes blinked up at her. It would be an utter miracle if they obeyed, but it was worth trying.

Bentley opened the door for her, and she paused, turning back to where her dogs sat, their tails wagging behind them on the gravel. "And no more chasing chickens." Rosie lowered her head, laying down, and Daisy barked once.

If only Lucy could have watched that interaction, she would have been hard-pressed to argue her point further. The dogs could clearly understand Hattie.

"You have quite a way with animals," Bentley said, following her inside.

She shrugged. "I think you mean I have respect for animals."

"It's the same thing?"

"It ought to be."

The small entryway opened up to a dark, wood-paneled corridor. It appeared exactly like she imagined it would. The interior was tasteful but masculine, with navy window coverings and a long, burgundy rug lining the floor. Doors blended into the mahogany-paneled walls, and it was impossible to tell just how many there were. A man had clearly designed this home, and it smelled faintly of roasted meat and wood polish.

Bentley passed her, opening the door to his left as a tall, white-haired man appeared from another room.

"Egerton," Bentley said, "our neighbor has sustained an injury to her arm. Would you send for Mrs. Notley and whatever supplies she might need to clean this up?"

Egerton glanced at her arm and nodded before turning away.

"Right this way." Bentley led Hattie into what appeared to be a parlor. Light streamed in through open windows and fell on the blue carpet in the center of the wood-planked floor. A seating area before the fire contained a brown sofa opposite leather armchairs, and Bentley directed Hattie toward one of the chairs.

She paused on the carpet, her attention stolen by the magnificent painting hanging above the mantel, its simple gilded frame encompassing a lovely seaside image. A sheer white cliffside curved around the top corner and dropped into a tumultuous ocean, pale sand spreading forward from the shoreline and out of sight. The detail of the light reflecting on the waves was magnificent; one lone, black-headed gull perched on the sand, its faint footprints erased by a receding wave. Hattie noted the detail in the white-capped waves and the bird's charcoal shadow with awe. Such expertise was beyond her. Some could practice and hone their skill until greatness was achieved, and others were gifted their ability from heaven. She had a feeling the artist of this painting was the latter.

"Do you like it?" Bentley asked, patiently waiting for her to take her seat.

Nodding, she had trouble tearing her gaze away from the landscape. She wanted to study it, to learn from it, to use it to become better herself. "It's breathtaking."

A short woman bustled through the open door with a basin of water in one hand and a mound of clean rags in the other.

"Ah, Mrs. Notley, allow me to introduce our neighbor, Miss Hattie Green."

"How do you do, ma'am?" Mrs. Notley asked, bobbing a quick curtsy. Her gray hair was mostly covered in a white cap and thin, silver-rimmed spectacles perched on her pointed nose.

Hattie had seen this woman at church many times but had never had occasion to speak to her. The housekeeper's voice was warmer than she expected. "I'm well enough. Except for this." She raised her arm and Mrs. Notley clucked her tongue, scurrying across the room and taking order of the situation at once. She sat Hattie in the chair nearest the warm fire and set to work helping her remove her arm from the spencer's sleeve.

Bentley allowed them room, seating himself on the sofa opposite. His pale gray eyes were steady, alert. They were trained on Hattie as though she was a wild animal and he was curiously waiting to see what she would do next.

Hattie liked being in that position very much, indeed.

CHAPTER 6

*B*entley watched his stout housekeeper tend to Miss Green's wound. The wretched chicken had done a number on her arm, and he was surprised to find that the gash looked deeper than it had originally appeared. Mrs. Notley cleaned it thoroughly, though, and wrapped a small bandage around Miss Green's arm. Lifting the discarded spencer, she clucked her tongue again. He wondered if she realized that she sounded much like the animal who had inflicted the wound on their trespasser.

For Hattie Green was no guest of his. He would not allow his mind to classify her so amiably.

"Nasty rip, dear," Mrs. Notley said, her lips pinched as she inspected the torn sleeve. "Shall I have my girl sew it up for you?"

"No, I thank you." Miss Green reached for the spencer, an easy smile resting on her pink lips. "My maid is fantastic with a needle. She'll be able to do it justice, I am sure."

"If she is able to remove the stain," Mrs. Notley added.

Miss Green looked to the rust-colored blood stain drying on

the frayed edges. "I do hope she might be successful. This is my favorite short jacket."

Bentley cleared his throat, garnering attention from both women. "If not, you must allow me to replace it."

Miss Green gave him a curious glance. "You needn't concern yourself with this, Your Grace. My maid is quite skilled at removing stains." She grimaced. "The poor thing should be, since I've given her ample practice."

Mrs. Notley gathered the used rags and basin of water and busied herself with clearing them from the parlor.

"Removing stains from everything except gloves?" Bentley asked.

Miss Green's sharp gaze flicked to him, confusion clouding her dark, speckled brow. She was so uniquely beautiful, Bentley had a mind, as he had many times since first meeting this woman, to paint her. He'd come close to asking if she would be willing to arrange a sitting, but reason took hold, and he refrained—if only just. She was remarkably handsome, done over in varying shades of brown from her hair, to her eyes, to her freckle-covered skin. The combination was striking in an unusual way.

But he could not ask her to sit for a portrait without giving her false ideas of his motives, surely. How was a man to kindly explain that he only wanted to capture her likeness, that he did not have any designs on her, without sounding rude? He couldn't. He did not know how.

Her current confusion was entertaining. "My gloves? I do not know what you refer to."

"That day we met in the milliner's shop, she pressed you to purchase gloves on the basis of—"

"Oh, that." Miss Green waved a hand dismissively. "My maid Agnes was able to remove the chocolate stain from my old gloves. Well, mostly. It is *hardly* noticeable, you understand. I'm certain no one shall inspect my inner elbow at the next ball I attend, so I am not overly concerned."

"If your maid was able to remove the stain, why did you purchase the gloves?"

Miss Green blinked at him. He was no simpleton, but when she looked at him that way, he certainly felt like one. "Are you familiar with Mrs. Dawson?"

He shifted, recalling Egerton's positive report of the woman. "I've visited her shop a small handful of times."

"She has been forced to cope with losing a good portion of her clientele to Melbury the last few months. I would never offer the woman charity, for she is far too proud to accept it, but I can buy an extra set of gloves to help her, can I not?"

"You can." And here Bentley had believed Miss Green had allowed herself to be swindled. He'd misjudged her, and it caused him to wonder what else about this woman he'd misunderstood.

Her gaze roamed back to the painting above the mantel, and pride swelled his chest. He'd caught her looking at it time and again while Mrs. Notley had tended to her arm, and anxious energy skittered through his limbs. He wanted to ask what she thought of it but could hardly manage to bear an unfavorable answer. The result was his own heightened nerves and a very dissatisfied feeling.

It was best if he changed the subject. No, scratch that. What was *best* would be to remove this woman from his house and his life forthwith. It was not wise to mix with the locals. Bentley had spent the better part of seven years avoiding this very thing. His desire to paint this woman and her different features did not —*could not*—override his wish for privacy.

"Do you know the artist?"

Bentley stilled. "Yes."

Her eyes lit up, and he feared she would ask him to put her

in touch with the man. What would he say then? He would not lie.

Bentley stood. "May I escort you home, Miss Green?" Rude, perhaps, but it was time to put an end to this visit. Though in truth, he hoped she would deny him the privilege of walking her home. Less time for conversation meant less time to grow interested in the things she spoke of. And he was already far too interested in what she had to say for his own good.

"I thank you, Your Grace, but you needn't bother. My dogs are sufficient guardians. To be perfectly frank, I think it best if we are not seen together." She stood before sliding her arms into her ripped spencer jacket. Pausing, she glanced around the room. "Please thank your housekeeper for me. I did not realize she left the room. I suppose I was just so taken by the painting to see much of anything else."

Bentley fought the approval that burned within him, shoving it down and snuffing it out before it could grow. He looked about for a bonnet until he realized that she hadn't been wearing one.

"I will most certainly let her know of your gratitude." He motioned for her to precede him from the room, and she obliged, glancing over her shoulder when they reached the front door.

Her forehead was creased in thought. "I can understand why you feel you are an expert on matters regarding painting and colors if that is the sort of example you have to study." She chuckled. "I was rather put off by your commentary on my colors the other day, but even I can recognize such immense talent as that."

How would she feel if she knew that it was *his* talent of which she spoke? He swallowed against a dry throat.

Egerton stepped forward and opened the front door for them, and Miss Green moved past him and down the steps. Her dogs were running about the grass to their right, but no chickens appeared, and neither did that pesky cat.

When had his home become so overrun with obstinate animals?

"Perhaps I will even forgive you now."

Bentley nearly missed his footing on the front steps. "I hadn't realized I was in jeopardy of remaining unforgiven." The truth was that he hadn't even known she harbored ill feelings toward him at all. She had seemed perfectly at ease in his presence for the last half-hour.

Her nose wrinkled. "Can you blame me? It isn't pleasant to be told you didn't do something well."

Bentley closed the door behind him, stepping down until he paused on the gravel beside her. He might not be interested in a friendship with this woman, but he did not want to anger her, and being rude had never been his intent. He cleared his throat, hoping to convey his feelings without divulging too much personal information. "I have an…obsession, if you will, with colors. I've taken an interest in the process of blending paints, and my only intention was to help, not to criticize. I found your painting quite stunning."

"Except for the shadows beneath the house."

A chuckle rumbled his chest and slipped from his lips. Her quick responses caught him off guard but were not unpleasant. "They looked…fine."

"Yes," she said, grinning. "*Fine*. Not great."

He fought a smile. For someone who harbored ill will toward him, Miss Green certainly did not seem perturbed. Quite the opposite, in fact. She appeared amused. "I will keep my opinions to myself in future."

A breeze drew over them, lifting a lock of her brown hair and drawing it over her forehead. She tucked it away. "In future, you shall not have the opportunity to give opinions on my work, I should think."

He clutched his chest. "I am in your black books?"

"No, Your Grace. I'll forgive you with time, I'm sure." Her teasing eyes belied her grudge, and Bentley was nearly positive that she was saying it in jest. Nearly. "But we shan't have occasion to meet again, surely. Not unless my dogs take a shining to your chicken once more. I hadn't intended to return to your property."

He believed her. A week had passed since he'd come upon her in the woods, and his daily walks hadn't procured any more visits from neighbors straying from their land.

"Daisy!" she called. "Rosie, come!"

The dogs obeyed at once, crossing the lawn toward them. "They listen well."

"Sometimes," she said, her smile wide. "Only when it suits them, of course."

"Oh, of course."

She turned to walk away, and Bentley fought the desire to lengthen their conversation. Miss Green was quite willing to not press an acquaintance with him, and while it somewhat baffled him, he was grateful for it. Though learning her reasons wouldn't be amiss, he did not need more information about her. He was teetering dangerously on the edge of wrecking his perfectly situated life as it was.

"Good day, then," he called.

Miss Green dipped in a curtsy, throwing a smile over her shoulder. "Good day, Your Grace. And remember, you shan't eat that chicken. You promised."

"No, I shall not."'

Absently rubbing the brown head of one of the flower-named dogs—he didn't know which—Miss Green took off across the lawn without looking back. Her silhouette disappeared into the line of trees, the playful dogs flanking her until they could no longer be seen. Bentley fought the urge to call out to her, for he had no inclination *why* he should do so, or what he would even say to her.

Returning to his house, he encountered Egerton in the entryway.

"Do you plan to resume your activities in the blue room, Your Grace?"

"Yes, Egerton. I will need extra candles, for the light will soon be fading."

"Of course, Your Grace."

Passing Egerton, Bentley rolled up his shirtsleeves and let himself into the blue room. The tall, wide windows along the far wall were sparse of light now that the sun was beginning its descent, and he was momentarily irritated that he'd be forced to rely on lamplight now. Firelight was of a warm hue and tended to jump about, neither of which were ideal for painting. Perhaps he would be better off drawing for the rest of the afternoon.

He dropped the used brushes into the glass of turpentine and looked once more at the large canvas near the window, its half-painted scene vivid on one corner and blank on the other, appearing as though the cat he had begun painting was melting from the canvas. He planned to depict the cat sprawling as it often was of late on a chair near the fire. The cat itself was currently nowhere to be seen, but Bentley had come to expect that from him. He appeared when he was hungry then napped on the chair or disappeared for hours at a time.

Taking his notebook from the table, he selected a charcoal pencil from his implement drawer and lowered himself into a chair beside the window. His fingers began before his mind settled on a subject, and he watched an image take form on the page as though he was not creating it himself. Indeed, sometimes he wondered if the pictures formed of their own accord, for he did not feel himself consciously choose the strokes necessary to make the gentle slope of a nose or the dashes of dark eyelashes against a rounded cheek.

Miss Green appeared on the page through no fault of Bentley's, and he watched her take shape, looking down as she'd been at her arm as Mrs. Notley had gone about dressing her wound. He completed the drawing and stared at it, unsure of how to go about creating her freckles. A few light dots of the charcoal seemed to work well enough, but they were not exactly right.

Turning the page over, Bentley began again. This time he angled her face up as though she was looking at the painting above his parlor mantel. The painting *he* had done. He added the shine to her eyes, the slightly lifted eyebrows. He could see her face so clearly in his mind that it was easy to translate it directly to the paper. When he completed the portrait, he leaned back and studied it.

The freckles were still not quite right. Which was entirely frustrating. Bentley didn't often struggle with his sketching. It was a skill that had always come naturally to him.

"Your dinner is prepared, Your Grace," Egerton said from the doorway.

Gads, was it that late already? Bentley stared at the notebook in his lap, faintly aware of the flickering candlelight around him. His eyebrows were drawn together so tightly he was certain to bring on a headache if he was not careful. Closing the notebook, he dropped it onto the table beside him and rubbed his thumb and forefinger along his eyebrows.

"In the dining room?" he asked.

"Yes, Your Grace."

He nodded. "I'll be in shortly."

Egerton quietly left the room, and Bentley rose, crossing to the window. The darkness beyond the panes was only broken by flickering candlelight from the lamp behind him, and he looked out over where the treeline should be, his mind conjuring the image he'd seen earlier that day. He'd been standing just here, considering the brown he should use for the leather chair underneath the cat in his painting when the volley of barking and chicken squawks had pulled him from his activity.

It was with amusement that he'd watched Devlin try to manage the chicken while simultaneously beating off the dogs. But his feelings had quickly shifted to concern when Miss Green broke through the trees, vexation written on the freckled lines of her face. Bentley stared into the darkness now, picturing her outrage upon finding Devlin trying to keep her dogs away from the irascible chicken.

Bentley could have stayed away, allowed Devlin to—albeit, unsmoothly—deal with the situation, but once his eyes laid upon Miss Green's face, he had dropped the paintbrush and made for outside at once. His body had moved without his mind first determining it to be a good idea, and now he wondered exactly what damage his actions had caused.

He'd let the woman into his home, and she'd met his housekeeper. Mrs. Notley, Egerton, and the rest of the staff had done a decent job of attending church the last seven years without creating relationships within the parish. Their tight-lipped refusal to speak about their employer in the beginning had nipped any further attempts at gossip in the bud, and while he'd once felt guilty for what he'd asked of them, ultimately, it was their choice. Each of his servants had known exactly what they were agreeing to when they had come to Devonshire with him, and his wishes had not changed.

Scrubbing a hand over his face, he turned his back to the window. He'd been weak today, curious, allowing himself to indulge in the company of someone else for only a moment. But now his walls needed to be replaced, his protection reinforced. Bentley only hoped his carelessness hadn't jeopardized everything he'd spent the last seven years building up.

CHAPTER 7

*H*attie knocked on the door to her papa's study before running her fingers lightly over the scratch on her forearm. It had mostly healed over the previous two days, and now only a faintly raised red line remained. She found herself drawn to it, tracing it as her traitorous mind repeatedly returned to that day in the duke's house. She had a naturally curious bent, and the foray into his guarded, secretive house hadn't staunched her curiosity—it had only made her want to learn more about the man.

"Enter," Papa called.

She let herself in, turning the ridged, wooden handle and leaning forward in the doorway. "I only wanted to ask if you've seen Romeo, my cat?"

Papa looked up from where he sat on a chair near the fire, a line creasing between his thick, gray eyebrows. A gun sat on the low table before him, spread out in pieces over a large cloth beside a small bottle of oil and a rag. "Still can't find the thing?"

"No, I can't. And it's been over a week now." She shifted on her feet. She had half a mind to remind Papa that his study was not the best place to clean his gun—she wouldn't convince him to allow a servant to do it, for he *enjoyed* it, somehow—but he would not be bothered to move. It was his house, after all. And she wasn't there to reprimand. She was there on important matters. "I'm beginning to worry."

Papa lifted a finger and ran it over his chin, setting down a piece of the dismantled gun. "Have you asked in the stables?"

"Yes, but they haven't seen him."

"The old barn?"

She hadn't considered that. Shaking her head, she folded her arms over her chest. "Do you think Romeo would have gone so far? He's lived in this house since he was a tiny kitten. I'm not sure he would know how to reach the barn or possess the ability to make it so far as that."

"Maybe not intentionally, but if he got lost, he very well could have remained there. I'm certain the building has enough rodents to keep him alive and happy."

Hattie wrinkled her nose. "I will ride out there and look around."

"And take—"

"I know," she said, crossing the room to place a kiss on his wrinkly cheek. "Take Agnes with me."

"Or a groom would do in a pinch, but I don't like you traveling to the edges of our property alone."

"Of course not, I would never be so horribly ill-mannered as that." She grinned, and her father chuckled despite the falsity of her words. They both knew he was far too indulgent for her good, but at her age, she hardly needed a nursemaid. She was smart enough to know which things she could push her boundaries on, and which she shouldn't. Her brother had gone away to school so long ago that Hattie felt as though she and her father had lived alone together for most of her life. It wasn't the case, but she was hard-pressed to remember clearly living there with other people.

Hattie reached the door when Papa's voice stopped her. "I need to speak to you tonight about your brother and his wife."

Her hand rested again on the ridged handle, and she tightened her grip, the wooden grooves biting into her palm. She fixed a pleasant smile on her lips and glanced over her shoulder. "Can we not speak on the matter now?" She very much hated putting off uncomfortable things. Better to get them done and over with.

Papa looked thoughtful, his wrinkled skin forming deep grooves on his forehead. "I suppose, if your cat hunt can spare a moment."

"He's been missing for a week and a half. I'm certain forcing him to wait another half-hour won't be too horrific." Or, she rather hoped.

Papa gestured to the plush, maroon wingback chair beside his. Hattie closed the door behind her and took the seat, curling up and tucking her feet beneath her.

"Jeffrey tells me that you've been avoiding Lucy."

She wanted to retort that she didn't see the trouble with that at all but bit her tongue. Papa did not appear to be in a humorous mood today. "I do not find her pleasant company, Papa. Can you blame me for doing my best to spend minimal time with my sister-in-law? I am certain, were I to be around her more often, that I would say or do something which would make you very upset with me."

Papa smiled softly. "Yes, but I have faith in your ability to curb your tongue when it is absolutely necessary. Can you not make more of an effort to welcome her? Until you marry and leave me, you are the woman of this house, and that is your duty."

"I believe Lucy feels she has more right to claim that distinction."

Papa sighed, rubbing his hand over his face. "Hattie, I am only asking you to make a greater effort. Unless you would prefer to come with me to visit your Aunt Sadler, you must do better to act a proper hostess here while I am gone."

"A proper hostess," she repeated.

Papa nodded. "And it would not hurt to try and learn a thing or two from Lucy while she is here. She has experience that you could benefit from."

Lucy's experience was limited to embroidery and hosting dinner parties. Both of which Hattie had well under control. The only thing Lucy had done in her life that Hattie had not was get married, and *that* was not something Hattie was interested in actively pursuing at this time. She was wholly aware that her husband was out there somewhere, and she had faith she would find him—or the opposite, perhaps, if he found her first—when the time was right. Waiting had grown tiresome, it was true, but she would not press fate.

Her husband would arrive in her life in due time, without her forcing the issue.

"What if I persist in the belief that Lucy has nothing worthwhile to teach me?"

A knock came at the door and Papa looked up, his lips pinched in displeasure. Lowering his voice, he said, "You will alter your attitude toward Jeffrey's wife, or you will come with me to my sister's house."

Travel in the cold, wet, winter to sleep in a damp room? Hattie thought not.

"Enter," Papa called. He left her no room to argue. She could abide by his strictures or suffer.

Though in truth, both courses of action seemed full of suffering to Hattie.

The door opened, and their butler stepped forward. "Mrs. Fremont has come to see Miss Hattie, sir. I've directed her to the parlor."

"I shall come to her," Hattie said, rising. She wouldn't bother replying to Papa yet, not until she had fully thought through the situation. She was of half a mind to join him on his journey if for no other reason than that he did not expect it of her. But that was the rub. He'd chosen an alternative she rather despised.

It was an interesting predicament when the lesser of two evils happened to be *Lucy*.

"Thank you, Papa. I will think on it."

His thick, gray eyebrows raised a fraction. "I leave in two days, Hattie. You don't have much time to think."

"Then you shall receive an answer soon."

She leaned over and kissed his wrinkled cheek again before flouncing from the room and hurrying upstairs to change into her navy-blue riding habit. If she was lucky, she would find Amelia Fremont in the parlor alone and could convince her friend to ride out to the old barn with her before Lucy could waylay them. Lucy had been dropping little hints of her desire to attend Melbury's assemblies the last few days, and Hattie wouldn't put it past the woman to try and draw Amelia into the scheme.

After changing quickly with Agnes's help, she quietly snuck downstairs and into the parlor. Hattie was relieved to find Amelia alone, regally sitting on the pale pink settee. Her bright red hair was pulled back into an effortless, elegant knot, vibrant against flawless, pale skin. She was immaculate as ever, and her eyes lit up when they fell on Hattie. "I have something exciting to share."

"Come, quickly," Hattie said, crossing the room with haste and reaching for her friend's hand.

"But Hattie—"

"Shhh. We mustn't alert anyone else to your presence here." She motioned to Amelia's riding habit, the long, emerald skirt pooling on the floor at her feet. "I see you've ridden over. Fancy a ride out to the old barn?"

Amelia's red eyebrows set high on her forehead as she

allowed Hattie to pull her up from the settee. "That would be fine."

"You can tell me your news when we're safe."

"Safe from whom?" Amelia asked, startled.

Hattie leaned in and whispered. "Lucy, of course."

Amelia sighed. "You realize she is only trying to be your friend."

"No, she is trying to get me *married.*"

They slipped outside and crossed the drive toward the stables. The cold, November air seeped through Hattie's riding habit, and she considered returning to the house for a thicker protectant against the weather. The sky was cloudy but lacked wind, and it did not appear as though it would rain. She realized this was probably not how Amelia had wished to spend her afternoon, but they could be fast. A quick ride to the barn to check for Romeo, and then they could return and warm up beside the fire with a bracing cup of tea.

She could even reward Amelia with a plate of ginger biscuits if Cook had any remaining from yesterday.

"That would be such a horrible thing, wouldn't it?" Amelia asked when they rounded the bend toward the stables. "Oh, marriage—absolutely terrible."

Hattie shot her friend an unamused glance, ignoring her grin. Amelia had only been married for two months now, but she had glowed with happiness from the moment she agreed to become Charles Fremont's wife. It would have been sickening if Hattie wasn't so happy for the pair of them.

"You've made your point."

"I recall a certain event on Midsummer's Eve where you attempted to discover exactly who your husband was going to be. If that was not an effort toward marriage, Hattie, then what is?"

"That was *different.*" Hattie widened her eyes to beg Amelia's silence before stepping into the stables to request her horse and to have Amelia's brought out with it. Rejoining her friend, she continued to defend her choices. "I will not force marriage into my life, Amelia. My efforts on Midsummer's Eve were to gather information, nothing more." She scoffed. "I have a far greater respect for fate than that."

Lucy stepped from the stables, her fair hair pulled away from her face and hidden beneath a riding hat. The skirts of her violet habit were clutched in her fists and lifted from the damp earth. "Are you planning to ride now, too? What a lovely surprise."

Hattie gritted her teeth to avoid cursing. How had she not seen Lucy inside when she went to request the horses? Had the woman been hiding? No, that was madness. The only reason she would have to do such a thing was if she was trying to eavesdrop.

Well, perhaps not complete madness, then.

"Good day, Mrs. Green," Amelia said, dropping into a brief curtsy. "It has been so long since I've had the pleasure of your company."

"Good day, Mrs...." Lucy paused, glancing between the two of them. It was through no fault of hers that she did not recall Amelia's surname. It had changed more than once in recent years.

"Fremont," Amelia supplied. "I recently married Charles Fremont, one of our neighbors here."

"Ah, yes. I did hear of that." Lucy turned expectant, rounded eyes on Hattie.

Oh, drat. Hattie was going to have to invite her along. There was no way around it. "We were going to ride out to the old barn to look for my missing cat, if you would like to join us?" She would like to add the caveat that neither woman was allowed to speak of Hattie's marital prospects but bit her tongue.

"That sounds intriguing."

Of course Lucy would make her acceptance sound pitiful, as

though the only reason she was coming along was because she had nothing better to do. If she was truly that indifferent, she ought to search out her husband and ask him to devise a scheme to entertain her. Or better yet, return her to London.

The grooms brought their horses out and assisted the women in mounting, and Hattie informed them that Lucy would no longer need an escort, for she was joining Hattie and Amelia.

Lucy looked over quickly. "You think it safe to ride out without a groom?"

"I'm not sure what danger can befall the three of us when we remain together and within the bounds of my property." To say nothing of the fact that two of the women were married.

Lucy appeared unconvinced but did not press the issue.

They rode out past the lake and the duke's woods, over the rolling hills speckled with grazing cattle, and toward the old barn on the edge of the Green's property.

"If our hunt is unsuccessful, we can call on Giulia and inquire of their household," Amelia suggested, sliding down from her tall, dark horse when they reached the barn. She unlatched the door and let it swing wide, disturbing the dust and raising a cloud of dirt.

Lucy delicately coughed from where she sat upon her horse, yards away from the debris.

Hattie ignored her sister-in-law and led her horse inside, startling at the sudden sound of a bird in the rafters.

"It's been too long since we've come here," Amelia said softly. "I feel as though we've let the barn down."

Her friends had let *Hattie* down, but she would never admit so. Hattie and Amelia had come here weekly to meet with Mabel and Giulia under the guise of a literary society. As the women got married, pregnant, and—in Mabel's case—moved to the northern coast of Devon, a good two-hour ride away, meeting weekly grew impossible. Amelia, Hattie, and Giulia still met frequently, but their houses were more practical locations as

Giulia had grown pregnant and now had a small babe to contend with.

Standing in the middle of the quiet, secluded barn now, Hattie felt the bitterness of what had passed mixed with the sweetness of old memories. It was not realistic, but she wished for the earlier days again. Though, she would never wish for any of her friends to remain as unmarried as she was, so it was moot. Hattie wanted two things at the same time, which was both impossible and unreasonable.

"I will look about the horse stalls if you'd like to check the loft?" Amelia asked.

Nodding, Hattie made her way toward the ladder and climbed up to the raised loft area. She checked the cushions and blankets left behind, the corners and dust-covered floor, but nothing appeared disturbed by a cat. Though Papa was correct, and she could see the evidence of rodents having chewed around the edges of the wooden sofa legs.

She unlatched the loft door and pushed it open to reveal rolling lands and Giulia's castle off in the distance. Hattie hadn't painted up here in quite a while, and she had the sudden, overwhelming urge to do just that. She could return tomorrow in the morning light, set up her things, and spend the entire day up here lost in the silence. The prospect sounded lovely.

A shriek pulled her from her thoughts, causing Hattie to startle and her foot to slide on the dusty, wood-planked floor. Falling down on her backside, she hit the floor hard, and her feet shot out in front of her, dangling over the edge of the open loft door. She clutched the frame for support, her heart hammering.

"Hattie!" Lucy screamed.

"I am safe," Hattie called back, her body flushed with cold from the fright. "No thanks to you," she muttered under her breath. If Lucy hadn't screamed in the first place, Hattie wouldn't have slipped. She drew in a sustaining breath and sat up fully. "What is it? What did you see?"

"You were so close to the edge," Lucy called, still seated atop her horse, her gloved hand raised to block the sunlight from her eyes. To her credit, she looked absolutely stricken. It was touching to know Lucy would be so concerned if Hattie *had* been close to falling from the loft. She hadn't been in even the remotest danger, but that was beside the point.

"Any sign of Romeo?" Hattie asked.

Lucy shook her head. "Nothing down here."

Hattie's shoulders deflated. Where was that blasted cat? "I'll be down soon." Rising, she closed the loft door and descended the ladder, slightly shaken from her near fall.

"Any sign of him?" she asked, coming up behind Amelia.

Amelia shook her head. "It's too dim to really see much, but there's no sign of any cats." She reached forward and squeezed Hattie's forearm. "I'm sorry. I wish we were successful. Shall we call on Giulia while we are this close and inquire of her servants?"

Hattie nodded. "They'll find it odd, I'm sure. We've so many cats roaming our stables, why should one lost feline matter? But he's mine. None of them are *Romeo*."

"We'll find him."

Hattie tried to smile. "But first, tell me of your news while we have a moment alone. There's no telling when we'll have another chance with Lucy on our tail."

Amelia looked over her shoulder at the open door. Lowering her voice, she leaned in. "It is still early days, but I think I may be pregnant." A smile spread over her lips. "I wanted you to be the first to know."

Joy erupted in Hattie's chest, and she pulled her friend in for a hug. "What has Charles said?"

Amelia leaned back, her nose scrunching. "I haven't shared my thoughts with him yet. I wanted to be completely certain before allowing him to raise his hopes. You are the first I've told."

"You've not seen a doctor or a midwife, then?"

Amelia raised her eyebrows. "My brother is the only doctor nearby, Hattie. I think you know the answer to that already."

Hattie lifted a staying hand. "Yes, that is what I thought. So do not argue, because I know you are not fond of her, but have you considered going to see Mrs. Fowler?"

Amelia nodded. "I trust her midwifery. It is only the white magic that puts me off the woman. I would be glad to visit her, but I did not want to go alone."

"You don't need to. I will go with you." Horse hooves stomped as a shadow passed the open door, and Hattie lowered her voice. "But not today. Soon, perhaps? First, we must rid ourselves of Lucy."

CHAPTER 8

*H*alstead Manor was an ancient castle that had been misnamed long ago with the intent to deceive. The people who resided within the home now were, quite opposingly, immensely honest and good-hearted creatures. When they informed Hattie that they had not seen her cat, she believed them and was disheartened by another failed search.

"He's gone," she said, slumping against the tufted sofa in Halstead's drawing room.

Amelia stood nearby, swaying softly with Giulia's baby swaddled in her arms. Her news from earlier was most welcome, and Hattie knew her friend was going to make a wonderful mother. It was with equal parts joy for Amelia's news and disappointment that her sweet cat was still missing that Hattie sat amidst her friends and frowned.

Lucy perched on the wingback chair opposite them, her hands folded primly in her lap. "You do not know that, yet. Have you searched the woods near your house? I would imagine the cat is more likely to have ended up lost in those trees than this far away."

Hattie wanted to be annoyed at her sister-in-law for suggesting such a reasonable course of action when she was too focused on their failures, but that would be petty. Papa was right. Hattie needed to make a concerted effort to be patient with Lucy, particularly when the woman's only fault was being too overbearing. She closed her eyes, reaching for patience, and nodded.

"Beware of the duke, though," Giulia said, chuckling. "I've heard he is quite a surly man. You wouldn't wish to be caught trespassing on his land."

Hattie's eyes opened, and she sat up. "The Duke of Bentley?"

"Oh, is that his name?" Giulia shrugged. "I only knew he was your neighbor. He has quite the reputation for being unpleasant, does he not?"

"My brother met him a few years ago when his butler took ill and needed a doctor," Amelia said, continuing to sway as the baby slept in her arms. Her graceful steps carried her in a smooth oval before the fire, the long skirt of her habit trailing behind her like a train. "He could not be called friendly, but Andrew didn't find him rude, either. Merely uninterested in pursuing conversation."

"There is nothing wrong with that," Hattie said. Each of the women in the room turned to look at her, raised eyebrows or widened eyes adorning their surprised faces. Had she been too bold? She swallowed. "I only mean that he likely has a good reason for choosing such a secluded life. I'm certain he would not begrudge me searching his woods for my cat. But perhaps I will send a servant with a note to ask permission first."

"Or perhaps *he's* taken your cat," Giulia said, "and that's why you cannot find it."

Amelia laughed, and Lucy dipped her chin, her expression uncomfortable. Hattie knew that wasn't the case, though. She would have seen Romeo while she was in the duke's house if it was. It was on the tip of her tongue to say as much, but she caught Lucy's eye and stopped herself.

Her friends could be trusted to learn of her meetings with Bentley and not think anything of them, but if *Lucy* knew of Hattie's somewhat amiable encounters with him, she would not be able to let it rest. There was no knowing what Lucy would do to get Hattie married—particularly to a single man of such rank and distinction—not when the woman was so determined to do so.

"Shall we look in the woods on our way back to your house?" Amelia asked.

And risk seeing the duke while Lucy was with them? Not a chance. "I would feel better if I could send a note first requesting permission. We wouldn't want to be caught trespassing."

Her friends were correct. It was a good place to search. But it would be better if Hattie was able to first give Bentley her reasons for stepping foot back on his land. Another chance encounter and he was bound to believe she was wandering his woods hoping to be found by him. She might want to be married, but she was not so desperate as that.

Giulia nodded. "That's wise. Best not to cause any problems with your neighbor if you can help it."

Lucy looked between them. "Do none of you understand what you are saying?"

Giulia blinked, taken aback. "What do you mean?"

Lucy glanced between each of the women in the condescending way of hers, her head tilted back just enough that she could look down the bridge of her nose at them. "Your home neighbors the Duke of Bentley, and none of you have thought to utilize that connection?"

"There is no *connection* to utilize, Lucy," Hattie said, doing her best to sound reasonable. "The duke is a recluse and will speak to no one. He even refuses visits from our vicar."

In this case, mere proximity was not cause for celebration, not when the man was a recluse. Hattie had been Bentley's neighbor for seven years before meeting him, and even then it had occurred purely by chance. If she hadn't nearly fallen into Mrs. Dawson's mirror, they never would have interacted in the shop. There was no way to know for certain, but Hattie assumed that if they hadn't interacted then, Bentley likely wouldn't have spoken to her when he found her in the woods. The tiniest moment—her clumsiness, walking without looking at where she was stepping—had set into motion an acquaintanceship between herself and the duke. Regardless, she had promptly squashed it out of respect for him and to protect herself.

If Lucy thought seeking out a relationship with Bentley was worthwhile, she was mistaken. Before their chance encounters, the most Hattie had seen of Bentley had largely been from a great distance or as a shadow within the confines of his carriage as he came and went, seldom as that was. So much so that he'd been unrecognizable to her, and she was his closest neighbor.

He'd gone to extreme efforts to remain alone. He likely had his reasons, and they ought to respect that.

"I propose a different plan," Lucy said, settling into her seat as though she was warming to her idea. "What if we search the woods without permission? We have a good reason: the cat. And if we are found, that can provide us an introduction to the duke."

"But we don't *want* an introduction," Hattie said, her teeth beginning to ache from her forceful clenching. Did Lucy not realize how scheming and manipulative she sounded?

"Why not?"

Amelia's lips pinched together. "It feels like an invasion of his privacy."

Hattie nodded. "Exactly."

"But," Giulia said thoughtfully, "you really *are* just looking for your cat. What if that is all it takes to meet the duke and then you fall madly in love? You could marry your neighbor and never have to leave Devon again."

"Except this is not his ducal seat," Hattie reminded them. "He has chosen to hide here for a reason."

"That is a valid point," Giulia said. She gasped. "What if he is running from something terrible? Or perhaps he committed a crime in a different country and is hiding away now. Maybe you oughtn't try to meet him after all."

Lucy scoffed. "Everyone knows why the duke is hiding here."

All heads turned her direction.

"He ran away just days after his father's death and has never once stepped foot in lords. He clearly does not wish to be a duke and is hiding out here to avoid his responsibility. I would not be surprised if he doesn't allow his servants to address him by his title, even."

Hattie knew that was not the case. His butler had said *Your Grace* several times, as had she, and Bentley hadn't once flinched.

"All this is conjecture, and it does us no good to make assumptions about a man we do not know," Amelia said with steady reserve.

"How virtuous you all are," Lucy said. "I feel quite chastised now. Though I have a feeling you would perhaps not judge my methods once Hattie and the duke were wed."

Giulia grinned. "Likely not."

The women said their farewells shortly afterward and parted with Amelia on the lane. The day had moved into afternoon, the sun beginning its descent across the wide, open sky. A layer of clouds blanketed the earth, giving the cool day a faint grayish glow and blocking any potential warmth. Hattie shivered from the chill air as it reached through the gaps in her habit's sleeve and neckline.

"Do you truly believe it is so wrong to seek out an opportunity to meet a man?" Lucy asked from atop her borrowed mare.

"I've sought plenty of opportunities to do just that. But I won't try to *capture* anyone, regardless of their status."

Lucy scoffed. "Then why are you so opposed to marriage?"

Hattie's fingers itched within their gloves to slap her reins and urge her horse into a full gallop away from her sister-in-law. It was as though the woman intentionally did not hear the things Hattie said. She felt as though she could not have made her position on this matter more clear, and she was blasted tired of speaking about it.

"I will find my husband when I am ready, Lucy."

"Oh yes, of course," Lucy said mockingly. "You believe in *fate*."

"I do. Not that it should matter. My beliefs are my own, and they do no harm to you or anyone else."

Lucy's lips pinched together. "It is no secret that you do not welcome my advice, but if you would only stop to listen to me, you might understand that I do have more experience than you and could have some wisdom to impart."

Funny, Hattie felt the same in reverse. She gripped her reins tighter and forced the irritation from her face. "Very well, I promise to listen to you if you promise to listen to me in return."

"I can agree to that." Clearing her throat, Lucy slowed her horse. "I will go first. There is no harm in seeking a love match if that is what you desire. I am quite happy in mine, and it would be silly for me to suggest otherwise when I have experienced the beauty of it firsthand. But in order to make a love match, you have to put yourself in the position to actually meet gentlemen. For all you know, the man that *fate* has determined should be yours lives in Melbury. You could meet him at an assembly, fall madly in love, and be glad that fate thought to pair the two of you. But you will never meet him if you never leave your estate."

"I'm away from my estate right now," Hattie said, the words

spilling from her lips as though they chose to argue regardless of her intentions. She snapped her mouth closed.

Lucy chose to ignore her. "A concerted effort to put yourself in a position to meet gentlemen is not forcing fate, or forcing love, or whatever else you accuse me of wanting for you."

"*That* may not be, I will grant you that, but scheming to walk about the duke's woods in an effort to meet him most certainly is."

"Unless fate sent *me* along to ensure that you met the duke," Lucy quipped with a saucy smile.

Oh, heavens. The woman truly understood nothing of these matters.

They passed onto the Greens' property and skirted the lake, the grove of trees just beyond them looming in the ever-darkening afternoon. The clouds were growing thicker and the wind began to whip around them. Rain was coming. It was a blessed thing they were so close to home.

But what if Romeo *was* in those trees somewhere? He would be cold, alone, and in danger of soaking when the heavens opened. She needed to get home and write that note to the duke so she could search his trees.

"I think we ought to agree that our opinions on this will never coincide." Hattie could feel her horse growing restless under her, their slow pace grating on the mare's need to run. "And now it is my turn to explain—"

Lucy took off to the west, quickening her horse into a gallop as they moved in the direction of the woods.

Hattie watched her leave, mouth agape. Did the woman listen to nothing? They had made an agreement to each hear the other out, for heaven's sake.

Clicking her tongue, Hattie directed her horse to follow Lucy. She couldn't very well leave the woman alone in the woods or she would probably lose her way clear up to the duke's front door.

By the time Hattie reached the edge of the trees, Lucy had dismounted and ran into the dense woodland. She jumped from her horse and left it standing beside Lucy's at the perimeter of the woods, looping both horses' reins around a low branch.

The trees were too close together to make riding easy, and Hattie was glad to be on foot. She could run quickly, snatch her sister-in-law, and get back out before disturbing anyone.

And, if she was honest, she'd keep an eye out for Romeo.

"Lucy," she called as softly as she could. "Wait!"

Lucy glanced over her shoulder, smirking, but didn't respond or slow down. She moved deeper into the woods, jaggedly creating a trail that drove them closer and closer to Wolfeton House.

Anxiety skittered through Hattie as they passed the heart of the forest, every step edging them nearer to the duke's estate. If they were not careful they would soon be in his courtyard, face-to-face with Devlin, the man who'd appeared to manage the duke's livestock. Or, as luck would likely have it, the chicken itself.

"Stop!" Hattie called. "This is not funny, Lucy. Come back here!"

Lucy ignored her, seeming to pick up speed. Her easy ability to hike through the rough forest was almost more shocking than the way she deliberately went against everything Hattie had asked of her.

Clutching the long skirts of her habit, Hattie increased her pace. She would drag Lucy from these woods if that's what it took.

Lucy staggered to a sudden stop, and Hattie's heart plummeted to her stomach. Her entire body tensed when she looked beyond her sister-in-law and found a tall, dark-haired, devilishly handsome figure standing just beyond her. Hattie slowed her steps, pausing just behind Lucy.

Drat Lucy and her wretched wayward behavior. This was the

precise situation Hattie had needed to avoid. She would have been better off leaving Lucy to wander the woods alone. But then if she'd found Bentley on her own, whatever would she have done?

Lucy shot Hattie a brief, excited smile over her shoulder, her eyes bright with mischief. "See? Fate."

CHAPTER 9

*B*entley stood in the midst of his quiet, secluded woods, suddenly angry that he was no longer secluded, and neither was it quiet.

"Oh, goodness!" the woman before him said, her blue eyes rounding to such extent that she was certainly feigning her surprise. He took her measure at once. A well-tailored, violet riding habit fit her to perfection, and a matching hat sat at a jaunty angle upon her head. Blonde hair was tucked into a knot at the base of her neck, but the wisps that had escaped were a testament that she had been riding—though there was no horse in sight.

She turned her neck and said something over her shoulder, and Bentley's stomach constricted. Hattie Green was here, just behind the intruder.

It was not something he wanted to further investigate that his mind considered this blonde woman an intruder, but not the freckled beauty behind her.

"Forgive us," the blonde said. "We were only searching for—"

"My cat," Miss Green cut in, the long skirts of her habit

clutched tightly in her hands as she lifted her hem from the dirty ground. "He is missing, and we wondered if he might have escaped to these woods, but"—she clenched her teeth, sending the other woman a frustrated look—"we realize it was rude of us to trespass upon your property, and we should have first sent a note begging your permission to do so."

There was clearly something going on between the women, and Bentley was, despite himself, curious to know what it was. "That is quite all right, Miss—"

"Green!" she said, stepping forward again, her brown eyes wide as though she was trying to speak to him with her looks alone. Heavens, what was that about?

"Green," he repeated, cautiously.

She nodded vigorously, a strain of panic lacing her features. "I am Miss Hattie Green, your neighbor to the east, and I beg your forgiveness for imposing this introduction on you when you most clearly wish to keep your privacy."

The blonde woman's eyebrows pulled together, and she looked to Miss Green. "But, Hattie, surely—"

"This is my sister-in-law, Mrs. Green," Hattie said—for now he could think of her in no other way than by that name which suited her so well—grasping the woman's arm.

Bentley bowed, pretending as though he met them for the first time. Hattie clearly wished to keep their earlier interactions a secret from this woman. He could question her later—and he would find a way to do that—but for now, he could play along.

"The Duke of Bentley at your service. It is a pleasure to finally meet my neighbors."

Mrs. Green's eyes lit up, and she squared her shoulders. "Thank you, Your Grace. Do you mind terribly if we continue our search?"

"No, by all means." He gestured to the trees around them. "Though it will soon be growing dark."

"We will not trespass upon your kindness further, Your

Grace," Hattie said. "Though I will return in the morning if you are truly unopposed to the idea."

He nodded, holding her gaze. He hoped she could recognize that it truly did not bother him. Though...had she mentioned a *cat* was missing? He cleared his throat. "This cat wouldn't happen to be gray, would he? With dark stripes?"

Hattie's eyes widened with hope. "Yes. Have you seen him?"

"I believe he may be lounging in my study at this very moment."

Stepping forward, Hattie dropped her hem to the ground and clutched his sleeve. Did she realize what she was doing? Given the excitement radiating from her, he thought it likely not. "May I come—" She stopped, releasing his arm and moving back. Her gaze flicked away, suddenly conscious of her sister-in-law, it seemed, and she cleared her throat, her dark eyes working through something in her mind. "On second thought, our horses were left standing. We shouldn't leave them alone any longer."

He couldn't see her logic. "We are much closer to my house, Miss Green. I can send a man over straight away to locate your horses and return them to your stables."

"No, I could never ask that." She looked between Bentley and Mrs. Green, clearly torn about something. But *what*?

His curiosity grew. Holding her gaze, he lowered his voice. "Are you in need of help, Miss Green?"

She looked startled, tucking her chin slightly. Well, at least he could rule out immediate danger. She would not have been so surprised by the notion if she was in any trouble.

Mrs. Green stepped forward, sliding her hand around Hattie's elbow. "Come, Hattie. We should collect the cat while we are so close. The horses cannot go very far, anyway. You looped the reins over a branch, yes?"

Hattie shot her sister-in-law a disgruntled look. "Yes, I took care of that for both of our horses."

"If they untangled themselves from the branch, they would likely just return to their stables, would they not?" Lucy continued, unperturbed.

"I *suppose* they might. Or we could lose them as well."

"That is unlikely to happen; they are such large animals. Should we not fetch the cat while we are here?" Her eager expression put Bentley on edge, but he trusted Hattie.

Hattie nodded, but she seemed wary. So perhaps he would do to remain on his guard.

Sweeping his arm before him, he pointed in the direction of Wolfeton House. "If you would follow me."

"Of course."

The women fell into step behind him, and he strained to hear what they were discussing in harsh, rapid whispers, but he couldn't make out anything they were saying. Light continued to fade as the clouds thickened over the descending sun, and Bentley reflected on how close he'd come to missing Hattie and Mrs. Green completely, as he had almost chosen to forgo his daily walk completely due to the weather. His walks had grown progressively longer as he'd begun trekking back to the place he'd found Hattie painting just over a week before.

He hadn't even realized he was doing it, but when he happened upon the precise location where he could look through the trees and see a perfectly framed Green estate for the third day in a row, he noticed the unintentional consistency.

In truth, it frightened him. His need for human connection had never been very strong. Even as a boy at school, or when he went to university as a young man, he had never had large groups of friends, often preferring to spend time alone with solitary amusements. The only exception to this was his cousin, Warren. Though the man's occupation running his plantation often took him overseas, and their visits were few and far between.

The alteration of Bentley's lifestyle upon leaving his family home and coming to Devon hadn't been grand. He'd already kept to himself because he was most comfortable in his own company, and others, particularly strangers, made him nervous. When he'd learned the truth, discovered what his mother had kept from him his entire life and decided that he had no other choice but to cut ties and escape, choosing a life of solitude had not been a hardship. If he had not been grieving so deeply at the time, he likely would have found the prospect of a reclusive life immensely attractive.

But now he found himself thinking of Hattie often. There were no romantic feelings, of course, despite her beauty. He merely wanted to paint her, to see if he could do it. His drawings had proved insufficient, the concept of her freckles evading him, but he was certain if she would sit before him, he could capture them in color.

He would be lying if he tried to pretend that his interest ended there, for he was eager to speak to her about painting techniques. He did not know another soul so talented as she that he would be able to carry on a conversation with.

Still, it would not be wise to pursue any sort of relationship with her, whether she was amiable or not. Bentley was fully aware of the innocent nature of his interest in this woman, but that was all the more reason for him to keep his distance. He wouldn't wish to plant false ideas of anything more in her mind or give cause for rumors in Graton.

Despite his desire, he could not, in any capacity, become her friend.

A cold wind blew over them, lifting fallen leaves from where they sat upon the solid ground and dancing them across the path. The short lawn loomed ahead with Wolfeton's ivy-clad facade just beyond.

"How did Hattie's cat come to be here, Your Grace?" Mrs. Green asked, forcing him to slow his steps. Now that they'd broken free of the woods, he had ample room to walk beside the women.

"He was injured and hid in the hedgerow just there." Bentley pointed to the location beneath his study on the side of the house. "But he is perfectly well now. It was a minor scratch. Much like—" He motioned toward Hattie's sleeve where his chicken had scratched her. He dropped his hand and faced the house again.

"Much like what exactly, Your Grace?" Mrs. Green asked, appearing confused.

Gads, he wasn't cut out for this evasive secret-keeping. One would believe he'd had enough practice over the previous few years. Could they not just inform Mrs. Green of the incident with the dogs and his chicken? Surely she would understand.

But without knowing Hattie's reasons for maintaining secrecy, he couldn't very well toss her to the lions, could he? What Bentley wanted was an opportunity to be alone with the woman so he could ask her to explain herself.

He glanced at the Green ladies. Mrs. Green's hand wound tightly around Hattie's arm like the ivy that climbed Wolfeton's wall. This was certainly not going to be easy.

The front door opened as they approached, and Egerton held it, his passive gaze slipping over their guests. He refrained from revealing anything in his expression, but Bentley was certain the man was confused. He had never before brought visitors home in their seven years at Wolfeton House, and in the last fortnight, he'd done so twice.

"If you could direct our guests to the parlor, Egerton, I shall return shortly."

"Very good, Your Grace." He turned toward the women. "This way, please."

Bentley left them and made his way across the corridor to the blue room, waiting for the receding footsteps to fade before slipping inside. The tall windows were covered by the thick, navy drapes, and the fire had been built up, casting light across the room. But the cat was missing from his usual chair.

Bentley searched the room, checking behind the drapes and beneath the furniture. Nothing.

"Blast."

Scrubbing a hand over his face, he looked around the room for any other potential hiding place the cat could have used, but it was a fairly bland room. The bureau containing his paint supplies was too full of Bentley's implements to fit a cat, and aside from that, the room only held a small seating area before the fireplace, a desk against the wall, and a handful of easels holding his various works in progress between the two.

This wasn't completely shocking, as the cat had tended to disappear for hours at a time. He'd granted the feline free rein of the house, which had pleased them both, for Bentley did not appreciate forever being followed around, and the cat, while it liked to crawl onto his lap in the evenings, did not seem as though he would appreciate forever being coddled.

If Bentley was being completely honest, he would admit that he was a touch let down Hattie had come to claim her pet. But it was just a cat. He would overcome his disappointment.

He peeked into each of the rooms on the ground floor on his way to the parlor, but they all came up empty of any felines.

"You'll have to forgive me," he said, letting himself into the parlor. He paused across from where the women stood near the fireplace, lightly clasping his hands behind his back. "He's gone off somewhere, and I'm not quite sure where. The cat has been doing this for the entirety of his stay here. I'm afraid he'll be hiding until this evening if his habits prove consistent."

"You've lost him again?" Mrs. Green asked, her bottom lip jutting forward.

"Not exactly, no. I'm certain he's in the house somewhere. We haven't been able to figure out where he goes in the afternoons. I can send a man up to look in the attic if you are willing to wait."

Hattie's grim expression tugged at his heart. She squared her shoulders, holding his gaze. "If you are certain Romeo is here, then what is another day of waiting?"

"His name is Romeo? I wouldn't have guessed."

Hattie shot him a quick smile. "I am glad he's safe. Perhaps I can send someone to fetch him tomorrow if that suits?"

Discomfort fell over him swiftly, swirling in his gut like the tumultuous waves in his painting above the mantel. No, he did not want a stranger coming to his home. Having Mrs. Green in his parlor was bad enough. "I would hate for them to arrive and the cat to still be hiding. It is probably best if I send him home as soon as he's shown himself."

Hattie nodded, her eyes full of understanding. He wondered if it was merely his logic that she followed or more.

"We should be leaving," Hattie said. "It will be dark soon."

He wondered if he should send them home in a carriage, but how would that look? If they went quickly, they could get home while there was still light enough to see. "I can escort you back to your horses. Allow me to fetch a lantern."

"That is most kind of you, Your Grace," Mrs. Green said, simpering.

Bentley gave her a perfunctory nod and moved to leave the room when an idea stopped him in his tracks. He could...but no. If he *did* show Hattie the painting, then she would know. Surely a woman of her talent would piece together the similarities between the cat portrait and the one that hung in his parlor and realize that Bentley was the artist of the seaside painting she so seemed to love.

Of course, he would be kidding himself if he pretended he did not wish for her to know he was the artist. The prideful, human side of him wanted her to see his talents, to attribute something she loved to his skill.

"I do have a way we can perhaps confirm that it is *your* cat before you leave," he said, hearing the hesitancy in his voice. His fingers began to shake, the skittish feeling moving up his limbs until he felt as though his very core shook within. Thankfully, it was not noticeable to the others—or so he hoped.

"How is that?"

"Just give me one moment." He left the room, shaking out his hands as he went, and hoping the discomfort would fly away. Retrieving the small painting he'd done of the cat curled up in the armchair, he took it to the parlor, careful not to touch the still-wet paint. Mrs. Green had moved closer to the pianoforte, and he carried the painting to where Hattie stood beside the fire, looking up at his rendition of the Kent seaside.

He angled the painting so she could see it. "Is this him?"

Hattie lowered her gaze, and he watched her closely, eager for her reaction. She stilled, her lips parting and her brown eyes widening a fraction.

"Yes, that's Romeo...but *how*?" She reached for the painting and he moved it back slightly, her hand stilling midair.

"Careful. It's still wet."

"Still wet? So it was you."

The awe in her voice infused his chest with a piercing sense of accomplishment, and he could not dampen the smile that curved his lips.

"Indeed."

Her gaze flicked to the painting above the mantel. She was making the connection.

"What a lovely likeness," Mrs. Green said, coming to stand beside Hattie and utterly ruining the moment. "You mean to say you did that, Your Grace? My goodness, I did not know you were so talented."

Given that she did not know him at all before an hour ago, that was no surprise.

"That is Romeo," Hattie said, her fingers reaching again for the painting before she stopped herself and pulled her hand back. He wondered if she was fighting the desire to stroke the cat's fur.

"Indeed," Mrs. Green said. "I should think this is enough confirmation to put you at ease, Sister. Surely now you may sleep knowing he is safe."

Hattie turned grateful eyes on Bentley, and his throat grew thick. "Yes, indeed. Thank you for bringing him in and caring for him." Her hand went to her other forearm, her fingers grazing the area he remembered her scratch to be, now covered by her navy-blue sleeve. Was she thinking of the injury her cat had sustained? She appeared as though she wished to speak openly, but Mrs. Green's presence stopped her. Indeed, he felt the same.

"Shall we?" He propped the painting on the mantel beside the seaside depiction.

"Yes. I'm certain my Jeffrey is wondering where we are."

Hattie grinned. "There is no telling what sort of search party they would launch if they found our horses without us." The amusement slid from her face as quickly as it had arrived, and she looked to Bentley. "We must go at once. There really is no telling what my father will do if he deems me missing and in danger."

"Nor my husband," Mrs. Green reminded them.

Bentley understood Hattie's meaning. Unless he wanted a group of nervous men searching his woods, they ought to hurry.

"By all means, we shall go as speedily as we can." He led the way outside after informing his butler of his intentions to see the women to their horses, and then headed into the woods. The lantern cast light ahead of them as the sun slipped closer to the horizon and the shadows grew longer within the trees. They picked their way down Bentley's familiar path until they reached the eastern edge of the woods, and he turned toward the women.

"Do you recall where the horses were left?"

"Yes," Hattie said. "We can find them. Thank you, Your Grace."

"It was my pleasure." And oddly enough, he found that it *was* a pleasure to see her again. He watched the women step from the trees before turning away and pausing. His conscience would not allow him to let them walk away in the growing darkness, not until he ascertained their safe arrival home, or at least to their horses. Stepping quietly to the edge of the trees, he searched the spreading lawn for any sign of the women.

Two horses came into view, cantering toward the estate, the women atop them. They must have found a stump or fallen log in order to mount, but he was glad of it. When they reached the halfway point where they were nearer to the Greens' estate than the woods, Hattie turned, looking over her shoulder in his direction. It was too dark for him to see her eyes, to know where she was looking, but he felt as though she could see him, and he shrank back further into the shadows.

Bentley watched until Hattie rode out of sight before he turned and began making his way back toward his house. He had a habit of painting to relieve his feelings, and he had a feeling he was going to be awake late into the night doing just that.

CHAPTER 10

*H*attie stood beside the carriage on the front drive as the groom held the horses' heads and a footman loaded Papa's trunk onto the boot. She felt an odd sense of foreboding and looked over her shoulder to find Lucy approaching, Jeffrey at her side. Their clothes made them look as though they had just stepped out for a fashionable stroll down London's Bond Street as opposed to a casual day in Devon. Jeffrey had never been so meticulous about his clothing before he met Lucy, but Hattie owned that some things were bound to change when a person wed. Only, Hattie wasn't certain if the bright green waistcoat and dangerously high shirt points were positive changes.

A thin layer of fog sat upon the earth, slowly dissipating as the sun peeked over the horizon. Hopefully, the rest would burn off before Papa got too far on his journey.

"How terrible that Papa must leave only a fortnight after our arrival," Lucy said, jutting her lower lip forth.

Jeffrey cast her a glance. "We did know of his plans."

Hattie wanted to inquire why they were still here if Papa's

impending absence was no surprise, but she bit her tongue. This was just as much Jeffrey's home as hers. Less so, Lucy's.

She tried for a more tactful approach. "You needn't remain if you'd prefer to go home. I certainly wouldn't wish for bad weather to set upon us and force you to remain here longer than you'd intended."

"How very thoughtful of you," Jeffrey said dryly.

She thought so, but it sounded as though Jeffrey did not mean his words.

Papa came outside, followed closely by his dogs, a wide smile stretching over his mouth. "I will miss my girl," he said, pulling Hattie close as Rosie and Daisy danced restlessly at their feet. Hattie wrapped her arms around him, returning his warm embrace. She never liked when he left, and this time was no different.

Horse hooves clopped over the gravel as a man in vaguely familiar livery pulled up to the carriage. "Miss Green?" he questioned, straightening his powdered wig.

"Yes," she said, stepping forward.

He took a small folded letter from his pocket and stretched toward her, allowing Hattie to take it from him. She sensed the note was from the duke, and she stepped away from the servant and her family in order to read it.

Miss Green—

Romeo has at last deigned to make an appearance. Unfortunately, now we are having trouble enticing him to leave the house. My footman has sustained injuries in his attempts to convince the cat to do so, and I have decided that his indignant scratches are not something I am willing to risk.

We are left with two options: first, Romeo will now and forevermore be known as a member of Wolfeton House's staff, and I will put him to work keeping rodents from the attic. Second, you may come fetch the beast yourself. I would prefer, of course, that you do not send a man, for I value my privacy, as I am sure you are abundantly aware. But moreover, if that option is the favorable of the two, I would humbly request that you contrive to visit alone.

This situation is far from natural, as I am certain you must agree, but I have a mind to speak to you about things pertaining to our last encounter and believe it will be much more comfortable for all parties were we not forced to curb our tongues.

You must not feel the strain of an immediate response. I look forward to learning where our dear little friend will be living from here on out.

Yours,

B.

Swallowing, Hattie folded up the letter and pressed it between her fingers and thumb, reinforcing the creases as her mind worked the problem over. It would be difficult to get away from the house without Lucy's notice, but she believed her sister-in-law was the person Bentley wanted to keep away from Wolfeton House.

Nodding to the duke's liveried servant, she said, "That will be all."

He turned about and rode off, surely taking her meaning. She could not reply verbally in the presence of her entire family, and she needed time to think.

"What is it?" Papa said gruffly, his thick gray eyebrows pulling together. "Is someone hurt?"

Startled, she stepped back. However did he get to that conclusion? "Heavens, no. It is nothing. The duke found my cat."

"Oh, what a relief," Lucy said, her hand fluttering over her heart. "I've been so worried."

That could not be further from the truth. Hattie stepped forward and placed a kiss on Papa's cheek. "Safe travels. Give

Aunt Sadler a kiss from me, and please be mindful of the weather on your return."

His eyes sparkled with danger and mischief, and she knew her plea fell on deaf ears. If anything, inclement weather would be more of a reason for Papa to travel home, for he quite liked doing the opposite of what should be expected of him. She was very much like him in that regard, but while the feature was admissible in herself, it was quite vexing in another.

"Bah." Papa climbed into the carriage, shooting her a wink.

"Give our love to Aunt Sadler," Jeffrey added.

"Daisy, Rosie, come," Hattie commanded, and the dogs backed away from the carriage, sitting on the gravel beside her feet, their tails wagging behind them and disturbing the small rocks.

The coachman took his place as a groom climbed into a saddle, prepared to ride as a postilion. Wheels crunched over the gravel as the carriage rolled forward, disappearing down the lane and into the wispy fog. The dogs chased after the moving carriage until it reached the edge of the trees, and then they circled back to the house.

"Well?" Lucy's eyebrows rose, her hands clasped tightly around Jeffrey's arm. She bent into her husband as though she was cold, and a shiver spread over Hattie.

"They are having trouble," Hattie said, indicating the letter from the duke. If only the wretched servant hadn't arrived *exactly* when the entire family was gathered outside, she could have hidden the note, which Bentley undoubtedly hoped she would be able to do. He had risked much by sending it to her, foremost her reputation. She must now show the note to Lucy and Jeffrey or put them off somehow, and she had no notion of how to do the latter.

"Oh, dear." Lucy pouted. "The cat won't go with the servants?"

However was she going to get away with this? "Well, no."

"But surely they've located the animal now. Shall we fetch him?"

"Mrs. Notley, the housekeeper, is a caring woman, and she will undoubtedly make certain he is fed and cared for." She lifted the note, hopeful her brother and sister-in-law would take that to mean that the letter came from the servant and not Bentley. "I'm certain Romeo will be willing to come home quite soon."

"But surely we ought to retrieve him." Lucy's blue eyes bore into her, but Hattie would not relent. She'd already allowed Lucy's antics to put her in an uncomfortable position in the woods the day before. She would not permit it to happen again.

She shook her head. "I cannot. I planned to paint out at the old barn this morning."

"In this fog?" Jeffrey asked.

"It will likely lift soon. But if not, then I shall paint the fog." She pretended to contemplate this possibility. "Laying over the rolling, green hills. Subduing everything. It would make for a lovely setting."

Jeffrey eyed her with misgiving.

Lucy nodded in understanding. "Ah, well, that explains the gown, then."

Clenching her teeth, Hattie cast her brother and his wife a bright smile. She thought her dark blue gown was simple and tasteful, not akin to a work dress as Lucy had implied. Of course, if it did not come from a London modiste, completed in a fabric so gauzy and thin it was certain to tear without the greatest of care, then it was not up to snuff to Lucy. Which only made Hattie want to don her thickest, darkest dresses whenever she was in her sister-in-law's company.

Fortunately, her dark blue gown also happened to be her warmest. Fingering the thick, navy skirt, she turned for the house. "If you need me, you will know where to find me."

Strictly speaking, that was not true. But Jeffrey hardly ever had need of her, and if he *did* send someone after her, she could always claim that she had gone in search of a different scene to paint. Either way, if things went as she expected them to at the duke's house, she would be returning with her cat soon.

Bentley lifted the forkful of ham and took a bite before chasing it with a swallow of tea. Sending the note to Hattie had been risky, but no other option had presented itself. Romeo had already given Edwin enough scratches to make the man appear as though he'd just crawled through blackberry brambles, and Bentley was not about to grant himself the same treatment.

But neither could he allow just anyone entrance into his home. No, his privacy was of the utmost importance.

It was bad enough he was letting Hattie in. But she was different—she was an artist.

A throat cleared in the doorway and Bentley glanced up to find his butler, tall and void of any emotion. "A letter, Your Grace." He proffered a silver platter, and Bentley took the folded paper, at once disappointed that it had been marked from the post and was not from his neighbor.

He'd sent the note to Hattie hours ago and had yet to receive a response. Perhaps he'd been mistaken, but he'd been under the assumption that she was quite eager to have her cat returned to her. And Edwin, upon returning from delivering the note, had informed Bentley of how promptly he'd been dismissed after she'd read it.

Bentley tried to put Hattie from his mind, but nerves shook his body with slight tremors. It was ridiculous and quite embarrassing—or it would be if anyone else knew of it. The discomfort of not knowing precisely what was ahead of him was strong, taking over his body with a physicality that was frustrating. But Bentley could not help it. He had always been this way, which was part of why he'd turned to artistic and bookish pursuits in school, choosing solitary activities whenever allowed.

Turning the note over in his hands, he fought the urge to throw it directly into the fire. He might not want letters from his mother, but he *did* do her the courtesy of reading them before disposing of them. He held on to the fear that he would one day throw away an unopened letter that contained an apology—the one thing that could make him change his mind.

Taking the knife from the salver Egerton held, Bentley sliced through the wax seal and unfolded the paper, skimming the contents. He suppressed a sigh, his eyes tripping over more of the same. Requests for him to put aside his childish prejudices —as if *that* would make him inclined to forgive—and travel across the country to see Mother and her husband and mend old wounds. She even had the gumption to request that he set out at once.

But he wouldn't. Mother should know that. Dropping the knife on the salver with a clang, he crumpled the letter in his hands, balling it tightly as Egerton backed from the room.

Pacing before the table, Bentley continued to squeeze the paper between his palms while flashes of his father's final night ran through his mind. Had he not been subject to days without sleep, sitting beside his father's bed and watching life slowly drain from the person he loved above all others, he would not have dozed on the chair. If he had not been half-asleep, he never would have overheard the conversation that had completely changed his life.

And it never would have stolen the most important moment of his life from him, robbing Bentley of being at his father's bedside when he slipped away from this world.

No, Mother was guilty of more than just a lifetime of lies. She had taken much from Bentley, and he refused to speak to her until she admitted her faults and apologized for them. He could never respect a woman who refused to own blame for the sake of her pride.

The door opened behind him, and he paused at the center of the table, throwing the balled-up letter at the roaring fire with as much force as he could muster. It landed behind the flames, rapidly consumed by the fire until it was reduced to ash.

His butler cleared his throat behind him.

His chest heaving, Bentley's gaze was fixed on the fireplace. "What is it, Egerton?"

"You've a visitor, Your Grace."

A cool chill ran over Bentley's body, and he turned, his stomach dropping when his eyes fell upon Hattie standing just behind Egerton, her eyebrows lifted the slightest bit. She wore a simple navy gown, appearing to be made of thick and sturdy material, and her hair was loosely piled behind her head. She certainly had not been concerned with appearing to advantage, and somehow that made her even more beautiful.

Desire to paint this woman flooded him, and he clutched the back of the chair beside him, hoping to appear at ease, though he desperately wanted to ask her to sit for him.

"I've come for Romeo," she said. "But if this isn't a good time—"

"No, no, do not concern yourself with that," he waved a hand toward the fire as though he had not just been caught acting out like an errant schoolboy. He glanced over her shoulder, but the corridor remained empty. "And Mrs. Green, she is…"

"She did not accompany me," Hattie said, her gaze flicking to the butler.

Her words did much to soothe Bentley, the tightness leaving his shoulders at once. "Romeo is this way, if you would follow me."

"Of course."

Egerton left them, and Bentley stepped around his guest,

leading her down the corridor toward the blue room. His painting room.

He hadn't intended to allow her inside his sanctuary, but what choice did he have? He couldn't very well subject his servants to more of Romeo's sharp claws. And while he had offered to keep the cat indefinitely, he'd assumed Hattie wouldn't take him up on that.

Bentley hesitated only a moment, his hand resting on the cool knob as he swallowed his reservations. He'd never shown this part of himself willingly to another soul outside of his own minute household.

"Has he been very terrible?" Hattie asked, her voice traveling over him like a warm blast of air. "I feel I ought to reimburse you for your trouble, but I do not know how."

She could pay a fee in the form of allowing him to paint her...but those words died swiftly on his tongue. He'd done nothing for her cat that he wouldn't have done for any other animal in a similar situation. He hadn't known who the cat belonged to when he'd taken it in. Accepting payment now wouldn't be right.

"You owe me nothing. I am perfectly happy to have been of service."

Her lips tipped into a soft smile, and he found himself riveted by them. If it had been anyone else, he would have forced his thoughts into submission, but the more he looked at the woman, the better he would be able to recreate her later on paper.

Scrubbing a hand over his stubbled jaw, he tried to smile. He was aware of just how awkward his words were. What a blessing that they remained in his head, for him alone to stew over.

"Truly. It was my pleasure," he finally said.

She gave him an odd look, and he opened the door and motioned for her to precede him. Holding his breath, Bentley watched Hattie's eyes round as she stepped into the room, her gaze flitting from canvas to canvas, unable to settle on just one. A small gasp left her lips and his body pulsed with satisfaction. Perhaps allowing her into his sanctuary was not so bad, after all.

"You've done all of these?" she asked, awed.

"Yes."

Hattie stepped around the room, looking at each painting on display. It suddenly occurred to Bentley just how conceited he must appear for his walls to be so utterly covered in his own work, but he sloughed the feeling away. He enjoyed the things he painted, so what was wrong with displaying them? Nothing, in his mind.

"Such beauty," she whispered. Pausing before the bureau at the end of the room, she stopped and looked at him over her shoulder. "You mix your own paint?"

He nodded.

"Is that not a lot of work?"

"It can be." He shrugged. "But I enjoy it. It is something of a hobby for me."

Eyes bright, she clasped her hands together before her, and he felt a strong sense of foreboding.

"Will you teach me?"

CHAPTER 11

*H*attie's heart raced. She was shocked at her own impertinence, but she did not regret her request. It was clear from the paintings covering the walls and sitting on the easels before the windows that Bentley was extremely talented. Though, in truth, she'd known that just from the painting above his parlor mantel. To have the opportunity to learn from him would be prodigiously beneficial.

But he was not speaking. He silently regarded her from across the room, his hands fidgeting behind his back as he looked like he was attempting to read her mind. His beard had grown longer since their first encounter, his dark hair thickening, and it gave him a roguish appearance. His cravat was once again missing, a triangle of skin exposed where his shirt fluttered open.

"I've always struggled with mixing the correct colors," she explained, dragging her gaze away from his open neck. "Which is why I did not take well to our initial meeting in the woods when you pointed out how I'd erred. I've taken lessons from other painters, but those were years ago now, and I know I've reached the point in my skill where I cannot progress without help."

"I have never taught another person before."

"Oh, that shouldn't matter," she said easily. "I'm a quick study. I typically get along well with most people. I promise I shouldn't be too much of a burden."

His eyes narrowed slightly, and it occurred to Hattie that he could very well believe she was attempting to take advantage of his goodness. Rushing to reassure him, she crossed the room. "I do not have designs on *you*, Your Grace, I promise. Only your skills with color."

His mouth quirked into a smile. "That is a relief."

"I should think so." She laughed. "Honestly, what you must make of me. Sometimes words leave my mouth without my permission, and I should have thought through this first. But I do not expect you to give of your time and talents freely. Of course I would pay."

"I have no need of money."

Yes, of course he didn't. Drat. She had nothing else to give. "Is there a service I can offer you? I am not above average with a needle, but I *can* mend shirts or—oh! I've recently perfected a few embroidery letters. If you'd like handkerchiefs mono-grammed with a B, I am certain I could manage it."

Bentley chuckled. "That is quite all right, but I thank you for the offer."

"Well, I cannot very well expect free lessons. Is there nothing I could give you?"

His expression seemed to freeze, his eyes darting over her face. His voice was low, uncertain, and he said, "There is one thing."

Hattie's stomach flipped over at the hoarseness of his tone, the danger that seemed to seep from his lowly-spoken words. The way he watched her so intently was alarming, and she took a hesitant step back. If this man intended to suggest that she pay him in a less than savory way, he would receive her unadulterated wrath. She was far too self-respecting to even *consider* entering into any such engagement. Though truthfully, she hadn't expected something of this nature to come from the duke.

But what else could it be? If the man had something above board in mind, why wasn't he speaking?

"This is going to sound strange, I am sure…"

Hattie had heard enough. "No."

He looked surprised. "No?"

"Yes, I said no."

While tilting his head just slightly to the side, his eyebrows pulled together. "May I inquire as to *why* you've said no before knowing exactly what it is I have in mind?"

"I realize you hardly know me, Your Grace, but if you think it admissible to proposition a gently bred lady whom—"

"What? *No*," he said, putting his hands up as if the action would stop her words. "That is not…that is, I do not wish to proposition you to do anything of *that* nature. I merely wish to paint you."

Hattie blinked, stunned. Paint her? He wanted her to be the subject of one of his masterpieces? She was no rare beauty. There must be something else he was not telling her.

He ran a hand through his hair, agitated. "I cannot believe you thought…I can see *how* you came to that conclusion, of course. But I have nothing but respect for you, Miss Green, and I would never—"

"Yes, well, maybe we can pretend I never suggested it." A blush crept up her cheeks, and she turned toward the fire, hoping he would believe her reddened skin was due to its warmth. A flash of gray caught her eye and she knelt, coming level to Romeo's passive face. "There you are! Come here, you wretched cat. You've no idea what you've put me through."

Romeo slunk out from beneath the leather armchair,

climbing slowly onto her lap with his ears flattened like an errant schoolboy in need of a scolding. She arranged her skirts over her legs and stroked Romeo's head, sitting in the center of the rug before the fire.

"He may have some idea what he's put you through. He looks awfully penitent."

Hattie ran her fingers over the missing hair on his side, then looked up at the duke. "Was he injured badly?"

Bentley crossed the room and lowered himself in the armchair Romeo had been hiding beneath. "It was not unlike the scratch you sustained from my chicken, and it healed quickly. In fact, I'm certain that bird is responsible for both injuries."

"I believe it," she said, pulling Romeo closer on her lap. She looked up. "You haven't eaten her though, have you?"

Bentley smiled. "No, I have not eaten her. I am a man of my word."

Hattie had no trouble believing this to be the case. This handsome, titled gentleman was so unlike everything she had imagined whenever her thoughts had strayed to her reclusive neighbor in the past. He was immensely skilled and perfectly willing to pass some of his knowledge to her if she would allow him to paint her. It was so fantastical an idea, she had trouble discerning the man's motives.

"May I speak plainly?"

His expression was bland. "Have you not already been doing so?"

Hattie conceded this point. "I would be willing to make the trade you have suggested under two conditions. No, three."

"What are they?"

"First, I should like to know why I am a worthy subject."

She waited, and he ran a hand over his bearded jaw. "Perhaps you ought to lay out all of your conditions so I might determine if I am willing to meet them."

He was a smart man. "Very well. My second condition is that no one, under any circumstances, can learn what we are doing here."

He nodded. "And the third?"

"No one can ever see the painting you complete of me."

Bentley seemed to mull these things over before nodding. He was a recluse by choice, so the latter two should not be a trial for him.

Hattie stroked her cat's back as he fell asleep on her lap, and she shifted back on the rug so she could rest against the chair legs behind her. Putting a bit more space between her and the duke was an added benefit, too.

"Deal," he said at length. "When can we begin?"

She looked up. "I'll need to devise a valid excuse to get away from Lucy."

"Your sister-in-law? Does she stay at your house?"

Hattie sighed. "Yes. It was only meant to be for a fortnight, but my father left this morning to see his sister, and I have an inkling that he has persuaded my brother to remain at the house until he returns. As if I am a child in need of someone to watch over me."

"May I ask how old you are?"

"Not that it is any of your business, Your Grace, but I am five and twenty." She straightened her shoulders. "And perfectly capable of watching over myself."

"I think that is abundantly clear." He lifted his ankle and rested it over the opposite knee. "I wondered why you did not wish for Mrs. Green to know that we had previously met."

Leaning her head back and settling it against the armrest, she cast the duke a wry smile. "Lucy has it in her mind that it is her duty to see me married. I'm afraid she would press her advantage if she knew of our acquaintanceship and put us both in an uncomfortable position."

His lips flattened into a grim line. "Because of my title."

"Well, of course."

"You would never go after a man for the sake of his title," Bentley said, his statement sounding much more like a question.

Hattie's mouth turned down in disgust. "Heavens, no. I plan to marry for love."

"Love?"

"Yes, love. You oughtn't sound so disbelieving. I already know whom I will marry, so you need not fear that I will do anything to trap you."

He chuckled. "I had not thought that, Miss Green."

"Well, good."

"Who is the man?" he asked.

Hattie's fingers mingled with the soft, clean fur on Romeo's back. Had he been given a bath? He hated water. Turning her attention back to the duke, she said, "I'm not sure yet."

He paused before speaking. "Forgive me, but I thought you just explained that you do know whom you are going to marry."

"Well, yes and no."

He waited, and she hesitated to continue. She didn't very well wish to sound mad. Best to appear as confident as she was able. Straightening her shoulders, she smiled. "I obtained an incantation from a Cunning Woman just this last summer and performed it exactly as she instructed on Midsummer's Eve. When it was completed, I was to look over my shoulder, and the man I will one day marry would appear there."

He nodded, his eyebrows knitting together in apprehension. "And did he?"

"Well, no, not a *man* exactly. I saw a fox."

Bentley seemed to freeze, his whole body going still as though he was made of stone. Clearing his throat, he asked, "What does that mean?"

She scrunched her nose. "That is the trouble. I'm absolutely certain it means something, but what? Could the man have red hair, or be sly and cunning? I rather hope it is not the latter. But I'm positive I will know the significance when I meet him. The fox simply must be a symbol of *something* meaningful."

"Fox," he repeated.

Was the man having trouble understanding? She nodded but was grateful he had not laughed her from the room. "Well anyway, shall we complete our transaction? I would like to know why you would like to paint me."

He held her gaze. "Because of your freckles."

Her hand stilled on Romeo's back, and she looked up sharply. Was the man mocking her? "I realize I have an abundance of them, but if you think I could have any less if I was better about wearing my bonnet, then you would be mistaken. It's a curse, and they would be there with or without the blasted sun."

"I am glad of it. I think they are striking."

Hattie was not of the same mind, and she had an inkling that he was only being kind.

Bentley could clearly see her hesitation, for he dropped his foot back to the floor and leaned forward slightly. "Think of this from an artist's perspective, Miss Green. You present a challenge, and since I am relegated to my house and limited inspiration, I have exhausted the extent of painting what is available to me. I would like to try something new, and you offer something both new and ambitious."

She hadn't realized capturing her on a canvas would prove so difficult. But she could see his point and understand it. Limited to paint what was directly before her, Hattie struggled to find new content as well, and she had not chosen to seclude herself in one location. Besides, if all she had to do was sit and be painted in order to learn from this man, it was highly worth it.

"Very well."

His eyebrows rose. "You agree?"

"I agree."

A grin spread over Bentley's handsome mouth. Hattie moved to rise, and Bentley came before her at once, reaching to help her stand. She slipped her fingers into his and warmth spread up her arm as his strong, capable hand pulled her up with ease.

"Tomorrow, then?" he asked, leading her to the door.

She paused, and he came to a stop rather close to her side. "Can you be certain that your servants won't speak of our arrangement to anyone?"

He nodded. "They are the souls of discretion."

"Very good. Perhaps we might begin Monday? I promised a friend I would help her tomorrow, and I need time to develop my excuse for slipping away."

"Monday suits."

Hattie rearranged the cat in her arms. "Very good. I look forward to it."

Bentley led her to the front door.

She paused. "Oh, is there anything particular I should wear?"

"It shouldn't matter on our first sitting."

She was tempted to ask how many sittings he expected there to be but bit her tongue. She would not rush his expertise. And she believed the more meetings they had, the more she would be able to learn.

"Monday, then," she said, turning to cross the lawn.

"Monday," he repeated.

She left, hearing the door close behind her and bringing the cat closer to her chest. She crossed the small expanse of lawn and slipped into the trees, her body fueled by possibility and eager for what lay ahead. She had a feeling she was going to learn a lot.

Lucy was standing in the entryway when Hattie opened the door and let herself into the house. She paused, Romeo in her arms proof of her guilt, and sent Lucy a smile.

"So you chose to retrieve him after all?"

"Yes, actually"—Hattie bent, letting Romeo onto the floor, and he scampered off—"my painting hit a snag. I think I need a new subject."

Lucy already appeared to be mentally checking out. Any talk of artistic pursuits put her straight to sleep, in Hattie's experience. "Well, I'm sure you'll figure it out. In any case, I wrote to an old friend who recently bought an estate just south of Melbury and told her of our visit, and she's written back to invite us to dine while we're in Devon."

Hope lifted Hattie's chest, and she stepped forward, tugging at the fingers of her gloves to pull them off. "How lovely for you. I'm sure you'll have a wonderful time."

"*We* will have a wonderful time, you mean?"

"Right, of course." Hattie stepped past her to mount the stairs. "You couldn't very well go without Jeffrey."

Lucy turned, her voice forcing Hattie to pause on the stairs. "The invitation was extended to you as well, Hattie."

Of course it was. Fixing a smile on her face, she rested her hand on the banister. "Dinner?"

"Dinner *and* a ball." Lucy smiled sweetly. "Surely that is amenable to you. I am not *contriving* to find you a husband, but the opportunity has presented itself to attend a ball at a nearby estate. You must admit that there is nothing untoward in my actions."

Maybe not, but her steadfast insistence that she was completely innocent was certainly cause for alarm. "No, nothing at all."

"Then you will come with us Tuesday?"

What choice did she have? She pasted a smile on her face. "Of course."

CHAPTER 12

*H*attie sat on a wooden bench outside of Mrs. Fowler's cottage and waited for Amelia to finish her business with the Cunning Woman. She pulled her watch from her bodice and checked the time. It had been half an hour already. Surely Amelia would be finished soon.

A metal rooster sat atop the building opposite, spinning with the growing wind. Hattie tucked the watch back into her bodice and pulled her pelisse tighter about her neck to ward off the chill. Clouds gathered on the horizon, the gray sky overhead turning dark despite the midday hour. They'd ridden over on horseback and would need to leave soon if they were going to beat the storm home.

Voices filtered through the door and Hattie rose as they grew louder, crossing to meet the women. The door opened, and Amelia's radiant grin was telling. Hattie took her hand, squeezing it, and Mrs. Fowler followed her outside, a satisfied smile resting on her timeworn face. Her frizzy gray hair was pulled back in a loose knot, and an apron covered her thin, woolen gown. She looked exactly as she had the last time Hattie visited this cottage, though Hattie would prefer not to remember that day. Or, rather, the sheer desperation she'd felt.

It was only a few months ago that Hattie had obsessed so heavily over finding the man she was meant to marry, that she had put herself into something of a state. But she was doing better now. Understanding fate and timing beyond her own control had allowed her to take a step back from her husband-search and appreciate her life for what it was.

Lucy, of course, was not helping. But her presence in Devon was only temporary.

"I cannot thank you enough," Amelia said, unable to curb her smile.

Mrs. Fowler cast an affectionate glance over her. "You may come to me or send for me as often as you wish. This is a great blessing, indeed." Turning to Hattie, her steely, penetrating gaze seemed to sink directly through her skin and read her very soul. "And you, Miss Green. It has been quite some time since I've had the pleasure of a visit."

Hattie's mouth went dry, and she avoided looking at Amelia. When she'd come here in the past to obtain incantations from the Cunning Woman, she had told her friends that she'd sent her maid in her stead, believing it wouldn't do to worry them unnecessarily. Though anyone could plainly see that Mrs. Fowler, while accomplished at white magic, was also harmless; and she excelled in her capacity as a midwife.

"Have you found some contentment, dear?" Mrs. Fowler pressed.

Hattie was able to nod truthfully. "I have considered seeking more answers, but I fear knowing too much would put me into something of a nervous state."

"Yes, it very well could. Well, you are always welcome here. Both of you."

Amelia thanked her, and they mounted their horses with the help of the bench on the side of the house.

"We ought to hurry," Amelia called over the growing wind. "It looks as though a storm is coming."

Hattie nodded, urging her horse to go faster, and Amelia came level with her. "Good news, I take it?"

"Oh, Hattie," Amelia said, her eyes glowing with joy. "I dare not hope, not until I have the babe in my arms. But I am too excited to do much else."

Hattie's heart warmed. It was difficult not to be overjoyed and full of hope on Amelia's behalf after the years of heartache she'd endured. She deserved this. "Do you plan to tell Charles the news straight away?"

"Yes. Now that I have reasonable confidence in this babe, and not simply a hope, I will tell him." She gave a rueful smile. "I'm sure I wouldn't be able to keep this secret."

"I'm certain he will wish to celebrate with you."

A cold drop of rain fell on her cheek, and she swiped it away. "The rain has come. Shall we part at the road?"

"That is probably for the best." Amelia looked as though she wanted to say something more but stopped herself. "Thank you for coming with me. I'm not sure I would have had the courage to face that alone. If I'd received bad news, I would have needed you there."

"I was happy to be with you."

Amelia lifted a hand in a wave and turned off on the lane that led to Sheffield House where she resided with her husband. The rain began to fall in earnest, dripping over Hattie's face and running over her horse. She lightly slapped her reins against the horse's gray neck, moving into a canter. She didn't wish to be reckless on the increasingly slippery road, but she also wanted to avoid being caught in the rain.

Nearing the road that turned off toward Wolfeton House, she felt drawn toward the duke's home but fought the desire to follow the lane. They'd agreed upon Monday, and as eager as she was to begin their lesson, she needed to be reasonable.

Showing up on Bentley's doorstep with no reason and no appointment was anything but.

An orange creature darted across the road, passing in front of her horse and she pulled on the reins to avoid the animal. She stuttered to a stop, her heart racing. Had that been a *fox*? Surely it could be no coincidence that she would see the animal just after leaving Mrs. Fowler's house.

Jumping from her horse, she pulled it toward the edge of the woods and looped the reins over a branch. The rain was some-what stunted under the wilting canopy of leaves above her. It would have been much better coverage in the heart of summer as opposed to the autumn. She lifted the hem of her riding habit from the wet earth and followed after the fox, its orange coat easily discernible against the dreary backdrop of the woods, despite the speed at which it fled.

She felt no other reason for chasing the animal except that she'd been drawn to it, but as the rain fell harder, she began to question her sanity. Nearing the lane that cut through the trees and would lead to Wolfeton House, Hattie lost sight of the animal. She stepped onto the lane, her gaze sweeping the ground around her for any sight of it when a horse whinnied and she jumped away, throwing herself to the ground off the lane to avoid its rearing forelegs.

"Madam," a man called, his boots thudding across the lane to reach her. Strong arms turned her over, and she found herself looking into the handsome countenance of a stranger. "Are you hurt?"

"No, not at all," she said, pushing herself into a seated posi-tion. She had fallen awkwardly on her arm and it felt uncomfort-able, but she wasn't hurt. She was far more interested in learning who this gentleman was.

He blew out a relieved breath and reached for her, his hand coming around her waist as the other grasped her hand and pulled her up. The breath left her lungs in one strong swoop, her heart racing from the contact he'd made.

"Do you live nearby? I can help you home," he shouted over the growing rain. The heavens had seemed to open, a deluge of rain pouring down upon them.

Shaking her head, she raised her voice to be heard. Her hair had mostly fallen from its knot and was plastered against her face and the back of her neck. "My horse is just on the other side of those trees. But I thank you for the offer, sir."

He bowed as though they stood in a ballroom and not on a sodden country lane. "The pleasure, I assure you, was all mine."

"Good day, then," she said, lifting her hem in preparation to go in search of her horse.

The stranger looked at her, his eyes creasing under the dark brim of his hat. His caped greatcoat slicked water from his shoulders in streams and the rain appeared as if it was not going to let up. She wanted to prolong the conversation, to ask after his name and his business in the area. Had he been going to see the duke, or simply passing by in search of a place to wait out the storm?

"Good day, madam." Doffing his hat, he revealed a mop of startlingly bright copper hair before turning to leave.

Hattie gasped. This could absolutely not be a coincidence. That she had been practically led to this man by a fox directly after being at the Cunning Woman's house had to mean something. And it hadn't been just any man but one possessed of *red hair*.

"But wait," she called as he swung up into the saddle. He must not have heard her over the wind and rain, for he sent her a smile and continued down the road.

She could very well have just met the man she would marry, and she didn't even know his name.

Bentley sat at the chair in his small library and swirled the brandy in his glass. Rain fell hard outside, and he was undecided whether he would continue to attempt to read, or if he would break his resolve and go draw. He'd been unable, since meeting Hattie, to draw anything but her, and it was growing ridiculous. Surely he'd spent enough paper in his attempts to capture her likeness; he was afraid Egerton or Mrs. Notley would come upon his many sketches and question his sanity.

Or, worse, believe he'd fallen in love with the woman. For truly, what other reason would he have to be so taken by her? Well, her freckles, for one. They truly were striking. But that would be difficult to explain to the servants, and there was something more about her that drew him in. Something about Hattie's essence, her zest for life, that he wanted to try and infuse in his drawing but hadn't quite managed to do so yet. He was hopeful that painting her would be exactly what he needed to accomplish it.

Then there was the matter of her marrying a fox. Bentley had been stunned to learn of it but was certain Hattie did not understand how the word significantly related to him. He was not about to inform her of such. Silly nonsense, that's all it was. It meant nothing.

A large pounding sounded on the front door down the hall, and he sat up, anxious jittering filling his body at once. It had been years since he'd had an unexpected visitor at the house, and he remembered it vividly. A farmer had requested his permission to shoot in Bentley's woods, which Bentley had heartily declined. He'd not wished to be rude, but no one was permitted on his property. *No one.*

Craning his ear toward the door, he struggled to hear what was occurring in the entryway. Was it another farmer? The low, steady murmur of voices proved that a stranger was now in his house and alarm filled him. His eyes sought the box of dueling pistols on the shelf, and he contemplated the merits of taking them out to wave at the intruder. Though, appearing like a madman would likely circulate worse rumors than the truth he was attempting to conceal.

A knock at the library door made him jump in his seat and he rose, putting his back to the fire. "Enter."

Egerton opened the door and stepped inside before closing it behind him. "You've a visitor, Your Grace."

The butler did not look as concerned as Bentley felt. "I heard."

"It is Mr. Warren."

Relief sluiced through Bentley's body, relaxing his tightly wound muscles. Dash the man. Could he not have given warning? Or...perhaps he had. "Is it not still November, Egerton?" he asked. Sometimes the calendar got away from him, but he was nearly certain it was nowhere near Christmas.

"It is, Your Grace."

Then Bentley was correct, and Warren was early. A *month* early. But that was no reason to turn him away.

Egerton cleared his throat. "I will have the usual room made up then?"

"Yes, and see him in here if you will."

"Very good, Your Grace." Egerton nodded, backing from the room.

Bentley needed a minute to orient himself to the new plan. He'd been prepared to entertain his cousin around the end of December, but he shouldn't be too shocked that the man had descended on them earlier than expected. This wouldn't be the first time he'd done something like this.

The door creaked open and Warren appeared, a grin spread boyishly over his face.

Bentley crossed to the sideboard and poured two fingers of brandy for Warren before refilling his glass as well. He handed off the cup and sat in the burgundy chair, Warren taking the chair opposite him.

"This is unexpected."

Warren grinned unrepentantly before taking a sip from his glass. "We docked earlier than anticipated, and I decided to skip the trip home and made my way straight here instead. I knew you'd be home."

"Because I never leave," Bentley said dryly. "Of course I'd be here."

"You can always change that, you know. No one is forcing you to remain hidden away from Society."

Bentley lifted his cup, taking a swallow of the amber liquid. The idea of leaving Devon was so odd, it jarred him. He recognized that his isolation was self-imposed, but that did not lessen his need for it. He raised an eyebrow. "It is necessary. I think you recognize that."

Warren shrugged, his gaze tripping over the bookcase-lined walls before settling on the painting above the mantel. "I see you've replaced the Kent coastline."

Bentley emptied his glass and set it on the small table beside his chair. "No, that's still in the parlor." He indicated the painting above them now, the rolling green Devonshire hills depicted on a sunny day. "This is new, though."

Warren was clean-shaven, his bright red hair damp from the rain and pushed to the side as though he'd tried to tame it with his fingers. He looked up again at the painting above the fire and nodded. "I've always liked it here. I can see why you've settled so far from home."

"My father must have liked it too, or he wouldn't have purchased this property."

"Do you have memories of coming here with him?"

"No, but I didn't leave Kent much." Bentley ran a hand over his prickly facial hair. He really should shave. "Then it wasn't easy for him to travel later in life, of course."

Warren nodded, understanding. As Bentley's cousin on his mother's side, Warren was the closest thing to a brother he could claim. They argued and disagreed like siblings, but the familial bond which linked them also kept them together. It was just the sort of relationship that suited Bentley, for they went months, even years sometimes between visits, but cared no less for one another because of the distance. This friendship forged in the small years of boyhood and occasional summer holidays had been the only thing from Bentley's life that he'd gladly carried with him into his solitude. Well, perhaps not the only thing. He'd also brought along his most trusted servants.

"How long do you plan to stay? I hadn't expected you until Christmas."

"Just a fortnight or so," Warren said. "You remember Thomas Carter from Eton?"

Bentley clenched his teeth. Yes, he remembered the idiot and how relentlessly he'd picked on younger classmen or those who were different. Bentley escaped the privilege of being ruthlessly bullied because of his future title, but he'd watched on with disdain as Thomas Carter hadn't been so kind to others.

Warren was never one to join in either, but neither did he stand up for those who could not defend themselves. In fact, Bentley sometimes wondered if the reason he had not been bullied had less to do with the dukedom he'd one day inherit, and more to do with Warren's friendship with Thomas, for his cousin would not have tolerated any ill treatment of Bentley.

"Unfortunately, I do remember him," Bentley said.

Warren laughed. "Well, he's bought an estate just south of Melbury. I stopped in to see him on my way through and learned that he's hosting a little rout next week."

"How nice for him. I assume you will go?"

Warren swallowed the last bit of brandy before setting his glass down with a soft thud. "When I told him where I was headed, he extended the invitation to you as well."

"You'll have to devise some excuse on my behalf."

"Oh, come now," Warren said. "How long has it been since

you've ventured into Society? How long since you've set eyes on a woman?"

Just yesterday. But Bentley wasn't about to tell Warren of Hattie's recent existence in his life. It was bound to be short-lived anyway. "You know I cannot go, Warren."

Warren's lips flattened. "I know you think you are protecting yourself, but how many people will truly recognize—"

"No." Bentley's voice was cool, infused with steel. "I care not what Society thinks of me. It is my family name I wish to protect—my father's reputation."

Nodding, Warren let out a long, slow sigh. "Though I cannot think he would have expected you to go to such lengths, I do concede that it is a noble motive."

"There is nothing noble about doing my duty," he said smoothly.

Warren looked as though he wanted to argue further, but Bentley had had enough of this conversation. They did not have to agree on this matter. Even if he had determined that it was time to return to Society, he certainly wouldn't do so under Thomas Carter's presumptuous roof.

"You are welcome to come and go as you please," Bentley said. "And to stay as long as you wish. It is always good to see you."

"And you," Warren said warmly. His sincerity flagged at times, but when it really mattered, Bentley could count on him.

Crossing to the sideboard, Warren refilled his glass as Bentley's mind roamed over this change in plans and how it would affect his lessons with Hattie. He had agreed that it was imperative they keep the painting a secret. But he also was not willing to give it up.

He had a few days to come up with something, a way for them to proceed while avoiding Warren, and he was determined.

CHAPTER 13

*H*attie had managed to slip out of the house without seeing either of her family members. She left the feeble excuse with her butler that she was heading out to paint in case Lucy or Jeffrey found the need to inquire, and that was certain to keep them off her scent for the better part of the morning, at least. She couldn't imagine the lessons would last longer than that.

She walked through the woods, anticipation building the closer she grew to Wolfeton House. The smell of wet foliage and dirt clung to the air, and the earth was damp, her feet sinking into the ground with each step. The leaves were shiny from the rain they'd just endured and there was a freshness about the woods that could only be had after a rainfall.

Wolfeton House came into view and Hattie's heart stuttered. It was too much to hope that the duke's red-headed visitor would still be present. Given Bentley's isolation, she felt she could be nearly positive that the stranger had come upon that particular road by accident. But she would inquire all the same. It was merely too much of a coincidence not to carry some meaning.

The door swung open as Hattie lifted her fist to knock, and Bentley stood in the doorway. He wore a hesitant look on his face, and he glanced behind her as he motioned her into the house.

"Good morning, Your Grace."

"Yes," he said, his voice soft. "Good morning. Now come; we must not delay."

She allowed him to usher her into his painting room, and he closed the door swiftly behind himself.

"When I mentioned that I would like to keep these lessons a secret," Hattie said, "I had thought your servants would at least be made aware."

"They are aware." Bentley's eyes were unfocused as he pressed his ear to the door. He managed to look sophisticated in his green and black waistcoat, despite a missing jacket and cravat. As always, his open shirt at the neck combined with his unshaven face made him appear quite the rake. She swallowed hard, looking away. Well, she wouldn't know exactly what a rake was *meant* to look like, but she imagined it was this.

And Bentley was anything but. He looked at her. "I've got company," he said gravely.

Could it be her red-haired gentleman? Tamping down her glee, she cleared her throat and did her best to look only slightly interested. "I thought you avoided people at all costs, Your Grace."

"Some people cannot be avoided." He closed his eyes, running his hand down his face. "No, I do not mean that. My cousin has come to stay. He does this every few years, between trips to his plantation in Antigua. I am quite glad to see him, even if his timing could have been better."

Antigua. Hmm. She needed to ascertain if this cousin had plans to remain in England for good or if he would inevitably return to the Caribbean. But first... "If you are fond of your cousin, Your Grace, then what is the purpose of this secrecy?"

Bentley looked startled. "We agreed that no one would know of our arrangement."

"But if he is staying in your house, it is inevitable that he should learn of it, is it not?"

He cast her a confused look before crossing to a long bureau on the other side of the room. "We might avoid that if we try. He is not here at present, actually. He went out for a ride. I found the timing to be fortuitous and directed him to Graton. He'd mentioned needing to purchase a new pair of driving gloves, and I can only hope that his ride will be extended." Bentley shot her an unamused glance. "He didn't take well to being kept inside the last few days with the rain."

"Neither did I," Hattie said with feeling. Already they shared something in common. This was looking quite promising indeed.

Bentley began pulling things from the bureau cupboard and lining them up on its countertop. "All the same, if our intention is to keep these lessons private, it is best that my cousin does not know of them."

"Is he known as a gossip?"

"Well, no, but—"

"Then perhaps it is not imperative."

He turned and leaned against the bureau, folding his arms over his chest and casting a serious look her way. "Why do I sense that you *want* him to know of your presence here?"

There was something so comforting and trustworthy about the duke that made her feel as though she could tell him anything. Hattie crossed the room, clasping her hands tightly before her. Her gaze fell on the items Bentley had pulled from the cupboards. A flat stone, curved slightly in the center, sat beside vials of liquid and powders. "What are those?"

Bentley did not remove his gaze from her. "You wished to learn the art of making paint, yes? I figured I would teach you as

I blended paints, and then I could use them to complete your portrait."

"That does make sense." She touched the rough stone square. "Is this where you blend them? What do you add to the oil? And what exactly do you use for the color?"

Bentley chuckled, reaching over her for a tall vial of yellowish liquid. "This is linseed oil, and we'll mix it with the pigments shortly." He lifted a bottle of indigo powder. "I've already ground the pigments, so it shouldn't take too long after we've selected the right colors."

She lifted a bottle of bright red powder and held it up toward the light coming from the windows. "Is that not a lot of work?"

"It is, but I enjoy it. This way I can mix the exact shades I want to work with. To begin, I ought to make the color of your skin today."

Taking a bottle of white pigment and another of red, he uncapped them both, pouring a liberal amount of white powder on the stone and sprinkling in a bit of red.

"You will notice that your skin has a pink tone to it, so the sprinkle of red will give us that extra bit needed to make the color look exactly right."

"But will that not create pink?"

Shaking his head, Bentley reached for the taller bottle. "The oil has a yellow tint to it, so you must always take that into consideration. Though, you are correct. We likely need to add some yellow."

He proceeded to do so before lifting a long, slightly bell-shaped stone and further grinding the mound of powders. The powders mixed together, melting from incongruous pigments into the color of Hattie's forearm—the underneath, of course, which was mostly void of freckles.

Uncapping the oil, he let a few drops fall onto the powder. "You want to begin with a small amount and work it in with the muller, slowly adding more as you go until you obtain the right consistency."

"Surely if you know how much liquid you might need though you can add more than a few drops," Hattie argued. "You can quicken the process."

Bentley's gaze flicked to her. "It is easier to mix the powders without lumps if you start with less oil. Too much liquid makes the lumps difficult to work out. Once you have a sort of paste though, you can add more oil in. You'll have a much smoother paint that way."

She nodded, understanding. Hattie had spent enough time with her cook in the kitchen as a young girl to grasp this concept of mixing out lumps. Of course, her focus had been the biscuits' end result, but Cook always had her help through the whole process, and she'd enjoyed it. Though that was many years ago now.

Offering her the bell-shaped stone, Bentley raised his eyebrows. "Would you like to try?"

"Yes." She pulled at the fingers of her gloves, removing them and laying the pair on the bureau before wrapping her hand around the muller, the rough stone warm where Bentley had held it.

"Now move it in sort of a circular motion...yes, exactly like that."

Her chest warmed from his praise, and she continued to mix the paint as Bentley added drops of oil. He opened the top drawer and pulled out a paintbrush, and Hattie paused to allow him to dip it in the paint.

"Shall we test it against my skin?" she asked.

He looked surprised. "I think it is close enough. Even with all of my years of practice, I'm certain I could not get an exact match."

"Let us see how close you came." Hattie let the muller rest

against the slab and pulled her sleeve up to her elbow, exposing her forearm.

Bentley lightly grasped her arm, lifting it so light from the tall windows lining the wall rested on it. He pointed to the bruise spread up the side of her wrist. "What is that?"

"It's only minor. I fell the other day and caught my fall wrong with my wrist."

"Does it pain you?"

She shrugged. "Not really. You won't paint it into my portrait, will you?'

His gray eyes crinkled. "No, I won't." His gaze fell to the thin red line, mostly faded, where the chicken had scratched her arm. His finger brushed over it lightly before he pulled away, clearing his throat. "Are you ready?"

A shiver swooped over her arm, but she swallowed and smiled. "But first, we test the paint." She took the brush from where he'd laid it against the stone and lightly dotted it on the inside of her arm. She set the brush down again and rubbed in the small section, angling her arm toward the light again. Bentley was correct; it was not a perfect match. But it was pretty close.

"Not too bad," he said. "But don't get it on your gown. You'll ruin it."

She looked up sharply. "This is not my first experience with paint, Bentley."

His body stilled, his gray eyes searching hers. The air between them seemed heavy and fraught with energy until he turned away, snapping the tension. He retrieved a cloth from another drawer and wiped it over her arm, folding it and wiping again until the paint had all but disappeared. Her arm in his large, warm fingers was causing an odd sensation to run through her body, and she didn't know if she liked it or hated it.

Lightening her voice and hoping to sound unaffected, she shot him a bright smile. "Where shall I sit?"

Bentley gestured to a leather armchair set before an easel near the windows. It looked to be the same one in which her cat had been painted. That was fitting. "I was considering a pale blue for the background. Do you have a favorite color?"

"Yes, all of them," she replied, settling herself into the leather chair while he moved about, swiftly pulling things from the cupboards, pouring powders into the stone, and using the muller to make his paint.

"Why does that not surprise me?" he asked, sending a soft smile over his shoulder.

Hattie watched him move with surety and grace, quickly mixing the various paints. She wondered briefly if she should go watch over his shoulder, but she needed a bit of space to breathe for a moment. "You know, I made my requests when we devised this scheme, but I never asked if you have any conditions. Do you?"

"Only the one, and you mentioned it, so I did not feel the need to do so."

"Which was?"

Lifting a palette covered in paint, Bentley crossed the room and situated himself behind the easel across from her. He took a few moments to arrange his things before lifting his eyes to meet hers. "That we tell no one."

Ah, of course. The recluse would want this to remain a secret more than she would. "Including your cousin," she said, the words a statement to reiterate what he had earlier mentioned.

"Yes, including my cousin."

She could do this for Bentley. It was only fair, and in all honesty, it was much safer.

"Besides," he added, dropping his attention to the canvas. "As innocent as these lessons might be, I'm not sure it would benefit your reputation if they were discovered."

Cool fear slid into her stomach, sending a wave of prickles

over her skin. That was one implication she had not yet thought of. In her excitement to learn, Hattie had failed to consider what would happen if others discovered their lessons and made their own minds up about the arrangement. She had feared for Lucy learning of it because the woman was bound to take advantage of the situation or believe that Hattie had already been doing so. She hadn't thought of the rest of her neighbors doing the same thing.

But they would, of course. If it was known that Hattie had been to the duke's house multiple times, alone and unchaperoned, she would be completely ruined. Then what would happen if she was to meet a man and fall in love? He wouldn't have her, that was for certain. Not if she was tarnished.

She needed to come up with a way to protect herself from that possibility. But foremost, Bentley was right. "Indeed. No one can ever learn of this."

He nodded in agreeance and returned to setting up his station. It occurred to Hattie that she would likely benefit from watching his progress on the canvas as well, but that wasn't really feasible when she was the subject. She sat still, watching Bentley focus, his dark eyebrows etched with a faint crease between them as he cycled between looking intently at her and then with equal concentration at the canvas. She found herself wondering if his beard was uncomfortable. It *looked* scratchy, but that did not necessarily mean it was.

Time felt suspended while Hattie sat, patiently allowing Bentley to paint her. She could see why Romeo had liked it in this room. It was warm and cozy, the chair soft and comfortable. But above that, the duke was comfortable company.

"How long have you lived here?" she asked.

He did not remove his attention from the canvas. "Seven years or so."

"It is so odd that we did not meet before now."

Bentley shrugged. "It's not so strange. I seldom venture

beyond my trees, and you do not venture into them. Until recently, of course."

Her cheeks warmed, and he glanced up, a small smile flickering on his lips. Would she have been able to get away with it if the man wasn't painting her? He likely wouldn't have noticed the blush if he hadn't been focusing on her face so wholly for the last quarter-hour.

His even, smooth voice slipped over her. "I take that rosy hue on your cheeks to mean that the day I found you painting was not the first time you've trespassed on my property."

"*Trespass* sounds so awful, does it not? I merely stepped onto the edge of your land a handful of times, and very briefly at that."

"When you were searching for your cat, that was the edge of my land?"

She sent him a wry look. "Surely you must know that I was chasing my sister-in-law, not searching for my cat. I had suggested sending you a note to beg permission *before* trespassing." Hattie looked away from his penetrating eyes and muttered, "Lucy had other plans."

A sharp rattling of the door startled them, and Hattie jumped.

"Bentley, are you in there?" a deep voice called.

The duke wore a panicked expression. That didn't bode well. "My cousin," he said quietly.

"Did you not say that he was out for a ride?" she whispered hurriedly. "Surely he could not have gone to Graton and returned in so short a time."

Bentley shrugged. "I have no idea, but I can tell you one thing: he isn't going away."

CHAPTER 14

The door rattled again with Warren's efforts to let himself into the room, and Bentley looked to his guest, who appeared just as concerned as he felt. Clearing his throat, he called, "I'm busy at the moment."

Warren's voice was muffled through the door. "If you're painting, I won't bother you. I promise I'll sit quietly and drink my tea like a good boy."

Could he not do so in any other room, then?

"Just a moment," Bentley called. "I'm rather tied up at present."

Hattie stood, her arms spread out as if to ask what she was meant to do. Bentley hadn't the faintest idea of how to put off his cousin. Well...if he could draw Warren to a different room, perhaps that would give Hattie the opportunity to slip outside unseen.

"You know the longer you wait to let me in, the greater my curiosity grows. I'm simply dying to know what it is you are painting so secretly." Warren laughed, the sound booming. "It almost makes me question if you are painting at all, or if you are hiding a woman in there."

Hattie scowled at the door, and Bentley swallowed a chuckle. Her reaction was so charming.

"I'm wiping my hands clean," Bentley called.

Jumping to her feet, Hattie crossed to the window and unlatched it. She tried to slide it open, but it didn't appear to be cooperating. Throwing a glance at him over her shoulder, she widened her eyes. "Come, help me. How far is the drop, do you think?"

Surely she couldn't seriously be considering climbing from his window. That was the behavior of ruffians, not gently bred ladies. "Five feet at least, I'd guess."

Her nose scrunched up. "Can you get it open?"

The door rattled again, and Bentley rushed over to the window, taking it in his hands and doing his best to quietly slide it open. Cold air crawled through the space, and Hattie poked her head outside.

"You can't be serious," Bentley whispered. "That wouldn't be proper. We can devise another way."

She looked at him sharply, eyes wide. "What other way?" After one small moment of silence, she nodded. "Precisely. Here, help me down."

Bentley wanted to argue further but the minx was already halfway through the window, her leg thrown over the side.

"Do not injure yourself," he admonished. The distance to the ground was nearly as far as she was tall.

Hattie sent him a scowl before throwing her other leg over the windowsill, and Bentley leaned forward, sliding his hands around her waist and holding her, helping to lower her to the ground. The earth sloped downward slightly, and she jumped, freeing herself of his grasp. It was rather a blessing the shrubbery didn't extend to this point of the house. But even then, the walls were covered in vines and she was sure to have scratched herself.

Glancing up triumphantly, she lifted her skirts from the

ground. "Don't let him in until I've reached the trees," she said quietly.

"When will you return?"

Blowing a strand of hair from her forehead, she said, "I can come Wednesday at the soonest."

"And if my cousin is here?"

"I'll come up with something," she said, unbothered. "Next time we shan't be unprepared."

Bentley couldn't help but chuckle as Hattie turned and fled across the lawn, disappearing within the grove of trees. He shut the window and crossed immediately to the door, unlocking it and letting it swing open before he walked back to the easel. Gratefully, the thing was facing away from the door so Warren would be unable to see the beginning of Hattie's portrait.

Not that it was discernible yet.

"That was unlike you," Warren said, letting himself inside and crossing to the chair Hattie had recently vacated. Bentley hoped that the seat had cooled with the air from the open window.

"You know I am a private person," Bentley countered. "My art is no exception."

"So if I ask to see the painting that kept your door locked, you won't show me?"

"No, I won't. And I expect you to respect that."

Warren grinned, settling into the leather chair. "Of course I won't press you. I'm just having a bit of fun."

Bentley dropped the brushes in a cup of turpentine. Taking the rag he'd used to wipe Hattie's arm, he set to cleaning off errant smudges from his hands. He froze, his gaze falling on Hattie's gloves at the bureau, and he crossed the room. "Were you able to obtain gloves in Graton, then?"

"No," Warren said, sighing. "I changed my mind and went for a bruising ride over the countryside instead. Maybe I can stop in on my way to Melbury tomorrow."

Or Wednesday, and then he would be absent from the house. Bentley tossed his rag over Hattie's gloves, busying himself with gathering the pigment bottles and pretending to arrange them. He didn't need to put everything away quite yet, but he needed to look like he had a purpose on that side of the room, and had not just been covering evidence of Hattie's presence.

"How long do you plan to be away? Just for the night?"

Warren rubbed a hand over his face. "I had thought to stay a few days. I surely will not return the morning after the ball." He grew serious. "It is not too late to change your mind."

"You know I cannot go out in Society. Not without risking my—"

"Your good name, yes, I know. But with the beard"—he motioned to Bentley's face—"you're nearly unrecognizable. You could take on a false name, pretend to be a lowly...blacksmith or some such thing."

"A blacksmith."

Warren nodded, his lower lip curving downward as though he was warming to the idea. "Yes. No man of good standing would arrive at a ball with unkempt facial hair."

"But a blacksmith would?" Bentley crossed to the other chair and used his boot to drag it to face Warren before sitting. "I'm not sure I've ever seen a blacksmith at a private ball."

"Well, neither have I," Warren said. "But I'm certain if he was to come, he wouldn't bother with tasks like shaving."

Bentley ran a hand over his unkempt facial hair, as Warren put it, the coarse whiskers short enough to still be scratchy. He hadn't quite reached what he would classify as a beard, but he believed his cousin to be teasing him. "I take your meaning, but I'll have you know that I care not for your opinion."

"What opinion?" Warren asked, feigning confusion. "I am merely commenting on the fact that no self-respecting gentleman would be seen in public with scruffy, unkempt facial hair."

Bentley chuckled. "It's rather a good thing then that I don't venture into Society often, eh?"

"I rather thought you didn't venture out at all."

Bentley rose. He wasn't sure he liked the direction this conversation was taking. "You'd mentioned tea. Shall I ring for some?"

"Yes. But you cannot avoid the subject completely, you know." He took a breath, as if gathering courage to deliver a fatal blow. "Unless you wish to hide out here for the rest of your life, you shall have to face her at some point."

"Perhaps I do plan to hide out here the rest of my life." Bentley crossed to the hearth and pulled the bell rope, but his breathing was shaky. He did not wish to speak of his mother. Not to Warren. Not to anyone. "I don't see any other option available to me at present, and furthermore, I am perfectly content in my life here."

"Your life here?" Warren threw his arms out to his sides. "Bentley, is all this hiding away really *living*?"

Bentley paused, staring at Warren, unsure how to answer him. His jaw tightened against the criticism, and his impulse was to flee. But he clenched his hands into fists and stood his ground. "I've never been drawn to a social life. That is not a new development."

"No, it's not new. I grant you that. But to be wholly secluded is not the same thing as choosing to forgo most social engagements. In Kent, you had other people to speak to. Even if the interactions were seldom, at least you were not always alone."

He was not alone here, either. He had Egerton, Mrs. Notley, and even Edwin on occasion to turn to for conversation. There were others around, but none that he spoke to. He had a feeling that citing his servants as a source of conversation would only strengthen Warren's case against him.

The door opened to admit Egerton.

"Have Cook send up some tea," he asked, loosening the tightness in his hands.

"Yes, Your Grace." Egerton bowed, exiting the room.

"Just agree to think on my words," Warren said. "I have much more I could say on the matter, but I will hold my tongue."

The threat was not endearing Warren to Bentley in the slightest. What more could he possibly say? "Do not hold back on my account."

Warren waited a moment, then he sat forward in his chair. "You have had years to come to terms with what you learned that ghastly night. Do you not feel that you owe your mother some grace? Or at least the opportunity to explain herself?"

"She's had both in spades," he said coolly.

"I'm not certain you can count it as giving her grace when you've refused to speak to her since your father died."

Bentley shrugged. "I gave her ample opportunity to provide a reasonable explanation. She had none. I do not need to forgive a woman who has shown no remorse, nor taken the chance to apologize for how she's ruined my life."

"You are still the duke. Nothing can change that."

Warren didn't truly understand, and Bentley could see no way to show the man how very wrong he was. It went so much deeper than whether or not the dukedom was his.

He would have regretted confiding in his cousin all those years ago, but he'd been overcome with grief at the time, and Warren had proved a valuable confidant throughout his life. Indeed, he was glad that one man knew of his secret and had not cast him off for it. At least he could trust Warren.

He couldn't say the same for the rest of Society.

CHAPTER 15

The Green family carriage rumbled down the road as the sun slipped closer to the horizon. Hattie tugged her long gloves up over her elbow and ran her hand down her gown as they pulled into the Carters' drive.

"Don't fidget, dear," Lucy said, the wide feather in her hat bobbing along with the swaying motion of the carriage. "There's no cause to be nervous."

"I'm not nervous," Hattie countered. Which was mostly true. She had always loved balls and dinners and the like, but she'd also always known most of the people involved. Those present this evening would be friends of Lucy and Jeffrey, amounting to a roomful of strangers.

It hadn't helped that Lucy had presented her with a new gown that morning straight from London. A surprise, evidently, and one that implied how lacking the rest of Hattie's gowns were. But the gown was merely an excuse to be annoyed. In truth, Hattie was far more concerned with how Lucy would shove her unwittingly at eligible bachelors. She hoped her sister-in-law had enough sense not to be too obvious in her efforts, however well-intentioned they might be. Though the scene in the duke's grove gave Hattie cause to worry.

"Hattie is a natural in a crowd of people," Jeffrey said easily. His confidence in her was sweet.

"Do not worry over me tonight," she said, sending them both a reassuring smile. "You may focus your attention on your friends. I will be perfectly comfortable."

Lucy looked unconvinced, her mouth flattening into a thin line.

They came to a stop. A groom opened the door and let down the step before moving away so Jeffrey could first exit the conveyance. He turned to help Lucy and Hattie out, then led them up to the house. The looming Palladian structure was made of pale stone, and the inside was just as pristine as the exterior. They removed their coats, handing them to a footman at the door, and followed the butler down a corridor toward a room bustling with people and noise.

A raven-haired woman stood near the room's entrance beside a tall, languid-looking man, and Lucy clutched tightly to Jeffrey's arm as they crossed toward the couple. *Now* who seemed nervous?

Lucy performed the introductions between Hattie and their hosts, Caroline and Thomas Carter, but her manner was stilted, her voice oddly high, and she kept attaching an awkward giggle to the ends of her sentences. Perhaps her incessant chatter on the drive over had dried out her throat.

Hattie debated offering to fetch Lucy something to drink, but she let her gaze trip over the mingling guests and found that no one held a glass. She supposed it made sense, with the group preparing to go in to dinner shortly. Lucy's scratchy, awkward voice would just have to wait.

"Ah, the man I've been waiting for," Mr. Carter said loudly, causing Hattie to startle, alarmed that such a loud sound could protrude from someone so thin. "This is an old friend of mine, Mr. Warren."

A tall, broad-shouldered man with a mop of red hair stepped forward, and Hattie's mouth fell open. She snapped it shut and curtseyed to the gentleman she'd met on the duke's lane just a few days prior. Introductions whirled around her, and hope rose in her chest. She'd been unable thus far to determine how to obtain an introduction to this man—for she assumed him to be the cousin Bentley had spoken of—when her painting lessons were to remain secret. But now it seemed as though fate had, once again, chosen to step into her life and organize things to her advantage. How kind fate could be.

Mr. Warren seemed to remember her as well. Rising from his bow, his gaze fastened on her, his green eyes unyielding. "You come from Graton, I presume?"

"Yes," Jeffrey said, surprised. "How did you know? I'm sorry, have we met before?"

Mr. Warren's gaze flicked to Jeffrey. "No. I had the fortunate —or perhaps it was rather *unfortunate*—experience of seeing Miss Green on the road the other day in Graton. Though my horse was not as pleased with the situation as I was."

"Nor I with him," Hattie said. "Though you may put your horse at ease, for I did not suffer greatly. It is a pleasant surprise to meet you at last, Mr. Warren."

"The pleasure is certainly all mine." His mouth curved in a gratified smile. He was handsome, his thick, red hair in careful disarray, as though he'd intentionally mussed it into perfection.

She couldn't help but appreciate his kind, attentive smile as he listened to Mr. Carter speak to him. Hattie found herself watching him as the men drifted apart from the women, forming their own conversation. Mr. Warren was a nice, simple name. Certainly, Mrs. Hattie Warren rolled off the tongue. Or it would later, when Hattie was alone and able to practice speaking it aloud. For now, she smiled prettily at him and waited for dinner to be announced.

"We enjoy an informal dinner here," Mrs. Carter said, lowering her voice as if she was letting Hattie and Lucy in on a secret. "You may sit where you wish." Eyeing Mr. Warren a few paces away as he listened to Mr. Carter and Jeffrey make conversation, she made herself quite clear.

"Is the man unattached?" Lucy asked, lowering her voice and sidling closer to her friend, putting more space between them and the man they were speaking about. Her earlier anxieties seemed to have slipped away, replaced with a conspiratorial alliance with their hostess.

"Quite so," Mrs. Carter whispered. "In fact, he has returned to England with the express purpose of finding a wife, if rumor is to be believed."

Lucy's smile widened. "Has he shown a decided preference for any particular lady yet?"

Hattie felt she should step in and stop the conversation out of respect for Mr. Warren, but that would be counterproductive. For she very much wanted to learn the same things. The men were but a few paces away, deep in their own conversation, and it was all Hattie could do to keep her gaze from continually straying in Mr. Warren's direction.

Mrs. Carter leaned in, her narrow chin coming far too close for comfort. "He has not been in Devonshire long enough for that." Looking pointedly at Hattie, her eyebrows lifted. "But I would be wary of too much hope. He has been known to link himself with fair-haired women of porcelain complexion. It is very possible that he has a decided preference for such."

Hattie's stomach dropped like a heavy sack of flour on the kitchen floor. She could not be more opposite from that description in every aspect possible. Her freckle-covered skin would never be considered milky or smooth, her mousy brown hair was flat and plain—not rich or dark enough to be worth any notice, and certainly not blonde. She was wholly average.

But she had one advantage that buoyed her spirits: she had been led to Mr. Warren by a *fox*.

Perhaps the better question was why Mrs. Carter had swung like a pendulum, earlier pushing Hattie toward Mr. Warren, it seemed, and then dashing her hopes.

Dinner was announced and the crowd of guests moved toward the dining room. Hattie found herself seated across from Mr. Warren, and, for the duration of the meal, had great difficulty not watching him over the rim of her glass. Her table partners were courteous, but the conversation did not flow neatly, and she was quite glad when the lengthy meal came to an end and they were all led into the ballroom. The musicians warmed up their instruments, the sound of bows sliding over strings filling the vast ballroom as groups gathered and mingled. A wide chandelier hung above them flickering with hundreds of candles, and Lucy sidled up beside Hattie, a conspiratorial gleam in her eye.

"Shall we begin introductions?"

Hattie tucked her chin. "That entirely depends upon who you have in mind." The only man she was concerned with at present was Mr. Warren. He stood on the other side of a group of chattering matrons, his head bobbing along pleasantly as he listened to Mr. Carter. The two were clearly good friends, which certainly explained his presence here this evening.

Lucy clicked her tongue. "Mr. Newsom has recently returned from the Continent. He took some time to study in Italy, I've heard. Certainly that would be of interest to you. You could discuss painters and such."

"Unless he has an interest in sculpture or architecture." A visit to Italy did not immediately infer painting. Though it was sweet of Lucy to attempt to find some common ground.

Lucy lowered her voice and stepped closer. "The gentleman

standing beside that woman in the dark orange gown is Lord Kilgern. He recently became an earl, but he's not often away from London. We saw him only last month at a soiree and I learned that the woman he was meant to marry has run off with her solicitor."

"Scandal," Hattie breathed. "Perhaps it's best to stay clear of the earls."

"You would not wish to become a countess?"

Was that such a foreign concept? Hattie repressed her amusement. "I would much rather become a plain old Mrs. than don a title, I assure you."

"That is singular," a man said.

Hattie turned sharply, her eyes widening as they rested upon Mr. Warren's tall frame. He must have approached them silently. Which begged the question: how much had he overheard?

He dipped his head in a bow, and Hattie and Lucy responded with brief curtsies. "May I request the next set, Miss Green?"

"You may," Hattie said, a smile spreading over her lips. If the man had sought her out, did that indicate his interest in her? Surely the connection she felt could not only be one-sided.

"Are you in our part of the country for long, Mr. Warren?" Lucy asked. Trust her to act the part of the interested matron, doing her utmost to learn everything she could about Hattie's prospective partner.

"I planned to arrive nearer to Christmas, so I've yet to decide if I shall extend my visit so long as that or if it is best to leave after the fortnight we had originally agreed upon."

The musicians ceased warming their instruments and a quadrille was called out. Mr. Warren offered his arm, and Hattie placed her gloved hand over his blue coat sleeve. She enjoyed being led onto the dance floor by a man who carried such a bold presence. He strode confidently, his smile wide and easy to match. When he settled his eyes on her, she sucked in a quiet, short breath.

"May I inquire as to why you would prefer to become a mere missus?"

She lifted one shoulder in a dainty shrug. "There is no particular reason. I just do not have high ambitions when it comes to rank and marriage. I find much more value in a comfortable union than one that will raise my station."

"You are not actively opposed to a title, then. You merely do not seek one out."

"Precisely." The dance began, and Hattie refrained from looking too eager. She smiled at her partner, passing through the motions of the dance, and felt a thrill when her fingers clasped his. They danced in groups of four, moving through the motions with practiced ease. When the song came to a close, a country dance was called, and they lined up for the second half of their set.

If the quadrille proved to make conversation difficult, the country dance was even more so. But it was enjoyable, even without the chance to learn more about her partner, and Mr. Warren showed an aptitude for dancing that was rather attractive. When the set came to a close, he bowed to her, his eyes on hers as he bent at the waist. Hattie's chest heaved, her pulse thrumming from the exertion of the dance. She put her gloved hand over his bent elbow and followed him toward the area Lucy had recently been standing.

More guests had arrived throughout the first set, and the ballroom was teeming with people. Indeed, it appeared as though every gentry member in all of Devon had been invited this evening.

"Is it bold of me to inquire if you plan to return to the duke's house?" Hattie asked, hoping she did not seem so forward. It would be exceedingly easier to see the man if he was going to be staying at the house next to hers.

Mr. Warren's eyebrows lifted fractionally. "How did you know I was a guest of the duke?"

"Forgive my boldness, sir. I only assumed because we met on the duke's lane." It was as good an explanation as any. She couldn't rightly tell the man that Bentley himself had told her of Mr. Warren's relation as his cousin.

He nodded. "Right, of course. I will return to Wolfeton House on Thursday."

It was on the edge of her tongue to ask if she would see him again, but she did not wish to appear too eager. She settled for delivering a heavy hint. "I am Wolfeton's neighbor to the east. Perhaps I shall see you again."

Mr. Warren's eyes lit with interest, and he dipped his head. "Perhaps you shall." He returned her to Lucy's side, and Hattie was unable to dampen her smile as she watched him walk away.

Two things pressed upon her, calling to attention the hastening of her heartbeat: first, that Mr. Warren certainly sounded as though he intended to call on her when he returned to Graton; second, that his absence tomorrow meant she was free to see Bentley.

The trouble was, she could not figure out which of the two she was looking forward to with greater excitement.

CHAPTER 16

*B*entley analyzed the unfinished portrait, trying to determine the next step he should take. Currently, the blue background and the base of Hattie's shape were discernible, but not much else. He could teach Hattie about the varying shades of brown—the power of yellow or blue to change the shade so drastically—or he could focus on the contours of her face.

He grimaced. Better to focus on the hair. He was afraid of what would happen were he to fixate too heavily on the soft curve of her jawline or the gentle slope of her nose. Though he would need to eventually...he only needed a better handle on his thoughts first. He'd been thinking of Hattie far more than was reasonable these last few days—since the moment he'd watched her climb through his window and run away.

Swallowing hard, Bentley assured himself again that the implements he needed were set up on the bureau and ready to be mixed into paint before crossing to the window. He'd been waiting an hour now. They needed a much better system than this—how would he know if she could not get away? He could waste an entire day sitting by the window and watching for the lone female figure to traipse through the—wait, was that her? He squinted, leaning close to the glass until he felt the cool emanating from it in waves.

A woman stepped from the trees, and he could see by her recognizably jaunty walk that it was Hattie, but she was not alone. Another woman trailed behind her. Who had Hattie brought with her? Surely she would not have brought her nosy sister-in-law to his house a second time. Mrs. Green was not a welcome addition to their lessons, in his opinion.

By the time the women reached the midpoint of the lawn, it was quite apparent to Bentley that the additional woman was a servant. Her golden blonde hair was secured neatly at the base of her neck in a knot, and her gown and coat, while well-made, were dark and plain. His mind began to form an argument for why they should not allow another into their confidence, but Bentley's servants were aware of the situation and sworn to secrecy. He could not very well allow himself that privilege but argue against Hattie doing the same thing.

And anyway, the maid likely already knew at this point.

Bentley waited with rising anticipation as the women neared the door and the distant, soft thudding of their knocking could be heard. He quickly lifted a book from the stack on the table that he had always intended to read but somehow had never gotten around to and dropped into a chair. He flipped the book open to the middle so it would appear as though he had been making good use of his time as opposed to being entirely preoccupied with the idea that Hattie may not be coming.

The knock at the door preceded Egerton, who stepped aside to allow the women entrance after Bentley flicked his wrist, instructing him to do so.

"Good morning, Your Grace." Hattie bustled into the room, her arm around the other woman's as she all but dragged her through the doorway. "This is my maid, Agnes Morton. She's come to lend herself as a chaperone."

"How very kind." He forced a smile and closed the book, setting it back on the pile he would likely never get to. Not while painting took so much space in his mind, at least. Standing, he dipped in a brief bow. "Welcome, Miss Morton. I am grateful for your discretion."

"Just Agnes, Your Grace," she said meekly, her wide green eyes fixed on him with apprehension. Surely Hattie had explained how very amiable he was. He could now see how she would have taken umbrage at his behavior during their first meeting in the woods, but he'd since proven himself to be a decent fellow, he believed. Hadn't he?

"You may work in that chair near the fire," Hattie said, directing her maid about the room as though it was her studio they painted in. It would be obnoxious if it was not so amusing. "What color are we doing today?"

"Your hair."

She looked disappointed, her shoulders sinking just so slightly. "Oh. Brown."

"More than just brown. I think you know that it takes multiple colors to produce the correct shade. Your hair certainly has more than one color in it."

She raised an eyebrow, challenging him. "You must take me for someone else, Your Grace. My hair is quite as plain as a patch of mud."

He had never wanted to prove her wrong more than he did in that moment. "Come." He crossed to the window, gesturing for her to follow him toward the light. The sun was hiding behind a thin layer of clouds, the sky more gray than blue. But it offered them enough light for their purposes today.

Crossing her arms over her chest, she followed him, coming to a stop just before the wide center window. "Yes?"

He motioned to her hair. "Can you unpin it?"

Hattie cast a look at her maid, her mouth falling slightly open.

"Oh, of course." He smiled at the maid. "Agnes, would you assist Miss Green with her hair?"

"I can remove my own pins," she said testily, before reaching up and proceeding to do so. "But I will certainly need your help to fix it again," she called over her shoulder.

Agnes nodded before turning her attention to the small article in her lap. Was she sewing? Ah, she was.

"Oh, drat," Hattie said under her breath. "It's stuck." She turned slightly, exposing her neck. Her hair was a nest of messy curls with a pin hanging limp in the wisps loosely brushing her neck.

"I can see that."

"Will you remove it?"

"Your maid—"

"Oh, it is only one pin, Bentley. Just pull it free."

He swallowed hard, his shaky fingers digging into the messy tresses where Hattie indicated. He found the pin and pulled it free, brushing her smooth skin accidentally. Her shoulders shook as bumps appeared across her skin, and Bentley stepped back as her hair cascaded over her shoulder.

"You don't mean to paint me with my hair down, do you?"

He swallowed against a suddenly dry throat, shaking his head. "I am teaching you color, am I not?"

"Yes," she said dubiously.

"Well, take the colors in your hair." He hesitated only a brief moment before reaching for a lock of hair from her shoulder and holding it out into the light. Spreading it between his fingers, the silky-smooth strands dripped over his skin. The sun was hidden behind clouds, but the bright, white light pouring through the windows perfectly highlighted the multitude of colors in her hair. "What do you see?"

She looked up at him, her brown eyes confused. "Brown."

"Yes, there's brown. But look closer at the individual strands. What else do you see?"

She tilted her head further, her neck elongating as she peered at the hair he splayed in his fingertips. Glancing up, she held his gaze. "Gold?"

Bentley couldn't help but smile. "Indeed. I see gold. There is a soft reddish-brown too, just there." He pointed and she looked back toward the hair he held. "I think you'll see that things often look much more colorful on closer inspection. It is important not to take everything at its initial appearance but to look deeper. You will be more satisfied, I think."

She nodded. "Which colors do you intend to mix for the painting?"

"Well, a soft brown and a reddish-brown to start."

"And the gold?"

He looked into her eyes, brown with gold flecks that shone brightly as they soaked in everything he said and did. They were so round, so full of expression. "I will mix the gold too, yes. It will be useful when we get to your eyes."

She blinked. "Let me guess. You see more than just brown in my eyes as well?"

"I see so much more," he said, his voice low.

Hattie's eyes widened, and she stepped back, her hair sliding from his hand and falling limply against her shoulder. "Agnes," she said, louder than necessary. "We've finished analyzing the color in my hair. Will you put it up for me again?"

Bentley crossed the room to put more space between them. He needed to steady his breathing. "I'll begin to mix the paints. We oughtn't to waste this time."

"Do you have another engagement today?"

"No, but I am uncertain if my cousin will return early."

"Oh, that. You've no cause for concern," Hattie said, her head turned away from him as she handed her maid the hairpins. "He plans to return on Thursday."

"Yes, but..." Bentley paused, looking at her over his shoulder. "How did you come by that information?"

Agnes gathered Hattie's hair, twisting it and deftly slipping the pins back into place. She crossed the room toward him, patting her hair to check it. "Mr. Warren told me of his plans himself."

Bentley startled, pouring far more linseed oil onto the mixing stone than he intended to. Well, that just meant he would have to make a larger batch. It appeared that he would be tackling both her hair and eyes today. "Forgive me, but I do not understand."

"Mr. Warren was at the ball I attended last night," she explained, her voice soft and matter-of-fact. "We were introduced, and when I asked him of his plans, he explained that he will return to Wolfeton House on Thursday. So you needn't fear that he'll return early. We have all day at our disposal."

"I see. You met Warren at the ball. Did you...enjoy his company?" Bentley would have grimaced at the awkwardness of his question if his body was not pulsing with the need to learn what Hattie thought of his cousin.

She nodded, her brown eyes bright. "He is a most excellent dancer, is he not?"

They'd danced. Why did the image of Warren and Hattie dancing send a surge of revulsion through Bentley's stomach? He turned his attention back to the paints, eager to give his eyes something to focus on so they would not betray him. "I wouldn't know. I haven't had the pleasure of partnering the man myself."

Hattie grinned, a chuckle slipping through her lips, and she leaned against the sideboard, watching him mix pigment with oil and then transferring it onto a palette. "I can attest to his talent, then. Truly though, I wonder..."

Bentley told himself not to inquire. Whatever it was that the woman wondered certainly could not be something he had an interest in. It would be better for him not to question her, to allow her unfinished sentence to die. Clenching his teeth, he fought curiosity as it reared and grew, clawing up his chest until the words were out of his mouth regardless of his intent. "What is it you wonder?"

She turned, her hand resting on his upper arm. "You recall the story I told you of Midsummer's Eve and how I saw a fox? I wonder...well, your cousin has such *red* hair, I wonder if it could mean something."

Bentley's body stilled under her touch, and then further hardened beneath her words. She believed her ritual from a few months previous was enough to signify that Warren was the man she was meant to marry? The idea was sickening, but Bentley could not decipher exactly why it made him feel that way. Warren was a good man, if not somewhat narrow-minded at times. He would make any young woman a decent husband, surely, though his lengthy absences overseas could be seen as a hardship.

"I do not wish to make you uncomfortable," Hattie said. "I do promise I shan't haunt your property in hopes of a chance encounter."

"May I ask what you *do* intend to do?" he asked, carrying the palette toward the easel and busying his hands with setting up his painting station, all while his heart flapped like the wings of a flock of starlings.

"Mr. Warren is perfectly aware of where I live. I plan to do nothing."

She spoke with such confidence and pride that Bentley nearly wished he had chosen to accompany Warren to that blasted ball if for no other reason than to witness their interactions. But it was impossible for him. He could never attend a social function such as that. It would be dangerous.

"If you won't haunt my woods, then how shall we contrive another lesson?"

Hattie screwed up her nose in thought. "Do you have any

hollow logs in the woods? Somewhere I might leave a note if I need to?"

He thought on it. "Nothing hollow comes to mind, but there is a tree that was struck by lightning some years back. I'm certain it would be easy to slip a small note into the charred portion of the trunk."

"I know exactly the tree," she said, surprising him. "I noticed it when I ran home after our last lesson. Very good. Shall we plan to correspond through the lightning tree? I will check it every morning as I take my constitutional walk, and you may inform me on days when you know it is safe to come."

It was a good plan, he'd give her that. This way they could do their lessons only when the house was free of Warren.

"Shall I sit?"

"Yes," he said, gesturing to the chair that remained opposite his easel. He hadn't allowed her to mix any of the paint. He hadn't even explained his purposes in which colors he chose and how they brought out more red or deeper brown; he'd been so preoccupied with Hattie that he had failed her in her lesson.

Pointing out the various colors in her hair had been to prove a point, but she'd also learned something. He'd have to be satisfied with that today.

Bentley immediately began painting her soft, simple coiffure, streaking the obvious brown with reddish-brown and gold. His brush expertly mixed the colors, giving the painting the rich, luxurious hair color he saw when he looked at Hattie. Time passed silently between them as he worked, and he found himself getting lost in the comfortable repetition of dipping the brush and stroking it along the canvas.

"I hope you do not find me too forward," she said, drawing his attention from her portrait to her face. "I would never presume to imply that Mr. Warren has indicated any preference for me."

"But you believe he might come to do so?"

"I *hope* he might. I know this might make me sound mad, but when I saw that fox on Midsummer's Eve, I knew it meant something. It had to."

"If he does come to show a preference for you, what then?"

"Then I will tell Mrs. Fowler that her incantation worked, for I've found my fox."

Bentley nodded. Any desire to tell her of his own claim to the word died swiftly on his tongue. The very last thing he wanted was for Hattie to believe he was throwing his name in for consideration—despite his wish to do just that.

He turned back to the painting, allowing Hattie to continue telling him of the ball. The people who'd gone, the dinner menu, the superb musicians...all of it combined to put an image in his head of the night she had shared with Warren. It was easy to imagine, for most Society functions were quite similar, and he'd attended a number of them before his father's death.

He would still be doing so if he hadn't overheard that fateful conversation on the night of his father's death when he had learned the truth. Disgust rippled through him at the thought. If he hadn't learned of his mother's misdeeds, of his father's ignorance, would he have been at the same ball last night? Would he have met Hattie and danced with her?

No, likely not. He would have married one of the women his mother had lined up for him seven years ago and done his duty to the dukedom, as his father demanded of him. As he'd demanded of himself. But without Father, there was no purpose, no cause in doing so now. He would only bring ruin upon their name and spread scandal were the truth to be discovered. And for all his mother had done, they both owed it to the previous Duke of Bentley to end the line with him.

Bentley was firmly decided. He could not, under any circumstances, allow Hattie to discover that his name was Silas *Fawkes*.

CHAPTER 17

"Oh, Agnes!" Hattie said, falling back on her bed and covering her face with her hands. "However am I going to marry Mr. Warren if the man refuses to call on me?"

It had been a week since the ball, and still, Mr. Warren had not come. Even worse, it had been nearly a week since Hattie's last meeting with Bentley, and despite checking the lightning tree every morning, he had not once left a note telling her it was safe to come to Wolfeton House. Hattie was nearly mad with the monotony of her days. Bentley *had* left apologetic notes, however. They began as short, clipped little messages, such as "*Not today. -B*" or "*Sorry, today's no good. -B*" written in a surprisingly elegant hand.

Over the days, however, and likely due to Hattie's lengthy replies with little snippets about Romeo—she imagined the duke would appreciate updates on the cat, and indeed he had seemed to enjoy them very much—their correspondence had grown into much lengthier letters. It appeared that Bentley had some wit hidden away in his quiet mind. But regardless of his entertaining notes, he had remained unavailable for another lesson all week.

Hattie had allowed her hopes to build and grow as they moved closer to Sunday, believing she might at least see Mr. Warren at church services—she knew better than to expect the duke—but they were all dashed and disappointed when the man didn't show.

A small thought niggled in the back of her mind that she could very well inform Lucy of the whole of it, for if any outside forces could contrive to get Mr. Warren and Hattie together, it was her sister-in-law with all her scheming. But Hattie refrained. If it was meant to be, the relationship would develop on its own.

"Perhaps you must call on him," Agnes suggested.

"I cannot," Hattie said, puffing her cheeks and releasing the breath. "I've made my interest and my location very plain to Mr. Warren. If he has any intention of furthering a relationship, it is his duty to call on me."

Agnes pulled a rich blue gown from the clothespress and draped it over her arm before raising her pale eyebrows at Hattie. "What of the duke?"

"What of him?"

Agnes tucked a blonde lock behind her ear. "What if it's him that's the fox? He's sly, isn't he? Hiding out the way he is and going unseen for so long."

Hattie's stomach constricted as the words floated into her consciousness and out again, failing to find a sticking place within her mind. "Impossible," she said decisively. She would not allow her thoughts to travel that path. It was dangerous and useless, merely Agnes searching for something where there was nothing to find. "I should like to think that if my true love was living on the property beside mine for so many years, fate would have contrived to allow me to meet him before now."

"Maybe," Agnes said, shrugging. "But look at Mrs. Fremont. She's known Mr. Fremont all her life and only married him a few months ago."

"That is completely different," Hattie argued, though she could not exactly pinpoint how it differed. Best if Agnes wasn't given the chance to inquire. "Now I am meant to go to Halstead to meet with Giulia and Amelia for a literary society meeting, and I think I'll ride."

Agnes nodded, turning back to return the gown and fetch Hattie's habit instead. But despite Agnes's willingness to drop the topic of conversation and go through the motions of dressing Hattie for the day in pleasant silence, Hattie was unable to remove from her thoughts the seed Agnes had planted. Bentley was very sly, and his ability to remain hidden away, hardly seen for years, was very much like a fox indeed. She reminded herself that many men of her acquaintance had attributes similar to that of a fox, but she had not imagined them all to be her husbands.

But she had been led directly to Mr. Warren by the animal itself. That was much more telling than anything Agnes might say. She found herself growing increasingly eager for another painting lesson, if not for the skill she would garner than for the chance to ask Bentley what was stopping his cousin from calling on her.

Perhaps it was best if she helped move things along. When Agnes completed her toilette, pinning back her hair and affixing her hat atop the plain style, she dismissed the maid and sat at her writing table. Would it be utterly pathetic to plead with the man? Hattie dipped her pen in ink, and her hand hovered over the paper, an ink droplet spilling onto the page and bleeding as it widened.

"Your Grace," she began, quietly speaking the words as she wrote them on paper. "I shan't bother you with a story about Romeo. Indeed, he has been naughty and scratched up the bottom of my favorite drapes. I have, however, become quite eager to continue our lessons. If your house is not a viable option, would you consider meeting at the old barn on the far eastern perimeter of my property? It is an old building, equipped with enough supplies to be of some use. If that suits, I shall look forward to seeing you tomorrow at ten o'clock. Though I do hope you can contrive to rid yourself of your house-guest for an hour or two." Signing an H with a flourish, Hattie sanded and dried the note before folding it tightly. She licked a wafer and slid it under the flap, pressing it firmly with the wafer seal.

Satisfaction fell over Hattie as she slipped the note into her bodice and left the room. One way or another, she would meet with the duke, and she would gather information. If this didn't work, then perhaps she would just have to see what Lucy could contrive.

Bentley took note of the corner of stark white paper peeking from the blackened interior of the broken tree, and his heart sped. The sun had barely crested the horizon and light was scarce, the wet foggy air thick around him as he made his way toward the note awaiting him. He was prepared to deliver a letter indicating that today would not be good to meet, complete with an assurance that his haughty chicken had not yet been eaten for dinner, but he tucked it into his pocket and retrieved the folded missive.

Sweeping his gaze over the loopy scrawl, he chuckled, his shoulders shaking softly as his breath clouded before him. He could perfectly imagine Hattie's lively voice as though she was speaking the words to him. Well, thus far Warren had shown no sign of any intention to leave the house. He had taken to lounging about and making up for the lengthy time they'd spent apart.

For once, Bentley wished his cousin would not be quite so

familial—ironic, as Warren was the only family member Bentley wished in his life.

But he wanted to continue the lessons with Hattie. Indeed, he was eager to add to her painting. He'd done so once already in a fit of impatience, spending time on the colors in the hair and perfecting the rounded, joyful, smiling cheeks beneath her eyes. He could have captured her in a more reserved way, but that did not fit the woman at all. It felt much more natural to paint her smiling.

Well, he could not take the portrait with him, but they could continue the lessons in another way, and then he would not feel guilty working on the painting in his own time. Slapping the folded note against his other hand, he was decided. The barn would have to do.

Bentley made his way back to his house with sure, even steps, formulating his response in his mind as he walked. The cool morning fog gradually dissipated around him, revealing more of the woodland floor as the sun rose. Anticipation built within him. He was going to see Hattie today.

The house was quiet as Bentley penned a note confirming that the barn was agreeable—though what he wished to say was that it was better than not meeting at all, if only just—and left to deliver it to the lightning tree. He hadn't anticipated anything this much in quite a long time, and the fact that it was about the woman and not her painting was not lost on him. His mind wandered as he slipped between trees, the morning light spilling over their cold bark and giving the woods a warm glow.

Tucking the letter into the tree, he wiped his hands together and set off for his house. He could not imagine Hattie felt the same sort of anticipation at the prospect of seeing him. No, she'd been perfectly clear that her interest lay in Warren. The ungrateful, undeserving man that he was. He'd been returned from the ball for a week with no word of meeting any woman, let alone showing any indication that he intended to so much as take Hattie flowers.

Bentley passed the next few hours before his easel, paying proper attention to the lines and planes of Hattie's face. She was a beautiful creature, made more so by the fact that she did not believe herself to be so lovely. She could not see, it seemed, that the beauty of her heart outshone any natural, societal definition of the word. Her smile radiated joy, lighting her face in a way that only true goodness could. Bentley found himself craving time spent in her company. He counted down the minutes until he could leave for the barn in a way that was wholly unlike him and caused his heart to jump erratically in his chest.

Seated at the breakfast table with a cup of steaming tea and a plate of last night's mutton and rolls, he startled when Warren appeared in the doorway.

"What has happened to cause you to wake so early?"

"Early?" Warren asked, crossing the room and seating himself at the table. "Is it not past nine?"

Bentley cocked an eyebrow. "Precisely." Lifting the teapot near him, he indicated it in question.

Warren nodded, then served himself mutton and rolls. "I met a woman when I was at the Carters' ball last week."

Bentley's hand jerked as he poured, spilling tea onto the table. He filled the cup and set down the pot, tossing his napkin over the spill to sop up the majority of the mess. "A woman? And you only tell me this now?"

Warren accepted the teacup and took a tentative sip. "I cannot seem to remove her from my mind."

"It does not sound as though she made much of an impression if it took you a week to tell me of it."

Warren shrugged, taking a bite of his roll. "Is an impression really necessary? I'm not looking for a wife, Bentley. But a bit of fun has never gone amiss."

Bentley's body heated, anger ripping through him with swift

ferocity. The idea of anyone considering Hattie a *bit of fun* was enough to make him want to land his friend a quick uppercut to the jaw. Swallowing down his anger, he leveled Warren with a look. "I do hope you will think twice before taking any unsavory measures against my neighbors."

"I did not mean..." Warren paused, regarding Bentley. "I did not say she was your neighbor."

"Did you not?" *Oh, blast.* Bentley swallowed, searching for a way out of this. "You met this woman at the Carters' ball, yes?"

"Yes, but I wouldn't exactly call the Carters your neighbors."

Thankfully, neither would Bentley. "I only made the assumption from that. I gather she does live somewhere close?"

"Closer than you'd imagine, in fact," Warren said. "As luck would have it, she happens to live nearby. I was surprised to learn that others from Graton were in attendance."

Bentley lifted his teacup and took a sip. He hoped to sound off-hand, that this was of little worth to him. "Oh?"

"And I've a mind to call on her today."

Well, that was just...lovely. Simply lovely. "Who is the lady?"

Egerton appeared in the doorway, a silver salver in his hand. He cleared his throat, gathering their attention. "A letter, Your Grace."

Bentley motioned him forward and retrieved the missive, his stomach souring upon recognizing the hand his direction was written in. Bah. Not this again. He tossed the note on the table and turned his attention to cutting his mutton with more vigor than necessary.

"You don't plan to open it?" Warren asked, his gaze straying to the sealed missive.

"I'm not sure what more she could possibly say that might entice me to come."

"*She* is your mother, I presume? And she is requesting that you visit her?"

Bentley swirled his tea gently, the smooth, glasslike surface shaking from the motion before he took a large swallow to chase his mutton. The meat had become dry, and he could not seem to chew it enough. He reached for the letter, tearing it open and reading it swiftly.

Devil take it. He bought time by swallowing the remainder of his tea, allowing his gaze to trip over the words again before looking up into Warren's interested face. "Apparently, my mother's husband is dying."

Warren's mouth dropped open. "But Bentley, that means—"

"I know what it means," he said sharply, though the implications had yet to fully sink into his mind, wisps of potential darting through his consciousness without taking root. It could mean so many things, and yet, he could not allow himself to consider any of them. Chair legs scraped against the floor as he stood, marring the stillness in the room. He left half of his breakfast on his plate; his appetite had fled, and now so would he. "I am going out."

"For a lengthy ramble?"

"Yes," Bentley said, not allowing his cousin to shame him. The compassion lurking in Warren's eyes was frustrating, and Bentley wanted nothing to do with it. "I'm certain I'll be gone for quite some time."

"I shan't hurry to return, then."

Return? Bentley paused at the door, glancing over his shoulder only to find Warren cutting another bite of his mutton, seemingly unperturbed. Ah, Hattie. Warren was going to visit the woman he'd met at the ball, and Bentley would be with her somewhere else. Should he warn his cousin to go another day? No, it was an impossible task without giving himself and their lessons away, and that was simply something he was unwilling to sacrifice.

Turning quietly, Bentley let himself from the room. He gathered his hat and gloves, allowing Egerton to help him into his overcoat as his horse was sent for. He did his best to put Warren from his mind. It would be better for Bentley to warn Hattie of Warren's intentions first, before her heart became engaged.

CHAPTER 18

*H*attie arrived at the barn early, the confirmation note from Bentley tucked into her reticule, which swung from her wrist. It bumped against the rough, wooden ladder with each rung as she climbed up to the loft. She reached the top and swiftly crossed to the wide, open door on the end, unlatching it and allowing it to swing open. Cloudy, overcast skies spread out as far as the eye could see over coarse, green terrain, and she breathed in a deep, cleansing breath of Devon air.

"Miss Green," a deep voice called from below. Bentley appeared from around the corner atop a deep brown steed.

Hattie pulled the watch from her bodice. It was still a quarter-hour before ten. "Good day!" she called back. "You may stable him inside."

Bentley nodded and dismounted, the motion so smooth and quick it spoke to his many years of practice. She leaned against the open doorway for a few minutes longer before cautiously crossing the floor and peeking down at the mostly dark ground below. Light spilled through the wooden slats of the barn walls and dotted light over the duke's familiar form.

"Am I to come up there?" he asked dubiously.

"Of course. If I can climb that ladder in a gown, you can certainly do so in riding boots."

His deep, warm chuckle floated up to her, and she stepped away from the ladder. "That is a faultless argument, Miss Green."

"My father has always told me I have impeccable logic."

"Has he?" Bentley's head rose above the loft floor. He heaved himself over the side and unfolded himself, his height doing much to make the loft appear quite small.

"You needn't sound so doubtful," she said. "My father happens to have impeccable logic as well."

"Ah, well, then it stands to reason he would think the same about—" He stopped, his eyes crossing over the many paintings, sketches, and drawings tacked on the walls. "Are you the artist of everything here?"

She hadn't considered the walls when she suggested this barn. Indeed, she had not even noticed it when she'd arrived that morning, so familiar the sight had become to her. She and her friends had met in this space for years before marriages and babies had gotten in the way and turned them toward their drawing rooms for convenience, but throughout all those years, Hattie had brought her art to display here.

Originally, it had been done in an effort to brighten up the dreary barn, but over time she added to the space simply so her drawings and paintings would have somewhere to go. It reminded her much of the gallery in her own house, but instead of portraits of her ancestors, this one contained every stage of development Hattie had gone through as an artist, including those early ones she'd rather not show someone as talented as Bentley.

She noticed a particularly ill-done rendition of the old church in Graton and cringed. "Do not judge my ability on what you see here. I have been adding to this space for a decade now."

"But it was you?" he asked again, glancing at her over his shoulder as he moved closer to one wall. "All of this?"

"Yes." She tried to sound off-hand, but even she could hear the shaky uncertainty in her voice. It was terrifying to bare her soul onto the page and then offer it up to another's viewing pleasure; it welcomed Bentley's opinion on something dear to her, and it was all she could do to keep her heart from speeding so fast that it erupted. For currently, it felt as though it was about to pound directly out of her chest.

What made it even worse—worse than the long stretch of silence as he gazed at her work—was how deeply Hattie cared for his opinion. She wanted Bentley's approval desperately, but she couldn't pinpoint exactly why it mattered to her so greatly.

"Beautiful," he murmured, and her heart skipped a beat. Bentley slowly made his way about the room and looked at each individual piece of art.

She found herself following him, just a pace behind, her heart racing and lips flattened.

"I can see your growth," he said, stopping before a portrait she had tried to do of her brother when they were younger, before Jeffrey had left for university. "Your skill has greatly improved."

Of all her paintings, that particular one was undoubtedly the worst. There was a reason it was in the barn and not hanging among the other Green ancestors in the gallery—Jeffrey had forbidden it from hanging alongside the depiction of their father at the same age. Hattie did not blame him.

She came to stand level beside the duke. "Yet I still do not possess the skill of capturing the human form in any way that closely resembles the person I'm meant to copy. I keep mostly to animals and landscapes now."

Bentley's lips curved in a smile, a deep groove creasing the side of his mouth. "I noticed that." He opened his mouth to say more, but his eyes drifted back to the wall. "Have you considered giving it another try?"

She scrunched her nose in apology. "Jeffrey forbade it."

Bentley's smile grew. "Then perhaps a different subject?"

"My father isn't keen on the idea either." She tilted her head. "Can you not see how Jeffrey looks more swine than human?"

Bentley looked again, nodding slowly. "Yes, I can. But I think you've grown, and your skill has developed quite a lot since doing that. You should try again."

She shrugged. "Very well. I can try again. But when Jeffrey refuses to sit for me then—"

"Don't paint Jeffrey."

She paused, startled by the serious look in his gray eyes. They matched the stormy sky visible behind him through the open loft door. "If you are about to suggest Lucy, then—"

"Your sister-in-law? Heavens, no."

"Then who—"

"Me." He shifted to his other foot. "Paint me."

Her stomach dropped from the tone of his words and the vulnerable pleading in his eyes. Was it not the duty of the painting masters to capture a duke on canvas? "I could never do justice to your likeness, Your Grace."

His face tightened, and his stormy eyes turned to steel. "I did not ask you to paint a *duke*, Hattie. I offered myself as a man, a subject for your improvement. This is nothing but another lesson."

Swallowing, she considered his logic as he swiftly brought her back to earth. What had she been thinking? Of course Bentley did not wish to hang the painting. He merely wanted to teach her, to continue their arrangement. Warmth spread up her neck at the audacity of the direction her thoughts had taken, and she considered the situation anew.

If she could remove his status from her mind, he easily

became Bentley. Not the Duke of Bentley, but just Bentley. A kind man, generous with his time, and willing to help better her artistic abilities. He had no other motive. In fact, by spending time with her, she very much assumed he was fighting his own discomfort. He had been used to being alone for so many years.

"Very well," she said. "Shall we begin now?"

He nodded. "Though I can still help you with the colors."

"I'll have to begin with a sketch. I'm not certain I'll need any colors today."

He nodded, his expression understanding. She gestured for him to sit on one of the sofas in the center of the floor and she obtained her watercolor paint box, pulling the drawer open and selecting a charcoal pencil. She retrieved a blank canvas and wiped the dust away before sitting opposite the duke. Pulling her feet underneath her, she tucked in her skirts, settling the canvas on her lap.

Looking up, Hattie let the charcoal go limp in her hand as she surveyed Bentley. She took in the sharp angle of his jaw, his straight nose, the small half-circles that faintly creased beneath his eyes, and the whisper of a shadow that spread over his face where his beard used to be, revealing a distinct cleft in his chin.

"You shaved," she said. How had she not noticed before? She'd clearly been too caught up in worrying over what he would think of her paintings. But surveying him now, she realized how very handsome he was without the beard.

"Indeed."

"Whatever for?"

He cracked a smile. "Because I thought it was time."

"Hmm." She gazed at him a moment longer, analyzing the shape of his face and the width of his neck. She noted the thickness of his eyebrows that arched just past halfway and the tiny scar he had to the left of his eye.

She would focus on his face, she decided, and perhaps his

neck and shoulders, but not much lower than the knot of his cravat. Hattie was tempted to draw him without a cravat or coat, in merely a shirt and waistcoat as he so often was during their meetings. But that felt inappropriate.

"Do you prefer I *don't* shave, Miss Green?"

"You cannot call me Hattie?" she asked to avoid answering his question. "You did so just earlier, and I did not find it uncomfortable." She looked up. "Did you?"

He coughed, seemingly taken off guard, and shook his head. "No, it was not uncomfortable." Clearing his throat, he ran a hand over his smooth jaw. "That would be acceptable during our lessons, I suppose."

She quirked a brow. "There are no occasions in which we will see one another outside of our lessons, I assume. Unless you choose to start attending church."

"Have you gotten a new vicar?"

Hattie turned her attention to the canvas, lightly sketching the outline of Bentley's face and neck. "No. Mr. Conway is still the vicar. Has been for ages."

"Then I suppose I shall not have to go yet."

She laughed, looking up and tracing the shape of his face intently with her eyes. "You cannot mean to tell me you are waiting for a new vicar before you'll attend church. That could be years."

"No, I was not speaking in earnest. I merely...must you do that?"

She startled, her body jumping slightly. "Do what?"

"Stare at me in that way."

She waited to see if he was once again joking, but it did not appear so. She lifted her charcoal pencil again. "I am trying to take down your likeness."

"Yes, but must you *stare* in that way? It is unnerving."

Hattie grinned. "I must. I don't have the ability to remember things for long. Pictures and the like. I must paint or draw what is directly in front of me."

His eyes were wide. "And memorize it within an inch of its life?"

"Yes."

He scrubbed a hand over his face. "Carry on, then."

"Do you have a favorite animal?" she asked.

Bentley's lips turned down at the ends. "Not that I can think of. Why?"

Her gaze was trained on the image as she tried to get the right proportions of Bentley's neck. "Well, Jeffrey always had a fondness for one of our pigs, Betsy, when we were children, and I'm wondering if there's a correlation between that affection and his portrait."

"The only animal I can claim to like is Romeo. If you make me look like a cat, however, I'm bound to think you did it on purpose."

She lifted her hands in surrender. "I shan't, I promise. Not on purpose, at least. Besides, now that you've shaved you're far less hairy."

Shaking his head, Bentley crossed his ankle over the other knee. "I never quite know what to make of you, Hattie Green."

"I shall choose to take that as a compliment."

"Trust me," he said quietly. "It was meant as one."

Hattie returned her attention to the drawing, taking her time to get the curve of his ear just so while her heart pattered hard against her breastbone. The duke's words, his tone, had gone straight to her chest, hitting her as though with a physical force. No one had ever had such an effect on her, and it was as frightening as it was exhilarating.

But it was not wise to allow herself to enjoy the feeling, either. Not when the man was wholly unavailable: his status as a duke alone was proof of that, to say nothing for his unwillingness to leave his house. Swallowing down her confusion over the warmth that was spreading over her body, Hattie stared hard at the face she was sketching. It did not resemble Bentley in even the slightest way, but it was still very preliminary. Though Hattie had a feeling she would only be proving Bentley wrong with this exercise, she continued anyway.

"Do you *ever* intend to go into town?" she asked, emboldened by the intimacy of their lesson, Bentley casually sitting across from her and lulling her with a comfortable repartee.

"I have not been to London in ages, and I don't plan to return anytime soon."

"No, not that town. Graton. The people might not be what one is used to in high Society, but they are good and kind, and there is a lovely sense of community—"

"The very last thing I want is a sense of community," Bentley said, his words steady but laced with an edge. "My isolated life is exactly the way I want it to be, and I do not intend to make any changes."

Hattie looked up, holding his gaze. She wanted to ask about their lessons, their meetings, their exchanging of letters—were those actions not changing his isolated life? Broadening it? But the steel in his gray eyes was enough to stop her argument in its tracks, allowing it to die a swift, fruitless death.

She continued to draw in silence for a few minutes longer, her body tense and the strokes too hard, not coming out as she wanted them to. Finally, she put down the pencil.

"I did not mean to be harsh," Bentley said quietly. "My privacy is immensely important to me. It is about more than comfort, Hattie. It is imperative."

What reason could he possibly have for remaining so alone? "I take a lot of value in the comfort of others, so I'm afraid I do not understand."

"You need not understand. Suffice it to say that if I was to come to church and join this community you love so dearly, I would be putting my family name in jeopardy. The only way to keep the past behind me and protect my father is to remain hidden away."

"Your father? Is he not…"

"Dead?" he asked curtly. "Yes. But his name shall live on forever. He served diligently in parliament and spent many years closely advising the king. He has done much for our nation, and I owe him everything. I owe him my life."

"You are certainly giving him that."

"And I will continue to do so. It is the least I can do."

Hattie set the canvas and pencil on the cushion beside her. "I rather think it is quite a bit more than that."

He blew a heavy breath through his nose. "There is no way for me to make you understand."

"Then try," she said, rising and crossing the space between their sofas, coming to sit on the cushion beside him. She could see Bentley's body tensing, but she ignored it. She had no intention of touching him. "Perhaps I can help, or at least try to understand. I am a good listener. Have you had anyone really *listen* to you lately?"

He swallowed hard, his throat bobbing. "Not really, no."

Reaching for his hand, she wrapped her fingers around it. All sense of propriety and decorum had fled through the large, open loft door the moment they decided to meet in this loft alone. But this? The moment she touched his hand, a spark of heat warmed her skin and traveled all the way up her arm. Despite telling herself it was dangerous, she could not seem to let go, enjoying the soft, warm skin against hers.

"Do you trust me?"

He held her gaze, his eyes wide and vulnerable. "Yes," he whispered without delay.

She squeezed his fingers on impulse, her other hand wrapping over his wrist until she cradled his hand like she would an injured kitten in need of affection. "Then trust me with this."

"I…" Bentley swallowed, his gray eyes fastened on hers, and

he seemed on the verge of speaking. "I'm not sure I can. If I was to tell you of the things which keep me here—"

The heavens opened and rain poured from the sky, hammering against the barn roof and pouring on the other side of the open loft door. Cold, damp air curled in through the wide space, wrapping around their sofa and causing a shiver to run over Hattie's body.

"You're cold," Bentley said, though he didn't make a move to stand or remove his hand from her grasp.

"Not really," she argued. "We needn't leave yet."

But she could see that the time had passed for sharing confidences. Drat the rain for breaking the spell over them, for awakening the duke to the realities of their situation and cutting his words off.

"You should get home," he said quietly, unmoving.

"I would prefer to wait until the storm has passed."

"And if it doesn't?"

She grinned, her fingers warm over his. "Then I suppose I shall be waiting here for quite some time."

"You'll catch your death."

"My constitution is much stronger than that, I assure you."

"That is not difficult to believe." He hesitated a moment before slipping his hand free of her grasp. Cool air immediately replaced the warmth he'd provided, and an uncomfortable shiver ran over Hattie's skin. Bentley brought himself to a stand, towering over her.

She stood, disappointed, but did her best to shove the feeling away. "I think your constitution is stronger than you lead me to believe, as well. You are missing out on the opportunity of knowing wonderful people by your choice to remain sequestered in your charming little house."

"Oh, am I?"

He looked more amused than annoyed, so Hattie pressed forward. "You are. Furthermore, I think you could benefit from more acquaintances in your life. You would have much more material to paint."

"I tend to avoid painting acquaintances," Bentley said.

Hattie lifted an eyebrow. "Aside from those who are grotesquely covered in freckles?"

Shock lit his eyes momentarily. "You cannot honestly believe that about yourself."

She did not wish for him to attempt to convince her that he thought otherwise, that was for certain. "I think you are correct. The rain is not lessening. Perhaps we ought to go home."

Bentley seemed ready to argue, but Hattie didn't give him the opportunity to do so. She moved about quickly, putting her canvas and pencil away and pulling the loft door closed before climbing down the ladder first—at Bentley's insistence—so he could help her over the side. Not that she needed the help. She had been climbing up and down that ladder for years.

Hattie and Bentley led their horses out of the barn and Hattie securely closed the door behind them. Bentley offered assistance, but Hattie used her mounting block to gain the saddle.

"Shall we continue to meet here until my house is free of its guest?" Bentley called through the rain. In a matter of minutes, they would both be soaked, but the weather did not appear as though it planned to lessen anytime soon.

"That would be wise," Hattie called. "If this rain continues, it would soak anything left in the lightning tree."

Bentley pulled his hat lower on his forehead and nodded in agreeance before they took off in their different directions. They could have traveled together part of the way, but this was better. It wouldn't do to be seen together.

Hattie spurred her horse on, going as fast as she deemed comfortable in the wet, slippery grass. Mud rose with the galloping hooves, splattering her riding habit, but she didn't pay it any mind. Her thoughts were too clouded by Bentley and the emotions he'd stirred up in her. The dangerous emotions that made her feel unsteady.

She watched him slip away around the far side of the lake, his form blurring in the steady rain until he disappeared. If only she could remove him from her mind as easily as that.

CHAPTER 19

*J*effrey appeared to be waiting for Hattie when she stepped into the house, standing in the center of the entryway, a letter in his hand. She closed the large front doors, muffling the sound of the heavy rain.

He looked up, his eyebrows raised, and he lifted the note in his hand. "It's from Papa. But you'll soil it. Look at you—you're a mess."

Hattie slicked her hands over her hair, water dripping from her skin and gown and pooling on the floor. "I know. The rain is horrendous."

"Our floor is about to look horrendous. I will meet you in the parlor after you've had a chance to change into something dry."

She nodded, the plan agreeable to her. "Can you ring for my maid? Have her meet me upstairs."

"Of course." He made to move away and paused. "Where were you?"

"Riding home." She wiped more water away from her forehead. "I got caught in the storm."

"Evidently." He gave her gown a once-over. "Quite a storm

by the look of it. Were you alone?"

"No," she said on impulse. He waited for more and her mouth went dry. "I went to see Amelia."

The words slipped from her tongue before she'd had a chance to consider them fully.

"Ah, I see." Jeffrey turned away again, accepting her explanation with ease and disappearing from the entryway.

But Hattie could not so easily step away. She was rooted in place, her feet stuck to the slick marble floor as though they were turned to lead. How had she been able to lie so easily? Her stomach sank, and she rubbed at her eyes. That was the farthest she could go to conceal her meetings with Bentley. No, that was untrue. That was *farther* than she could go, and she would never do so again. The next time she was questioned, she would come clean and explain that she'd been drawing in the barn. It was reasonable, and it was true.

She would merely omit Bentley's presence. But at least she would not be lying.

After changing into a thick, warm dress with the help of her maid, Hattie sat on the edge of her bed and pulled on heavy woolen stockings.

"Forgive my dishevelment, Agnes."

"It's the rain's doing, miss. Not yours," she said, gathering Hattie's soaked clothing into a basket before setting it beside the door. "I can get that mud out of the hem, don't you worry."

Hattie had every confidence in her maid, but she didn't like to think that she'd caused her extra work. "It is not pressing." She looked to the window, the rain pattering steadily against it and running down the bubbled-glass panes in thick streams. "I'm certain I shan't need it for some time. This weather does not appear as though it will relent any time soon."

Agnes took Hattie's hair from its pins and began to comb through the snarled, wet tresses. "For your lessons' sake, I'm right sorry for it."

"You needn't be. I think we can still contrive to meet. Though I'm sorry you couldn't come today. Were you able to get through everything you needed to this morning?"

Agnes's mouth turned up in a soft smile. "Nearly, miss. I shall have time later today to finish up."

Hattie nodded, her mind growing distracted as Agnes continued to work through her snarly hair. Rubbing her fingers over her hand, Hattie could not dispel the feeling of Bentley's skin on hers. It was so unlike anything she'd ever felt before.

When Hattie was once again presentable, she went and found Jeffrey in the parlor, his wife beside him with her knitting needles working away at an oblong, bright yellow object. Rosie and Daisy lay idly before the roaring fire. Hattie lowered herself on the settee opposite them and smiled brightly. "You have something to tell me?"

"How is Amelia?" Jeffrey asked, lowering the book to his lap. "I did not see her at church this last Sunday."

"She's a trifle unwell," Hattie said truthfully. When she'd seen Amelia last at Giulia's house during their literary society meeting, Amelia had quietly admitted that her stomach had been unsettled for days. It wasn't cause for alarm. They both knew it was typical.

Lucy frowned. "I do hope it is not contagious."

"It is unlikely," Hattie said. "Now what is it you wished to discuss?"

Jeffrey closed his book and set it aside, reaching for a folded letter on the table nestled against the end of the couch. "Papa has written. He must extend his stay at Aunt Sadler's."

"Did he give an explanation?"

Jeffrey stood, passing the letter to Hattie before reclaiming his seat beside his wife. "Evidently, an old friend of his in the area has taken ill. He feels a responsibility to remain."

Hattie scanned the contents of the letter before lowering it in her lap. "By the sound of it, Papa does not expect his friend to survive this illness."

Jeffrey nodded.

"Well, allow me to put you at ease," Hattie said. "You needn't remain solely for my sake. I know Lucy would like to return to London before the weather turns, and I am perfectly capable of keeping house here."

Lucy looked to the windows, pouting. "It would appear that we are already too late for that."

"Oh, nonsense," Jeffrey said bravely. "We can certainly travel in the rain. It is snow we wish to avoid. Blasted hate the stuff."

Lucy didn't look quite convinced. "Do you recall the day our carriage nearly slipped from the road into that ditch when we were leaving London? The road was more water than mud."

"Yes, well, that was a horrid, wet winter. I do not think one day of rain will yield the same results."

"Then perhaps you ought to go tomorrow," Hattie said.

Jeffrey shot her an unamused look before turning to comfort his wife. "We will not be leaving tomorrow. Please recall the reasons we came, and that I will not intentionally do anything to put us in harm's way."

Lucy nodded, her worried, round eyes fixed on Jeffrey.

Oh, gracious heavens. It wasn't as though *Hattie* wished to put Lucy in harm's way either. Must Jeffrey really say it like that?

"I did hope to host that dinner party before we left," Lucy said, her voice regaining a steady tone. "We would need at least two weeks to prepare and give our friends ample time to plan. You mustn't forget that we also spoke of seeing them at the Melbury assemblies next week. I would hate to leave before that."

"Of course, dear," Jeffrey said in soothing tones.

Hattie raised a finger. "Pardon me, Lucy, but did you mention hosting a dinner party here?"

"Well, yes, of course."

Of course? No, it was *not* a given. "Whatever for?"

Lucy looked taken aback. "We must invite the Carters to dine, Hattie. We cannot simply ignore that they invited us to their ball and do nothing to return the gesture. It simply isn't done."

"Then by all means. My house is yours."

Jeffrey shot her a warning look, and Hattie snapped her mouth closed.

Lucy chose to ignore Hattie's rudeness, smiling instead. "What is the name of that gentleman you danced with? The man with the red hair? I've forgotten his name. Maybe we can send him an invitation, too."

Hattie's shoulders tightened. She'd intended to ask Bentley why his cousin had yet to call on her, but she'd gotten distracted, and the subject of Mr. Warren had never come up during their lesson. If she was being honest with herself, she wasn't certain she wanted him to call on her any longer, anyway.

Rubbing her temples, she tried to relieve the multitude of thoughts battling for precedence. She felt a decided headache coming on, and Lucy's floral perfume was not helping her situation.

"Hattie?"

She looked up. Jeffrey and Lucy were looking at her with confusion. "His name?" Lucy said.

"Mr. Warren."

"Do you know where he came from?" Jeffrey asked.

Lucy nodded. "He is staying with his cousin in Graton. The only thing I failed to learn was his cousin's name. But perhaps if we put our heads together we can discern who it is."

"Unless," Jeffrey said, looking at Hattie, "my sister already knows."

Drat the man! How could he tell? She began to form a favorable lie when her entire body revolted against the very idea. She couldn't lie to her brother. Not again. It made her sick just thinking about it. Small, white lies were one thing. But intentionally deceiving him? That was another thing entirely.

"I do know," she said cautiously, "but I'm afraid I cannot tell you."

Lucy's back straightened. "Whyever not?"

"Yes, Hattie," Jeffrey echoed. "Whyever not?"

She set her gaze on the ceiling to avoid sending her brother a glare. "Well, I have made a promise not to disturb Mr. Warren's host, and I think that if I tell you of Mr. Warren's whereabouts, you shall cause me to break my word."

"The duke!" Lucy clapped her hands together, her face radiating joy. "Mr. Warren is a cousin of the duke, isn't he?"

"How in heaven's name did you figure that out?" Jeffrey asked, looking impressed.

Lucy lifted one dainty shoulder in a minuscule shrug. "Hattie is overly concerned with not bothering the duke. It stands to reason that *he* would be the only thing keeping her from such a handsome, eligible bachelor." She sucked in a breath, looking to Hattie with shock written on her features, her mouth hung open and eyes wide. "You mean to tell me that Mr. Warren has been just across the woods this entire week, and you've done nothing about it?"

"Yes," Hattie said proudly. "You know I do not approve of your methods for obtaining husbands."

"Then don't employ my methods," Lucy said. "But you can still do *something*."

Jeffrey looked confused. Again. "What is this? I do not understand."

"What exactly am I meant to do?" Hattie asked, ignoring her brother. She had a feeling he would not appreciate Lucy's methods either, or how his wife had run through the duke's woods in an effort to meet the man for Hattie's benefit. "I cannot call on him, nor can I write him a letter without inciting a scandal should I be discovered. He did not come to church, and I have not seen him riding about. For all we know, Mr. Warren has already left Graton altogether."

Lucy stilled. "That is true. What *could* you do?"

Fear crept into her stomach, tightening it against the expression on her sister-in-law's face. "Whatever it is, I will do it, Lucy. Is that understood? Not anyone else, just me. I cannot condone bothering the duke. I've expressly promised him I would do no such thing."

"Yes, yes of course." Lucy flapped her hand at Hattie as though warding off an irritable insect.

"Do I have your word?"

"Hmm?" Lucy asked, quite clearly distracted. The woman was concocting a scheme, and Hattie did not have the mental capacity to withstand this conversation any longer. Her temples throbbed, the cloying floral scent emanating from the sofa enough to swirl her stomach.

"Lucy," she repeated. "Do I have your word?"

Jeffrey stood. "Hattie, you look unwell."

"It is just a headache. Your word, Lucy?"

"Very well, you have my word!" Lucy's fair eyebrows pulled together. "But I must agree with Jeffrey. You look unwell."

She was. Rising, she warded off Jeffrey's advance with a lifted hand, the other resting against her nauseated stomach. "I think I shall go lie down."

"Would you like dinner sent up?" Jeffrey asked.

She gave her thoughtful brother a sweet smile. "I'm going to send my maid for a headache tonic. She can fetch me dinner when I'm ready for it."

He nodded, and Hattie took her leave of the room, noting Lucy's distracted farewell. Climbing the stairs toward her room, she could not fully stem the rising panic within her. Lucy was up to something, make no mistake. And Hattie was going to have to find a way to stop her.

CHAPTER 20

*B*entley pulled on his leather riding gloves as he made his way toward the front door. It had rained for four continuous days with no reprieve. But now that the sun was finally shining again, he planned to take advantage of the fine weather and ride into town to visit the apothecary before the storm clouds descended once more. He'd felt a decided shift in his mood these last four days. A melancholy had settled upon him that he couldn't seem to shake, and he imagined it had much more to do with the lack of painting lessons in his life than the lack of sun. Hattie's sunshine could permeate any gloomy day, he was certain, and he'd been disappointed when she'd sent a footman over with a letter explaining that she had come down with a nasty headache and it would be better if they put off their barn meetings while it was raining so heavily.

Wouldn't wish to catch our deaths, she had said. She'd signed the letter as Jeffrey—her brother, Bentley believed—in what was likely her attempt to keep them free of trouble if it was discovered that they were passing notes. Her handwriting had become known to him through her recent letters, however, and he knew the true author of the missive.

But nevermind that. Bentley had passed the rainy days working on Hattie's portrait, and it was coming together quite nicely. He was nearly finished; he just needed to add the freckles. Though, that was not something he could do without her sitting in front of him, he decided. He also needed to wait for the paint to dry a little more, but it was getting closer.

"Bentley," Warren called from the stairs, causing him to pause before the door. "Where are you off to?"

"The apothecary. I need more pigments." He would usually ride to Melbury for this errand, but he was eager to return to his painting. One small trip into Graton wouldn't cause him trouble, surely.

Warren sauntered down the stairs, a lazy smile on his mouth. "You do realize you can order paints already mixed, yes? I know a number of people who do so. Saves them heaps of trouble."

"Yes, but I prefer to mix my own. Would you care to join me?"

Warren wrinkled his nose. "I'd prefer to have breakfast."

"At one in the afternoon?"

Warren's laugh echoed through the wood-encased corridor that led to the entryway. "Yes, breakfast at one. You know I had a late night last night."

"I did assume as much. Though I never heard you return." He swallowed. "Just having a bit of fun?"

"Not really. I went down to the pub. Jolly's, was it?"

"Yes, that would be the inn. The only taproom we have around."

Warren scrubbed a hand over his face. "Small crowd, but it was lively enough."

"Quite an astute description of country living," Bentley said.

Warren barked a laugh. "Right you are." He yawned. "Oh, while I have you here. What are your thoughts on that dinner invitation? How shall we reply?"

"What dinner do you speak of?"

"Did I not tell you? The woman who lives just on the other side of those woods—Green, was it?—invited us to dinner on Tuesday next."

Bentley's stomach clenched. Hattie had extended an invitation to dine? To both him and Warren? "Miss Green invited us? Are you certain I was included?"

"Yes, quite certain. Though it wasn't Miss Green who penned the note. A Mrs. Green, I believe. I can't recall meeting her at Carter's, but I suppose I must have done."

Bentley's mind whirled. The sister-in-law was up to something, but what? He knew Hattie better than this. She would never have put him in so uncomfortable a position as to be forced to decline an invitation.

"You can do whatever you wish," Bentley said.

Warren came closer, a soberness to his expression. "Have you given any thought to what would happen if Mr. Humphries was to die?"

"Yes," Bentley said, though his throat went dry regardless. "I can hardly think of anything else. But his death wouldn't change much. My mother has still yet to apologize, and—"

"But your fears, Bentley. They would no longer be necessary. You could go out again, join the Lords, and do all that good for the world that you always spoke of when we were young."

"Those dreams were dashed the night my father died," Bentley said. "I no longer carry aspirations of any grandeur."

"I'm certain grandeur of any sort has never been on your agenda, Bentley. But I won't press the matter further." He paused, his eyes sweeping over Bentley's face. "If you do not go to them, will you regret it later?"

That was the question that had plagued Bentley since receiving his mother's letter just four days prior. He did think that attending his mother's husband on his sickbed would only end badly for all involved. Bentley could never forgive them, so what was the purpose of going?

He didn't answer Warren, instead, stepping back.

Warren seemed to understand. "I'll say no more. The apothecary, did you say?"

"Yes, have you changed your mind?"

"No." He grinned. "Breakfast awaits."

The apothecary was empty when Bentley arrived, and it took less than ten minutes to select the pigments he wanted to purchase. He intended to go directly home and grind them into powder, for he needed something to expel his extra, anxious energy, and working with the muller and stone to grind his pigments to dust was as good a way as any. He hadn't been lying to Warren earlier—his mother's letter and the information about her husband's failing health had been on his mind quite a lot recently. But moreover, the potential of regret burned his chest, worrying his mind. He'd heavily regretted his anger the night his father had died and how his choice to argue with his mother had made him leave the room just moments before Father took his last breath.

After weeks of sitting vigil at his side, Bentley had missed being there, had missed holding Father's hand when he'd needed Bentley most. Bentley's regret was still acute, and the years had only slightly dulled it. Above all else though, he did not wish the added burden of additional regret to plague him for failing to allow Mr. Humphries the chance to speak for himself.

Did Bentley owe the man that much? He genuinely did not know.

"All set," the man said behind the counter, sliding a wrapped parcel over the smooth wooden countertop and pushing spectacles up his nose.

Bentley counted out what he owed the man, shaking coins in his hand to find the correct sum. The door opened behind him, bringing with it a rush of cold wind, and his body tensed on impulse. He'd spent so many years closeted away, worried that people would see him, note his distinct nose, his cleft chin, and the way his eyes were set back just so, and know at once the secret his mother had kept from him his entire life. He couldn't risk being seen, couldn't risk forming relationships with others. What if they knew his father, his mother, or her newer husband?

Then the game would be up. Father deserved this, for Bentley to make every last effort to conceal the truth and protect their name. He should have just gone to Melbury.

"Certainly," a female voice said as the shop door closed. "We are here anyway, so I do not see why Lucy should be so bothered by a quick visit to the apothecary. It is not as though she needs my help choosing between pink and dark pink for her gown. I should think it won't be the last headache I endure while she remains under my roof."

Bentley's pulse thrummed. He would recognize Hattie's voice anywhere, and his heart jumped at the sound, his chest warming and his fingers shaking around the coins he delivered into the apothecary's waiting hand. He thanked the man and lifted his package, unsure what he should do.

Well, he would allow Hattie to take the lead. If he was lucky, she only had her maid with her again. A smile formed on his lips. He was eager to catch a glimpse of Hattie. Due to the rain, he'd been starved of the woman and greatly anticipated feasting on the sight of her.

Bentley dipped his head to the apothecary then turned. Hattie stood beside her maid near the door, her gaze fixed on him. She must have recognized him when she entered the shop and was waiting, as he was, to see how they should react to one another. They'd never determined how to act in public, having written off the possibility of meeting. But here they were, more than a month after their first meeting in the millinery, and accidentally seeing one another in a shop again.

"Good day," he said, breaking the silence. That was typical behavior, was it not? Certainly strangers bid each other good day quite often. It was only polite, and anyone looking on would not suspect that they were friends from a simple greeting. Regardless, Hattie had been staring, and he would have given his entire package of pigments to know what she'd been thinking.

"I shall retrieve the tonic," her maid said quietly before bobbing a curtsy and skirting Bentley to approach the counter.

Hattie seemed to regain her bearings and dipped in a curtsy. "Good day. Quite a cold day, in fact."

Bentley could hear voices quietly behind him as Hattie's maid spoke to the apothecary. "Indeed," he said. "Nearly frigid, in fact."

"Much too cold to...um..." She looked to be casting about for the proper words before her gaze narrowed in on him again. "To spend too much time with horses. In a *barn*."

"Ah, well, I'm certain if one was to wear a thick enough coat, one could visit their horse in the barn for a short period of time."

Hattie looked to be fighting a smile. "Provided it does not rain."

"Well, naturally. The rain would be a deterrent from visiting a barn. But if it was sunny..."

"Then there would be no reason *not* to visit your horse. In the barn. Regardless of the cold. Even on a day like today."

Bentley had to work to keep his grin from spreading. The amusement dancing in Hattie's eyes was reflected in the warmth filling his chest.

He glanced over his shoulder and found the apothecary's focus wholly on Agnes. Lowering his voice, he shot Hattie a significant look. "Do you happen to be aware that your sister-in-law has invited my cousin and me to dine at your home next week?"

Hattie's eyebrows pulled together. "Drat the woman. I told her to leave you out of it."

That stung, though Bentley believed she had meant it as a kindness.

Stepping closer, she spoke quietly. "Mr. Warren may accept the invitation alone. Do not feel as though you are slighting me by refusing—I understand that you cannot come."

But the idea of Warren attending dinner at her house without Bentley, spending time with her, inciting her wicked laughter and sparkling, amused eyes, was enough to set him on edge. He did not feel the least inclined to allow Warren that luxury and surprised himself by shaking his head.

The shop door opened, and an older woman stepped inside, a wide black bonnet covering most of her gray hair. Her wrinkled face shifted into surprise as she looked from Hattie to Bentley, and he could see the calculation shining in the older woman's eyes. Hattie had stepped too close, and they were in much too intimate a position to hide the fact that they knew one another. He needed to act quickly.

Hattie, it seemed, had come to the same conclusion. "Oh!" she said softly before falling against Bentley's side. Her body pressed against him, and he was so caught off guard by her action that he delayed response, standing limply beside her like a simpleton.

"Put your arms around me," Hattie hissed quietly. "I'm *ill*."

Bentley complied, sliding his arms around Hattie's waist just as she fell fully against him. He dropped his package of pigments on the floor and slid his free hand under her knees, lifting her in his arms and pulling her close to his chest. Her head lolled against his shoulder, and her warm breath puffed on his skin, sending a wave of shivers over his neck.

"Smelling salts," she murmured quietly, so softly he hardly heard her.

"Smelling salts!" he called in his most authoritative tone. "The woman has fainted. Does anyone have smelling salts?"

"Oh, miss!" Agnes said, jumping to his side and taking Hattie's hand, chafing it between both of hers. "I don't have my salts!"

"I do." The matronly woman near the door crossed to them quickly, her gray eyebrows raised high on her forehead. She pulled a vial from her reticule and popped the cork from the top, waving it under Hattie's nose.

Hattie immediately stirred, sucking in a quick gasp as her eyes fluttered lazily.

Bentley looked down at her, the gold flecks shining so brightly within their copper brown depths. Or perhaps that was due to how close he was to her. His heart hammered in his chest, and he was certain Hattie could feel it, so fast and hard it was pumping. Bentley hoped she believed it was from the fear of nearly being caught in an intimate conversation with her and not the truth—that he was overcome by the perfection of holding this woman in his arms.

"Miss Green!" the woman said. "What has come over you?"

"I'm afraid I do not know," Hattie replied in an alarmingly convincing manner, her tone faint and weak. "I am so embarrassed."

"Hush, child. There is no cause for that." The older woman looked up at Bentley with mild disapproval, her mouth pinched. "You are fortunate to have been so near this capable man when you felt weak."

"Indeed," Hattie agreed, closing her eyes again.

"Shall I fetch Mrs. Green?" Agnes asked.

When Hattie spoke, her eyes remained tightly closed. "You may go for the carriage. I don't wish to spoil Lucy's shopping. I can await her in there."

The older woman sputtered. "But surely she—"

"Right away, miss." The maid bobbed a curtsy and hurried outside.

Hattie looked up at Bentley meekly, her voice soft. "Would you be so good as to put me down, sir?"

The older woman sputtered. "But Miss Green, *really*, do you think you can stand on your own?"

Hattie looked at the woman. "Mrs. Naylor, I am so grateful for your consideration, but I do think I can manage it. With help, of course."

With some hesitation, Bentley lowered Hattie's feet to the floor, his other arm remaining around her in the guise of support. He was exceedingly aware of his hand on her waist, and he found that he'd enjoyed holding her far, far too much. Swallowing hard, Bentley glanced over his shoulder at the man behind the counter, who appeared slightly bewildered, as though he was uncertain what had just taken place.

Bentley felt somewhat similar.

Hattie stepped forward, leaning heavily on Bentley's arm, and he helped her outside, Mrs. Naylor following closely behind them.

"Where is your carriage?"

She glanced down the street. "I'm assuming Agnes will direct it here."

Bentley nodded.

"Oh, dear, look at the time. I really must be returning home," Mrs. Naylor fretted. "I've yet to make my purchases." She hesitated.

"I am in perfectly good hands," Hattie said.

She was *literally* in Bentley's hands. Something which did not go unnoticed by the older woman's beady eyes. Was that the reason she seemed unwilling to leave?

Carriage wheels alerted them of the approaching conveyance, and it rolled to a stop just before them. Mrs. Naylor looked inordinately relieved. "Good day then, dear. Take a nice, restorative nap when you return home, and you will feel much more the thing."

"Yes, of course, Mrs. Naylor," Hattie replied dutifully. She waited for the older woman to return to the apothecary to complete her business before climbing into her carriage and settling herself on the bench beside her maid.

Bentley stood at the door, his hand resting on the enamel siding as he leaned in slightly. "I needn't ask, of course, but—"

"No, it was not real." She grinned. "But there is no saying how long Lucy will be with the modiste, so I'm uncertain when I can get away."

"I am a patient man," Bentley replied quietly. He dipped his head to Hattie, then her maid, before leaving. He'd dropped his package of pigment supplies on the floor when he'd sprung into action, so he slipped back inside the shop to retrieve them.

"And the *man*," Mrs. Naylor was saying to the apothecary, leaning forward against the counter with her back to the door. "Never seen him before in my life. But my, what shoulders. Did you see the way he lifted Miss Green so easily? It begs the question—"

The apothecary cleared his throat. Blast. Bentley was really interested in learning exactly what question his lifting Hattie had begged.

He bent to retrieve his package from the floor where it had fallen, and Mrs. Naylor looked at him over her shoulder. Two bright spots of color formed on her cheeks and he lifted the package to show exactly why he'd re-entered the shop. Dipping into a bow, he bade them a good day and left.

Gossips. That was all these country folk were—or *any* folk, truly. Was it any wonder he'd remained hidden away for so long?

The Green carriage sat idly where he'd last seen it, and he

glanced through the window as he passed, noting Hattie speaking to her maid.

He was so impressed with her quick ability to fall into a ruse. He never would have considered fainting in order to draw attention away from their nearness. Bentley quickened his pace with growing anticipation. He merely needed to stop home to leave the package of pigments in his painting room, and then he was going to see Hattie. Nothing in the world sounded more enjoyable than that.

CHAPTER 21

*H*attie pulled her gloves from her fingers, eager to rid herself of her gown and don her habit as she followed her sister-in-law up the steps and through the front door of their house. Lucy had taken an extraordinary amount of time in the modiste's shop, and Hattie feared she was keeping Bentley waiting for her in the frigid barn. She had warned him of the potential, however. She could only hope he had waited a good amount of time before leaving the warmth of his house.

The butler stepped forward, his hands gripped behind his back. "You've a visitor, ma'am. He's in the parlor with Master Jeffrey."

"Who is it?" Lucy asked, stopping behind her.

"Mr. Warren."

Hattie's heart leapt. *Finally*. Thanking her butler, she stepped around him, Lucy doggedly at her heels.

"What do you intend to say?" Lucy asked.

"A greeting, I expect."

Lucy's irritated chuckle sounded. "But how shall you present yourself?"

"As myself."

Lucy tugged at her arm, pulling her to a stop in the corridor outside of the parlor door, her eyes wide. "You cannot step into that room without a plan, Hattie. This is your chance to make an impression on the man that will entice him to return. Quite a lot is riding on this." She lowered her voice, stepping closer. "Are you nervous? You seem nervous."

"Well, *now* I am. Heavens, Lucy. If he was not enticed to come visit straight away following the ball where we met, then what hope do I truly have?"

Lucy looked disturbed, her chin tucking. "With that sort of attitude? No hope at all." Seizing Hattie's hands, Lucy gazed at her fiercely. "But you can incite his interest. I have faith in you. Is it not worth a smidgen of effort in order to secure the potential for future happiness?"

Hattie's body froze. Was it worth the effort? Up until now, she had firmly believed love would find her, that her true love would come into her life when the time was right, and she oughtn't fight it. That had been the case for her parents, had it not? They'd met and married after they both had passed their thirtieth year, and they were blissfully in love. Hattie hadn't felt as though she was losing chances and running out of time to form a connection, but what if Lucy was correct, and Hattie's true love was Mr. Warren?

She *had* been led to him by a fox, after all.

Drawing in a deep breath, she pressed her lips together and nodded.

Lucy looked inordinately relieved, and she tried not to read too much into that. "What is your plan?"

"Plan?" Her plan was to speak quickly to Mr. Warren and then escape to the barn. She couldn't very well leave Bentley waiting for her much longer.

Lucy pressed her lips together and breathed through her

nose, annoyance written over her drawn eyebrows. She opened her mouth to speak when the door opened, and Jeffrey appeared. He stopped himself before running directly into his wife.

"Gads, darling. What are you doing?"

Lucy strung her arm through his and affected an innocent smile. Goodness, she had that down to an art. "Just discussing tedious things. Did I hear you have a visitor?"

He nodded. "Mr. Warren came to visit. I was just coming to see what was keeping you. We saw the carriage arrive home."

Hattie shot him a blank smile before skirting her brother and gliding into the room. Mr. Warren stood at once, doffing his hat and sending her a grin that sent butterflies to her stomach. Which was odd, for hardly anything made Hattie nervous.

"Have you enjoyed your visit to our beautiful county, Mr. Warren?" she asked, rapidly considering her options. She lowered herself into the seat nearest his and waited for Lucy and Jeffrey to claim the sofa opposite them.

"Indeed, it has been a restful respite."

"The country is good for that," Jeffrey agreed. "But I find myself eagerly looking forward to returning to Town."

That came as a surprise to Hattie. She'd thought Jeffrey adored Devon. It was their home, the place they were raised.

Lucy tittered, her voice reaching an unnaturally high tone. "Of course that must be because our friends are in Town, and all the best shops. Nothing compares to being in the company of those one finds comfortable."

Jeffrey shot a glance at his sister, and she valiantly smiled. Did Lucy imply that she did not find it comfortable in Devon generally, or just in Hattie's house? It was true that they had never been particularly close—Lucy and Hattie were much too different for that to be possible—but Hattie had never made a concerted effort to push Lucy away. They simply did not appreciate the same things. Lucy enjoyed sifting through fashion plates and discussing gowns at length, and Hattie preferred to paint. Lucy loathed the sun and the freckles it could mar her skin with, and Hattie was so covered in the little beasts she had long since ceased trying to limit them, much preferring any activity which took her out of doors and allowed the sun to warm her skin.

Lucy cared for the strictures of Society, and Hattie valued her own ideas and opinions above those of others. The two were simply water and oil. But it hurt all the same to learn that Lucy did not wish to be there. Hattie would have assumed her home was the most comfortable, welcoming house in all of England. Her sister-in-law should feel likewise.

But then, as hostess, it was Hattie's duty to *make* it so, and she had failed in that regard.

"I only stopped by to thank you for the invitation to dine," Mr. Warren said.

Lucy straightened, inclining her head. "It was our pleasure. May I presume to guess that you shall be joining us?"

"Indeed, I would be delighted. The duke and I are both honored to accept the invitation."

Hattie sucked in a quick breath. "But surely the duke would prefer to speak for himself on such matters."

Mr. Warren's face betrayed nothing, but he tilted his head just slightly to the side. "I can assure you I have his blessing to relay this bit of news. He is quite looking forward to it."

Given Bentley's reaction to learning of the invitation in Graton, Hattie very much doubted that to be the case. Lucy stared at her hard though, and Hattie closed her mouth before she said anything she would later come to regret. If nothing else, Bentley could beg off later by his own hand, and Hattie would make certain he was given the opportunity to do so.

"You must have such an exciting life, traveling to and fro."

Mr. Warren nodded at Lucy. "It has been quite the adventure,

I'll admit. Though I do wonder at times if I am too old to keep it up much longer."

Lucy's tittering laugh grated on her nerves, and Hattie clenched her teeth. She wanted to speak to Mr. Warren, of course she did, but she could not remove from her mind the image of Bentley waiting in the cold barn loft alone. Her toes tapped the plush carpet as she did her best to appear interested in the conversation circulating around her, all the while wishing it would end.

Lucy had been right; Hattie had certainly needed a plan before entering the parlor. Instead, she was wasting this time by wishing she was elsewhere. She believed herself adept at slipping away from unhappy scenarios. How could she manage to escape this one?

"Miss Green is quite the dancer," Mr. Warren said, nodding as though he was agreeing with Lucy on that score.

Lucy's eyes were wide, her head tipping toward the gentleman. She could not be more obvious if she made an effort to be so.

"I enjoy dancing quite a lot," Hattie agreed.

"But not nearly as much as painting," Jeffrey said, chuckling. "I believe my sister was born with a paintbrush in her hand."

"Oh, it was nothing of the sort," Hattie said. "I developed my immense skill much later than that."

Jeffrey barked a laugh. "And she's humble, to boot. But we love her just the same."

Hattie grinned. "Speaking of painting, I do have a project I would like to return to—"

"Say no more," Mr. Warren said, rising. "I've overstayed my visit."

"No, no." Lucy rose, seemingly desperate to force him to remain. "You are quite welcome here, I assure you. We are practically starved of company so far out here, and it is a blessed thing to have one so comfortable to speak to."

Hattie closed her mouth against further arguments, unable to keep her brow from furrowing. Was she truly such horrid company?

Mr. Warren would not be deterred, however, much to Hattie's relief. "I have remained far longer than I should have, and I thank you for your kindness and hospitality."

"It was nothing," Jeffrey said, motioning toward the door. He left to see their guest to the door.

When the sound of footsteps had receded, Hattie moved to go upstairs, and Lucy followed close behind her. "Well, that could have gone better, but I do think it wasn't a complete failure."

"Thank you, I think." Hattie mounted the stairs toward her bedchamber, Lucy continuing along just a step behind her.

"He seemed eager to see you again. I do think it is a good sign that he was willing to wait such a length of time just to speak to you. There could have been no other reason for waiting as long as he did."

"No other reason except a delight in Jeffrey's conversation, of course."

Lucy was quiet for a moment before agreeing. "Well, yes. There is that, too."

Opening the door to her bedchamber, Hattie was happy to find Agnes there smoothing the gown of her habit over her bed. Her maid was such a gem.

"If you will excuse me, Lucy, I think I shall go for a ride."

Lucy's face screwed up in confusion. "Did you not say you wished to paint?"

Hattie paused. "Yes, and my supplies are at the old barn."

Lucy looked from Hattie to her maid. "I do not think you should go alone. Would you like for me—"

"I will not be alone," Hattie said quickly. She would not allow her sister-in-law to ruin this for her. She wanted to see Bentley, to speak to him. Lucy's presence would make that impossible. "Agnes will come with me. Do not forget that our customs here differ from what you are used to in London. No one would consider it odd to find me alone on a ride on my own father's land anyway."

Lucy's mouth opened before she closed it, looking to the ceiling in thought. "I suppose you are correct."

Hattie bit her tongue before she said something she regretted, instead shooting Lucy a bland smile.

"Allow me to get out of your way."

Hattie didn't argue, only waited for her to leave. Once Lucy was gone, she turned quickly. "Hurry, Agnes. Bentley is likely waiting for us right now. We must make haste."

"Not us, miss. He is waiting for *you*."

Hattie paused in her efforts to free herself from her gown as Agnes swept behind her and deftly unfastened it. Agnes was not wrong in her statement, but it was jarring, nonetheless.

"Are you all right, miss?"

"Haste, Agnes," Hattie said, unsure of the answer herself, her thoughts like a jumble of yarn in her brain. "Haste!"

When Hattie and Agnes reached the barn, she jumped from her horse and tossed the reins to her dismounting maid, who caught them with agility. Hattie lifted her skirt from the muddy barn floor and stepped into the dim interior, relief flooding her when she spotted the duke's horse neatly tucked into a stall. She looked up to the loft.

"Bentley?" she called.

He stepped toward the edge, leaning over and fastening his gaze on her.

She had never before been so happy to see a face. "I am so glad you're here!" She crossed to the ladder and climbed toward him.

"As am I."

The rough wood was cold under her gloves, and even the old walls did not protect her from a chill wind. It would soon become too cold to continue meeting here if this weather persisted. She stilled at the top of the ladder, resting her arms against the top rung. "Please tell me you haven't been waiting long."

"Define *long*." He reached to help her up, and she slipped her hand into his.

Oh, drat. Should she tell him that he owed his waiting to his own house guest? "Are you completely frozen now? I wish we could build a fire up here, but I fear that would only end in disaster."

He chuckled, his hand lingering on hers. "I would thank you to keep from lighting any fires in here."

Hattie grinned. "So you say, but would you be glad of the warmth?"

"For a minute, perhaps. Then fear for my life would take over."

Agnes climbed over the top of the ladder and Bentley released Hattie's hand in order to assist her maid.

A duke assisting a maid. Never had Hattie expected to see such an occurrence. But it did not surprise her—not with Bentley. He seemed to treat his own servants better than a lot of her acquaintances did who were half his rank. It was refreshing and spoke volumes about the type of man he was.

"Did you have a visitor?" Bentley asked, following Hattie toward the sofas. There was an array of blankets thrown over the back of the ratty couches and she offered him one before taking another for herself. They smelled as though they had been in a barn for quite some time, but Hattie preferred the warmth.

"How did you know?"

Bentley shrugged, arranging the blanket over his lap, the

frayed, aged quilt at odds with his well-put-together appearance. "Warren wasn't home when I returned from Graton, so I made the assumption that he'd gone to visit you."

How was she meant to take that? She wanted to know what Mr. Warren had said to lead Bentley to reach that conclusion, but she bit her tongue. Bentley had mentioned his distaste for gossips, and he certainly wouldn't appreciate it if she attempted to engage him in the activity. Hattie retrieved her sketch and charcoal before sitting across from Bentley, pulling her feet underneath her and tucking a blanket around her legs. Agnes did the same, sitting on the end of Hattie's sofa and covering herself in a blanket.

Bentley cleared his throat. "Did he stay long?"

She scrunched up her face in apology. "He waited for a good deal of time before I arrived, so I did not feel I could leave without visiting with him."

"I understand."

She drew in a breath, focusing on the drawing instead of Bentley's face. "Mr. Warren accepted Lucy's invitation to our dinner party next week."

"I would expect nothing less."

"He accepted on behalf of both of you."

The loft grew silent, the only sound was the whistling wind traveling through cracks in the walls and the horses huffing down below. She hazarded a look up and caught him staring at her intently, his mouth in a firm line.

"You may write to Lucy today and explain the misunderstanding," Hattie suggested. "I think she would understand."

"No," Bentley said softly. "I don't think that will be necessary."

Hattie put down her pencil. She said nothing, only stared. He was going to attend? Had he gone mad? "Do you realize the implications of attending this dinner? There is more to the party than just my household."

He shifted in his seat. "Is it a great number?"

"No more than a dozen, but is that not a great number when you've spent so long in isolation?"

Bentley ran a hand over his face, then he speared her with a look. "I think it is time I put an end to my isolation."

CHAPTER 22

*B*entley could not deny the very real warmth pulsing through his body, despite the frigid cold surrounding him. He had just told Hattie that he would come to her house for a dinner party, and his heart was beating so hard he feared it would soon escape his chest. It was quite a lot for his brain to wrap around—the idea of going out in Society again. But Warren had been correct. Once Mr. Humphries was no longer around, there would be little threat to Bentley's secret being discovered.

He could attend dinners or balls again, or even church. He could openly call on Hattie.

"You are considering going out in Society again?" Hattie asked, her eyebrows raised. "That is wonderful news."

"Well, there are a few contingencies." In truth, he was questioning the sanity of such a notion, despite the benefits. Should he not wait for a confirmation letter from his mother before believing himself safe? Pain sliced through his heart, and he closed his eyes briefly.

"What is it?" Hattie asked, her tone dropping at once as she shoved her pencil and portrait at her maid and crossed to his sofa. The gesture felt oddly familiar and comforting in its familiarity.

He tried to smile. "It is nothing."

"You are distressed." She waved a hand about his torso. "None of this strong-willed *it is nothing* business, if you please. I am the soul of discretion, and Agnes is quite as trustworthy as I am."

Bentley glanced to the maid, and her brief smile was all he needed to believe Hattie's faith was not misplaced. He could well imagine that the maid had a strong loyalty to her mistress. How could anyone not feel that way in relation to Hattie?

Hattie gazed up at him, her eyes as wide and open as her soul, and he very much had the desire to cease speaking and draw her into his arms. She fit so perfectly there, and her warmth would do much to heal his aching heart.

"You are beginning to worry me," she whispered.

Bentley pulled himself from his musings. He needed to focus. It was as though holding Hattie in the shop earlier that day had unlocked a portion of himself he'd vowed to keep hidden away. Bentley had chosen not to pursue marriage out of respect for his father and subsequently dismissed the thought of obtaining a wife, giving it very little thought. But now... he looked at Hattie's open, caring face and the subject was very much on his mind.

What he lacked, at present, was the knowledge and ability of how to go about addressing it. How did one discover if another cared for them in equal measure? Was he just meant to tell her of his feelings and hope she returned the sentiment? It was impossible to know how to proceed, and quite a terrifying prospect. Bentley had avoided vulnerability for so long, he was uncertain if he contained the strength to make himself so vulnerable now.

But he could try.

"It is not worrisome, merely..." He cleared his throat, uncertain how to begin. Should he tell her of his mother's deceit? Surely that was too much for her innocent ears.

"What are the contingencies you speak of?" she asked. "Are you in danger?"

Her concern buoyed his spirits. "No, nothing of the sort. I merely…" He swallowed. He could not very well say that he must wait for his mother's husband to die. The very thought made him feel foul. "It is rather complicated. You see, I do not have an easy time in company, and being around groups of people has always made me uncomfortable. As I aged, my mother sought to drive that abnormality from me by exposing me to as many social functions as she could. It did nothing but heighten my desire for solitude."

"You have chosen to remain hidden for your own comfort?" Her tone was compassionate, not condescending, and he appreciated her desire to understand.

"No, that merely made my choice easier. I hid away because I deemed it necessary to protect my father's good name from scandal. If it was discovered that I…well, I do not wish to reveal the sordid details. I fear they are too much to lay upon your ears."

Hattie glanced to the sofa opposite them where her maid sat. Bentley had forgotten the woman was there.

Laying a hand over his, Hattie squeezed his fingers. "You needn't tell me anything."

He blinked, noting the authenticity of her words and realizing how deeply he *did* want to tell her everything. But she rose, stepping away from him and crossing to the other sofa, reclaiming her seat nearer her maid. Her attention was drawn back to the portrait she was crafting, and the mood in the room shifted, as though the very atmosphere recognized the time for sharing had passed.

"You know," Hattie said, glancing up at him before looking

down at her canvas. "I never noticed the cleft in your chin before you shaved. Your beard hid it well."

"That was my intention," he said, without thinking. Or perhaps that was the lie he told himself, and the slip up had been entirely intentional. He wanted her to know. Bentley believed Hattie would be different, that she wouldn't cast him aside.

She chuckled. "Whyever would you want to do that? It is so handsome."

He warmed from her praise, his heart skipping a beat. "Because if anyone spotted the similarities between me and my mother's second husband, my father's good name would forever be tarnished. Gossip tends to spread through the *ton* like a barn caught in flames."

Hattie looked up, dropping her hand onto her lap. She was clearly surprised, her mouth hanging open before she clamped it shut. "You mean to say that your father, the duke—"

"Was not my natural father."

Silence descended on the barn loft. Hattie recovered quickly. "Your mother married your...natural father...after the duke died?"

Bentley had made a mash of this. He'd wanted her to know the truth, but his delivery had felt more like a confession than bringing her into his confidence. He suddenly wondered at the wisdom of this plan. It was out there now, and there was nothing he could do to take it back. He had trusted this woman—blindly, perhaps—and now his fate lay in her hands.

After seven years of guarding this secret, how could he lay it bare? He was a fool.

"Indeed. I learned of it too late to inform my father, but I wonder if that was a blessing. He was on his deathbed and needn't know that his heir didn't carry the blood of his ancestors."

"But your father would not have loved you any less, surely." Hattie's voice was low, thoughtful. "It was not your fault."

He shrugged. "I will never know."

His mother's face flashed in his mind, fear in her eyes when she'd realized Bentley had overheard her conversation. But what had she expected? It was foolish to speak so openly when he was nearby, regardless of his appearance to be sleeping.

"The man who is your natural father, do you speak to him?" Hattie asked gently.

"I do not speak to him or my mother. It has been years since I have done so."

Hattie glanced to her maid again before looking back at Bentley. "May I ask why?"

"Of course. I'm certainly telling you more of my history than you sought to know." He gave her a brief smile. "She lied to me and my father my entire life and is not sorry for it. My mother never apologized, and the man she married has no bearing on me. I care not for his opinions or his failing health."

Hattie sucked in a breath. "Bentley."

He could say nothing in response to this. Her admonishing tone was warranted.

The maid rose. "Shall I prepare the horses?"

"Yes. Thank you, Agnes."

Prepare the horses? Were they not left in the stalls already prepared? Bentley watched Agnes shoot her mistress a look before climbing down the ladder. Hattie rose, coming to stand directly in front of him, and he began to ache from the burden he had just relieved. It was an odd thing for Bentley to bring another into his confidence, for it seemed to sap him of energy and buoy him up simultaneously.

"This is why you've hidden away all these years? To keep your mother's secret and protect your father's name?"

He nodded. It felt odd to look up at Hattie. Particularly given her compact height. "If you were to see my mother's husband…

well, the similarities are astounding. Same eyes, same cleft, same eyebrows, even... It is a wonder no one has yet to make the connection."

"But to hide yourself away for all those years... what a toll that must have taken on you." He could tell that she understood the gravity of his situation. If anyone were to discover and spread word of his questionable legitimacy, there was little they could do to remove him from the dukedom, but his father would be shamed. They would speak ill of the dead—of a man unable to defend himself.

"If one loses their good name, what do they have?" he asked, looking up into Hattie's compassionate eyes. He had been right to trust her, to know that she would understand and not judge him for it.

"Oh, Bentley," she said, anguished. She reached for his hand and tugged him up until he stood before her. Slipping her hands around his waist, she pulled him close, fisting the back of his coat in her hands and pressing her cheek against his chest. "What a burden you've carried and for so long."

Bentley stiffened, but Hattie's warmth soon thawed his fear and he melted into her, his arms surrounding her and pulling her tight against him. He hadn't felt an embrace in years, not since he had lived at home. Even then, his mother had never been the type to show affection. It was simply not the way things were done.

Hattie breathed in deeply and let the air out slowly, pressing further into him as though she meant to squeeze the negativity away. He closed his eyes, his pulse thrumming in his neck, and he imagined her heartbeat matching his.

Leaning back, Hattie bent her neck to look into his eyes and he wanted to still time, to memorize the moment so he could recall it always. He cared about this woman, and he was going to make it so he was in a position to tell her so.

She shook her head fractionally, her brow furrowed. "But what has changed? Why do you now wish to go into Society?"

Could he tell her now? He drew in a quick breath, his voice low and hoarse. "Do you really not know?"

Hattie seemed to freeze, her body growing still. Time seemed to pass slowly as he painfully awaited her response. He was woefully out of practice wooing young ladies, and he didn't know if there was another way about it. But he was allowing his heart to lead him, and it was presently guiding him to Hattie.

"I'm not sure I know what you mean," she whispered.

Bentley lifted a hand to her face. Brushing aside a lock of hair, he revealed her beautiful, freckled cheek. He wanted to lay a kiss upon each speckle.

Swallowing, he held her gaze, his thumb brushing her blushing skin. "Surely I have made myself plain."

Her eyes widened a moment before they darted to his lips, and she bit hers. Bentley suppressed a groan. He wanted to kiss her, but she had yet to respond, to say that she returned his feelings.

"If only you were a fox," she said softly, an awkward chuckle leaving her chest.

Bentley stiffened. He looked at her a moment longer before shame flooded his body. Did she harbor an attraction for Warren? Surely she could not love the man, not when they had only spent a few hours in one another's company. But if she was attracted to him, imagined a life with him...should Bentley tell her now that it was all for naught? That Warren was not interested in a wife?

No, he couldn't. It would only appear as though he was trying to strengthen his own suit. Dropping his hand from her cheek, he released her waist and stepped back, clearing his throat.

Hattie looked pained. "I realize that you were hurt by your

mother's dishonesty, but if her husband is dying, will you not regret missing the opportunity to speak to him just once?"

"I think I will," he said. He agreed, and it was a decision he had not made lightly. "I leave tomorrow at first light to see them. I shall return before the dinner party, so you may tell your sister-in-law that I am happy to attend."

"You mustn't feel an obligation, Bentley. Not when you have so much to attend to now."

"I will return," he said, trying for a light tone when all he wanted was to escape. "You needn't fear for your painting lessons."

"I should think those painting lessons are the least important thing at present."

Bentley felt as though she'd taken the end of her pencil and stabbed him in the heart. "On the contrary," he said softly. "They are one of the things I look forward to most."

Hattie regarded him quietly as he busied himself with replacing the blankets they'd used, then stood near the ladder to wait for her. He felt her eyes on him, but he was ashamed he'd lain himself bare for her and had been summarily rejected. Could he call that exchange anything else? If the woman had feelings for him, she would have allowed him to kiss her. His blatant staring at her lips could have meant nothing else, and that was something even she should have picked up on.

They climbed down the ladder quietly and mounted their horses. Agnes closed the barn door and mounted her horse, directing it toward the Green estate. The cold wind whipped around them, softly pushing them toward their homes and away from one another. Before meeting Hattie at the barn Bentley hadn't entirely decided on when he should leave for Kent, but now he was determined to rid himself of Devonshire as quickly as he was able.

"Goodbye, Hattie," he said, before turning his horse and urging him into a canter. He wanted a bruising ride and a way to forget his forwardness. Perhaps Hattie's Cunning Woman had an incantation he could use. He chuckled to himself and urged his horse to go quicker. The sooner he put her behind him, the better.

He wanted her to want *him*, not settle for him just because his name was Fawkes.

He wanted to be her Bentley, not her fox.

CHAPTER 23

*H*attie swirled the cream into her tea, lifting the spoon and letting the liquid drip back into the cup. She lowered it again, and the spoon clanked against the fine porcelain as she stirred it further, mesmerized by the tiny ripples in the cup. It had been nearly a week since the meeting with Bentley in the barn, and she had been unable to think of much else since. He hadn't responded to the letter she had left in the lightning tree. She hoped he had gone to visit his mother as he had claimed, and not simply chosen to ignore Hattie.

But the events of the last meeting they'd had left a confusion within her, an uneasiness that she hadn't been able to shake. She needed to see him again, to make certain they were still friends. She heartily regretted turning to humor during such a vulnerable moment, but Bentley had implied feelings for her, and she'd panicked. She should have been kinder in her response, not made a jest about foxes.

"Hattie, have you gone mad?"

"Hmm?" she asked, looking up at four sets of eyes blinking back at her. She returned to the present, her thoughts drifting away from Bentley and back to the Fremonts' drawing room and the friends gathered around her. Amelia and Charles Fremont sat on the couch beside her, while Giulia and Nick Pepper were comfortably ensconced across from them.

What had they been speaking of? Oh, yes. The assemblies.

Giulia cradled her babe in a blanket, a smirk on her lips. "Or is there a different reason you've chosen to attend a Melbury event?"

"Melbury?" her husband asked, his blond eyebrows lifting. "Why would you want to go there?"

"For the assemblies," Amelia said, settling close to her husband's side. "She merely wants to dance. We shan't begrudge her that."

"We can have a dance," Charles said kindly. "You need not soil yourself by going to Melbury for it."

Hattie sipped her tea, fighting the smile on her lips. "You sound like my father."

"Rightfully so," Nick said, scoffing. "Melbury cheated at the cricket match. You were there, Miss Green. I'm surprised you are willing to overlook the event."

"And they stole our horses," Charles put in, bringing his teacup to his lips. "That was only a few months ago now. Have you so easily forgotten?"

"I should think your father would be adamantly opposed to you attending any function within Melbury's boundaries," Nick agreed.

Giulia reached over and gripped Nick's hand. "It is only a dance, gentlemen. One which I propose we all attend."

The men groaned good-naturedly.

"Indeed," Amelia said. "We cannot send Hattie into Melbury unprotected."

"I should think not," Nick said with feeling.

Hattie swallowed the remainder of her tea. "You needn't come if you don't wish to. My brother shall accompany me, rest assured. It is Lucy who wishes to go, after all. I am not being thrown to the wolves."

There was a general murmur of assent in the room. She did share her friends' opinions, but she couldn't very well refuse Lucy the assemblies. Not after learning that coming to Devon to visit was such a chore for the woman, the company here so thin.

"Fear not," Giulia said. "We shall come."

"Indeed, we will," Charles agreed, "but Amelia will not dance."

Quiet settled over them. Giulia looked up sharply, her knowing eyes falling to Amelia's hand resting on her stomach. "Do you have something to share with us?"

The smile which spread over Amelia's lips brightened her face. "Charles and I are going to become parents."

Charles's broad grin displayed how excited he was, and Hattie was happy for them.

Amelia's face grew apologetic. "It is still early days, but I'm not sure I could stomach the motion of dancing yet."

"But you will still attend?" Giulia asked.

"Of course."

Relief poured through Hattie. If she had to go to the assemblies in Melbury to appease her sister-in-law, at least she would have her supportive friends by her side. She was particularly grateful to have their husbands to claim as dance partners, for she was not in the mood to flirt. From the moment Bentley's fingers brushed her cheek, Hattie's body had erupted with the desire to kiss the man, and it overcame her with such a powerful force that it frightened her.

She couldn't very well throw herself onto him when he was in such a vulnerable state. She had only embraced him because his story had broken her heart, and she had been able to see from the pain in his eyes how his own soul was tormented and broken in kind. He'd needed to go to his mother, to see to his stepfather and put the past behind him in order to heal.

They had spent quite a lot of time together of late, and it was clear to Hattie that Bentley believed himself to have feelings for her on some level. But surely that was only because she was the first woman he had interacted with for years.

If he had regularly interacted with other women, he would not be choosing a short, freckle-covered Hattie who spoke far more outlandish things than was proper and possessed too many faults. She knew she was odd for putting so much store in the Midsummer's Eve fox sighting...but what if she wasn't crazy? What if Mr. Warren *was* her true love? How could she know?

Surely the warmth that filled her and the way she ached for Bentley's touch had only been because she craved love so deeply. She would likely feel that when any willing man held her so tenderly. She glanced up to find Nick looking at her and shuddered.

Well, not *any* man. Definitely not her friends' husbands.

"The only thing our party is missing is Mabel," Amelia said. "Do you think we can fetch her in time?"

"The assemblies are not until tomorrow night, yes?" Charles said. "I should think that would be entirely possible, only, she is still in her confinement, is she not?"

Hattie shot up in her seat, grateful her teacup was empty so she did not slosh liquid onto Amelia's carpet. "Oh, please do try."

Charles and Amelia shared a look before he cast her an apologetic smile. "It is not possible, Hattie. She only had little James just a few weeks ago. She's in no fit condition to ride such a length of time."

Hattie slumped back against the seat. "You are right, of course. I wasn't thinking."

Amelia reached over and squeezed her arm. "I was joking when I suggested it, Hattie. I wouldn't have, though, if I'd realized how much it meant to you."

Her friends cast her pitying looks, and she put on a brave face. "I should probably be going. Lucy will wonder where I've gone."

"Of course," Amelia said.

Giulia passed her bundled Olivia to Nick. "Can we accompany you part of the way?"

"I think I will cut through the fields, actually," Hattie said, eager to be alone. "It is far too cold to take the roads the long way around."

She meant to cut through Bentley's estate and check the lightning tree once more. She'd looked that morning, but her letter had still sat untouched, wedged into the charred bark of the broken tree. That had been hours ago, though. Perhaps Bentley had returned home now and had had the opportunity to write her back.

Anticipation slowly filled her, and she followed her friends to the door, distracted as they said their farewells and the Peppers loaded into their carriage. A light touch on her elbow drew her attention and she found Amelia's concerned gaze on her.

"What is troubling you?" she asked.

Hattie shrugged. "I am only distracted."

"But the Melbury assemblies? You've never once wished to go before."

"And I don't wish to go now. I'm appeasing Lucy. I haven't been the greatest of hostesses, I fear. It is the least I can do to recompense her for my distraction this last month."

Amelia nodded in understanding. "When will your father return?"

"Soon, I hope. He was meant to come home weeks ago, but then discovered that an old friend of his was nearby and deathly ill. He wrote again a few days ago to let us know that he should be home within a fortnight, he believes. It could be sooner."

"I'm sorry to hear it." Amelia paused, her pale red eyebrows drawing together. She searched Hattie's face. "Will you tell me if something is troubling you?"

Hattie looked into her friend's soft, blue eyes and held her breath, running over her concerns in her mind. They were so jumbled, she wouldn't know where to begin, and she could not reveal anything about Bentley. She had made him a promise.

But without speaking of Bentley, there was nothing to unburden to Amelia. Shaking her head, Hattie focused on her horse, gripping the saddle and climbing onto the mounting block before seating herself and arranging her skirt over her legs.

"I am well, Amelia, and I look forward to dancing."

Amelia's face betrayed how little she believed her, but what could Hattie do? She wouldn't betray Bentley, and she knew from experience how Amelia did not believe in any of Mrs. Fowler's white magic. Hattie had never before felt so alone in her troubles. But that was precisely where she would stay. She had no other choice.

"Be safe," Amelia called, and Hattie lifted a hand in recognition as she rode away.

The sun was high in the sky but did little to counteract the cold wind that rushed over her as she rode toward home. It was unfair of Bentley to put her in this position where she questioned everything, and then leave. But it was more unfair of her to be angry about it, so she shoved down the warring emotions and allowed her horse to lead her toward the achingly familiar lightning tree. It came into view and her heart leapt when she found it empty. Her note had been taken.

Jumping from the saddle, she rushed to the tree and searched the crack for a response, but nothing was there. Had Bentley returned home recently and taken the note but lacked the chance to reply yet? Hattie's heart beat steady and quick as she searched the ground in case her letter had fallen, but it was nowhere to be seen.

Taking her horse's reins, she led him toward a fallen tree and used it to regain the saddle. She was equal parts nervous and excited to see Bentley again. Surely he would have much to tell her after his recent trip.

When Hattie turned her horse in the direction of home, she screamed at the sight of a man on horseback just two paces away.

"Forgive me," Mr. Warren said, lifting his brown hat in greeting before placing it back on his copper hair. "I did not intend to sneak up on you. I thought you could hear my approach."

Hattie's gaze shot to the tree before she swallowed and turned a bright smile on Mr. Warren. "I was distracted."

His brow was puzzled. "Yes, I see. Now, was I mistaken, or did you just—"

"Are you coming to the assemblies tomorrow?" she asked quickly before he had a chance to finish his question. She didn't wish for him to ask about the tree. She couldn't lie to another person.

His impatient horse stamped his hooves. "I did not know of it."

"In Melbury, tomorrow night at the White Hare. It's on High Street. You won't miss it."

"I will be there," Mr. Warren promised. He watched her closely, and she grew uncomfortable under his stare.

Hattie nodded. "Tomorrow then," she said, trying to sound airy. She turned her horse about and headed for home, uncertain why she was so discomfited by the interaction. Mr. Warren showed every sign of being interested in her. She should be glad of their chance encounter.

Well, not entirely chance, of course. He was staying with the duke, and they'd met on Bentley's land.

She sucked in a quick breath as her horse cleared the treeline and broke onto her father's property. If Mr. Warren was still nearby, she could ask him to extend the invitation to Bentley. Glancing over her shoulder, she searched for motion but did not see anyone.

Surely he did not need her request in order to make sure Bentley was aware of the assemblies. He had said he planned to rejoin society, had he not? She urged her horse to go faster, eager to return home. She wanted to look her best tomorrow night. There was a probable chance she would see Bentley then, and she needed him to know that they could put the awkwardness of their last encounter behind them and remain friends. She wasn't ready to lose his lessons or his company. She'd grown too fond of them to sacrifice them yet.

When she returned her horse to the stables and let herself into the house, she snuck upstairs and allowed Agnes to draw a bath to warm her chilled body. She did her best to remove Bentley from her mind, but it was much harder to do than she expected. There was nothing for it. They would need to discuss what had happened.

Preferably at the assemblies, while she looked her best. Then she could ease the discomfort of the conversation with a friendly dance. The prospect was enticing, and she warmed to it the more she thought on it.

Sitting at her dressing table while Agnes combed through her hair, Hattie couldn't dampen the smile that curved her lips. She was going to see Bentley.

CHAPTER 24

*B*entley stood on the rounded portico of his ancestral home in Kent, the pillars behind him blocking shafts of weak sunlight as rain poured down in sheets. He was drenched, unable to escape the rain during the last few hours of his ride and unwilling to prolong the trip any longer by stopping to wait it out. He'd been at it for far too long already, and uncomfortable on an unfamiliar borrowed hack he'd been forced to use when his own steed grew too weary.

But now that he stood on the steps of his home, the house his father had raised him in, where his mother had now lived with her husband for the last seven years, he could not bring himself to go inside.

The servants knew Bentley was there. They'd taken the horse and promised him a hot bath would be waiting in his old room. It had been a shock to the old groom Wiley and the stable master, Jeeves, when he'd shown up in the stable's doorway, and Bentley hadn't realized how glad he would be to see their familiar faces after so long.

He would be satisfied if he could change out of his wet clothes and warm his chilled body before facing his mother. But managing to slip upstairs unseen could prove tricky. The enormous house towered above him and he wondered at the feeling of contentment that had settled over him when it had first come into view. He was home. This was where he would always feel a connection to his father. Though in truth, after his many years at Wolfeton House, this mansion now felt far too big.

The door swung open and he straightened, staring into the shocked, wrinkled face of Haskett, his old steward.

"Master Silas, is it really you?" The man's mouth gaped like a trout. "The servants are in a bit of a flutter, and I had to see it for myself."

Bentley slicked water from his hair and nodded.

"Dashed rain. Come in, sir." He shook his head quickly, his jowls shuddering from the motion like a shaken jelly mold. "No, forgive me. Your Grace. You're Bentley now, aren't you? These old bones will take some time to get used to that."

He'd been Bentley for seven years but knew none in his household likely saw him that way. How could they? He'd left as soon as the dukedom had fallen on his shoulders. To them, he'd always been Master Silas.

"I requested a bath," Bentley said through chattering lips.

A woman appeared behind Haskett, and Bentley stiffened until he recognized the timeworn face beneath the white cap. Mrs. Ramsbury, an old maid. Was she the housekeeper now? She was certainly dressed as such, the chatelaine jingling from her thin waist. She clicked her tongue. "Your Grace, come in. You must be frozen through."

"Nearly," he said, allowing the older woman to usher him inside. The house was much warmer than he remembered the chilled halls being as a boy, and he at once recalled that it was his own income and resources going to heat it. The sourness in his gut built and swirled as Mrs. Ramsbury led him up the familiar stairs in the waning light and toward his bedchamber.

He'd clearly spent too long waiting on the portico, for a bath was already prepared alongside a few footmen he didn't recognize.

"Philip and Ralph will assist you with whatever you need, Your Grace. Can I send for a tray or will you be joining the duchess for dinner?"

She was no longer the duchess, not to Bentley. When she married Mr. Humphries, she lost any right to call herself that. Instead of voicing his thoughts, however, Bentley tried to smile. "A tray would be grand."

"I'll see to it at once, Your Grace."

Mrs. Ramsbury scurried from the room, Haskett just behind her. He sat stiffly in the ladder-back chair and allowed the footmen to begin removing his boots.

He hadn't seen Mother yet, but she likely knew he was there. The meeting loomed ahead, and he forced himself to think on other things, like sweet Hattie's slender arms doing their best to comfort away his sorrows. She was the most giving, compassionate person of his acquaintance and he wished she was with him now. He could manage anything with her by his side, he was certain.

And she'd been correct. He needed to see his mother again, to allow her one last chance to apologize. Surely if he did so, he would not carry any more guilt for the remainder of his life. He certainly could not handle more than he had now.

Bentley was decided. He would bathe, then sit before the roaring fire and warm himself while he considered the best way to go about this. Once he was warm and his belly was full, he could probably stomach the idea of facing his mother.

He would just have to pretend Hattie was by his side.

Hattie stepped into the dimly lit White Hare Inn and looked around the crowds for a familiar, dark-headed duke.

"I know who you're looking for," Lucy said, leaning close so a cloud of rose-scent descended upon them both.

Hattie struggled to draw a fresh breath of air and trained her face into a bland expression. How could Lucy know? "Who?"

"Mr. Warren, of course." Lucy leaned in closer, an excited light in her eyes, and lowered her voice. "I see him just over there."

Oh. Hattie tried to rally, tamping down the disappointment snaking through her. Lucy took her hand and led her across the floor to where Mr. Warren stood beside Mr. and Mrs. Carter, leaving Jeffrey behind to speak to a neighbor.

"Caroline," Lucy purred. "I didn't expect to see you here this evening." Though she spoke in a tone that sounded as though quite the opposite was true.

Caroline dipped her gaze over Lucy's gown before looking at Hattie and giving them a slight smirk. It was so subtle, her disapproval, and delivered with such a slight flick of her eyes and chin that Hattie nearly believed she'd imagined it. But Lucy's bright red cheeks told her she hadn't, and Caroline Carter was exactly the sort of unkind woman who would judge another based on the cut and style of her clothing.

It made Hattie wish she had one of Cook's delicious berry pies to accidentally press against Mrs. Carter's pristine pale blue gown.

"Good evening, Miss Green, Mrs. Green," Mr. Warren said, dipping in a bow as the women greeted him. "I had no idea Devon boasted such fantastic company."

"Does this mean you will grace us with your presence more often?" Mr. Carter asked.

Mr. Warren shot Hattie a look. "I'm not sure yet." Clearing his throat, he smiled. "Miss Green, may I claim you for the next set?"

"I would be delighted."

Lucy squeezed her arm tightly, and Hattie wanted to pry the

woman's fingers loose, but she couldn't stomach the thought of embarrassing her sister-in-law in front of her wretched friends. If one could even call such a dismissing minx a friend. In Hattie's experience, friends were meant to uplift, support, and protect. This woman seemed more inclined to compare, degrade, and criticize.

"Will you fetch me something to drink?" Caroline drawled to her husband. "I'm absolutely parched."

"Of course." He left to do so, Warren just behind him, and Caroline's gaze flitted over the group. "I'm not sure what Mr. Warren could possibly mean. All I've encountered in Devon are countrified gentry who think they're better than they are. Gallivanting about the countryside like unkempt farmhands, even. They wouldn't last two minutes in a London drawing room."

Hattie gritted her teeth, forcing her mouth closed so she wouldn't speak her unkempt, countrified mind.

"Perhaps in Melbury," Lucy said diplomatically, taking Hattie by surprise. "But I have met many fine people in Graton."

Caroline's eyes sharpened. Had she been made aware of the childish rivalry between the towns?

"Hattie!" a sweet voice called, buoying her up with its familiarity. Giulia crossed toward her, Nick on her arm, and released her husband in order to pull Hattie into an embrace. She turned her grin on Lucy and took her by the hands. "How good to see you again, Mrs. Green. You look absolutely stunning tonight."

Lucy's cheeks pinked, and it was altogether superior to the way Caroline had brought roses to her cheeks. This time the color was born of pleasure and kindness.

"You look lovely as well, Mrs. Pepper."

"I thank you." Giulia turned her grin on Hattie. "Nick has promised to dance with me all night, even if it makes us look quite horrid to these Melbury folk. I think it's wicked of him, but I can't quite refuse the treat."

Nick stepped forward. "I would love to claim a dance from both of you, if you have space."

"Are you quite certain you're free to do that?" Hattie asked.

Nick shot his wife an indulgent smile. "I'd love to shock the people here, but I don't truly wish to embarrass my wife."

Of course not. He was a gentleman of the highest order.

A gentle throat clearing caught their attention, and they all turned toward Caroline, who stood against the wall with a plainly irritated expression.

"Oh, forgive me," Lucy said, appearing slightly flustered. "Mr. Pepper, Mrs. Pepper, allow me to introduce an old school friend of mine, Mrs. Caroline Carter. She and her husband live just south of Melbury."

Greetings were exchanged, and the Peppers subdued their jests.

"Amelia is not feeling well so they were forced to remain home, and she was sorry to miss it," Giulia said softly, so they weren't overheard.

Hattie scrunched her nose. "I'm only sorry she isn't feeling well. How is little Olivia?"

"Perfect, as always. Now I am quite ready to dance until the sun comes up. I hope you brought your most comfortable pair of dancing slippers."

Hattie nodded absently, looking over the growing crowd. She recognized most people, but none of them wore the half-day's shadow of a beard to cover their perfect cleft chin or wore dark hair just slightly too long over an open-necked shirt. She shook her head. She was clearly looking for Bentley, and he was absolutely not here.

The music began, and Mr. Warren approached her to claim his dance. His hand slid over hers as they moved into position, and she spent the next quarter-hour essentially wrapped in his arms in various motions of the dance. They stepped apart and came back together, his eyes fastened on her deliberately. But the one thing she felt through the duration of the dance was that this man, this red-haired, kind, handsome gentleman, did not ignite even a spark of heat within her chest. Absent was the feeling of warmth and anticipation she felt when Bentley was nearby, the feeling of wholeness she had in his arms.

Maybe...well, she did not wish to sound mad, but what if she was missing those feelings because she had yet to embrace this man? Certainly if his arms were wrapped around her, she would feel *something*.

She needed to get him alone.

CHAPTER 25

*B*entley picked at the roasted fowl congealing on his plate, but his appetite had long abandoned him. He was warm, dry, and restless, but the door to his bedchamber remained closed. Somehow, he had imagined his mother would break down the door and force him to speak to her, but she hadn't.

Though if he were being honest, she never had pressed herself upon him, had she? She merely sent him letters at a rate that even a spendthrift would balk at. One would believe she wanted nothing to do with him if it wasn't for her incessant requests for him to come and visit her, or to put off his ideals and return home to his rightful place.

Ha. His *rightful* place. What a joke that was.

Scrubbing a hand over his face, he blew a long breath through his nose. He needed to gather courage and go to her, but he was afraid.

What would Hattie do if she was there with him at that moment? He imagined her plain, guileless smile and knew at once what she would do. She would simply allow for the opportunity to talk. She would not walk into the dining room and demand answers. She would be compassionate and kind, and he would do his best to emulate the behavior he knew she would respect.

Before he could talk himself out of it, Bentley left his room and walked the corridor toward the small parlor he knew his mother had once favored. Dinner was long over, and he hoped to find her there. But when he reached the room, it was empty. The lack of fire in the grate indicated that she certainly wouldn't be entering it at all that evening.

"May I help you, Your Grace?" a timid voice said behind him.

He turned to find one of the footmen standing there nervously. Was it Philip or Ralph? He couldn't recall which name belonged to which man. He would usually have remembered easily, which was a testament of how jumbled his mind was.

"Where may I find my mother?" he asked.

"In with Mr. Humphries, Your Grace."

Well, that certainly wouldn't do. He thought over his options. "Will you inform her that I request her presence? I will meet her in the dining room. Unless there is another room warmed at present."

"Afraid not, Your Grace. We warmed more rooms for Mr. Humphries's guest, but he left yesterday to see to a family matter and shan't return until tomorrow. Mrs. Humphries doesn't go anywhere but the dining room and her own bedchamber when there is no one else to attend to."

How touching and revolting at the same time. Could Mother not have been half so dutiful when his own father lay on his deathbed?

"The dining room will suit well enough," he said gruffly.

Philip or Ralph, whichever he was, nodded and walked toward the mistress's suite, and Bentley left to await her in the dining room. His heart raced, but he did his best to breathe calmly and deeply, reminding himself to be level-headed and kind.

The door opened, and his mother stepped into the room, resplendent in her royal blue gown, her dark hair immaculately coiffed. Bentley's heart leapt to his throat. It hardly mattered how old one was or how horribly dishonest their mother had been, there was something quite soothing in the familiarity of seeing one's mother. It was quite at odds with the anxious fretting in his stomach.

"Silas," she breathed, stepping further into the room. Her face was more lined than he recalled, her skin looking soft and shinier with age, but her eyes were very much the same, and her bearing had not changed at all. She was still the regal duchess.

The darkness of night beyond the glowing windows made the room dim, with only the blazing fire beside him for light, bouncing from the walls and ceiling and illuminating his mother's face with a warm sheen. The table sat between them, a comfort to him as it would keep some space there.

"Mother," he said, and unfortunately the word sounded strained. He cleared his throat softly. "Are you well?"

She tilted her head to the side. "No. But you haven't come here to ask after me."

Indeed, he hadn't. "I came to give you one last opportunity to apologize."

She looked surprised at this, her thin eyebrows rising. "Apologize? I've done little else."

Bentley swallowed back a harsh retort, doing his best to sound even-tempered despite his emotions jumping about like a wild hare. "On the contrary, I'm not certain you have even once."

She scoffed lightly. "What do you make of those letters I've sent you over the last seven years?"

"Requests."

"Of *forgiveness*."

"No, Mother. You merely requested I travel to Kent, or retake my seat in Lords, or reclaim my rightful position as the duke. You ask for all these things from me, but you have never once admitted your fault."

She was quiet, staring at him as though he had turned into a horse before her very eyes. "Well, I hadn't realized an apology was still needed. Will you forgive me now?"

"Will you apologize?" he countered. So much for his well-intentioned plan of doing his best to emulate Hattie. It had surely worked, of course, just not in the way he'd planned. Bentley was *never* this sassy of his own accord.

Mother stepped forward, resting her hand on top of the polished table. "Silas, I never meant to hurt you."

He scoffed. "You did not realize I could possibly be awake that night and hear your lies?"

"No. We always meant for you to know the truth, but not then. Not in that way. The timing was horrible. I was overcome with grief."

"Why, Mother? Did you not think perhaps I should have known earlier?"

"I did." She held his gaze steady. "It was your father who believed otherwise."

Anger pierced him, and his voice lowered to a dangerously low tone. "Do not call *that man* my father."

Mother looked startled. She stared at him, her chest heaving, until something appeared to connect in her mind. "To whom do you think I refer?"

He swallowed. "Mr. Humphries, of course."

A slow, sad smile spread over her face. "Silas, when I speak of your father, I speak of Daniel Fawkes, the Duke of Bentley. I would never devalue his memory by doing otherwise."

Bentley felt as though the wind had died a little on his argument. He struggled to recall her words, and when he did, the impact felt like a punch to the gut. "When you said you always meant for me to know the truth…"

"I meant Daniel and myself."

Bentley pulled out the chair he had been standing beside and sat heavily upon it. The room spun, his chest heaving as though he'd just finished a bruising ride. "You are implying that Father knew of your indiscretion."

"Of course he knew. You arrived six months after our wedding, robust and healthy. It would have been an actual miracle if Daniel had been your father."

Bentley closed his eyes. This changed everything. Father had known from Bentley's birth that he was not his natural son. "But he never treated me differently. I thought you had kept this from him, that he never knew it was not Fawkes blood which inherited his dukedom."

"It's unlikely that your father himself was possessed purely of Fawkes blood. There was a long line of infidelity in your family, Silas." She paused, her mouth pinched in a firm line as she stood on the other side of the wide oak table, her hands resting upon it. "But that does not excuse my behavior. I am not proud of my indiscretion, but I cannot regret it. Not when it gave me a son."

He scoffed. "You can hardly expect me to believe that, Mother. You married the man the moment your mourning was complete."

"Because I love Patrick Humphries. I have loved him my entire life. I did my duty and married your father, and he was wholly aware of where my affection lay when I did so. It was no secret. Ours was not a love match, but a merger of two families, combining an ancient title with much-needed money. *My* family's money."

"It all sounds so cold," Bentley said with a hint of disgust.

Mother straightened. "You do not have to approve of my actions, Silas, and you certainly do not have to understand."

He looked up, suddenly overcome with the overwhelming desire to know everything. "But I wish to."

Mother looked at him, her mind working behind still eyes, before she nodded once and lowered herself into the dining seat across the table from him. "You already know I grew up on an estate on the other side of the county, much closer to Sussex."

He nodded.

"Well, I was raised knowing I was intended for your father. It was never a question. I was to be a duchess, and I was trained for it, but that couldn't stop me from falling in love with Patrick. Both of us knew that we could never marry, but that did not stop us from spending time together in our youth." She closed her eyes briefly before settling them on the fire just behind Bentley's chair. "I did my duty, knowing I would have to cut Patrick from my life when I married your father. We said goodbye before the wedding, and I never intended to stray once I'd said my vows, but I had been foolish in my youth and did not know that I came to my marriage already pregnant."

Bentley's jaw hardened.

Mother continued. "When your father found out, he was furious. I told him as soon as I realized I was pregnant and gave him the option of seeking an annulment. He left me for a week, and it was the longest, most horrible week of my life. But when he returned, it was with the decision that we would remain married, but live separate lives. The only thing we would share was you." She smiled faintly. "We were fortunate that you were a boy, for it meant Daniel had his heir."

The information sat in the room like thick, heavy fog. Bentley did his best to make sense of it, to alter the assumptions he'd made and recognize the truth of his history. This changed so much. He'd spent seven years fearing that his father wouldn't have loved him had he known the truth, but he'd been wrong. "Father truly knew?"

She nodded. "He asked me not to say anything. He did not want you to be burdened by feeling as though you did not belong. You were always Daniel Fawkes's son."

Bentley had felt that way. His father had raised him to be a duke, to take over in his stead, to lead the people. And what had Bentley done? Hidden away to protect the secret of his birth from the world.

He swallowed against a dry throat, his entire body feeling parched of energy. "If he felt that way, then why hide it?"

"You've met Patrick, Silas. You are so similar in appearance, you could be twins. There is no mistaking your paternity, and your father had his pride. Especially as you aged, it became crucial to keep you and Patrick from meeting. But when your father became ill, Patrick believed it safe to come. He arrived without my invitation or knowledge, and that was the argument you overheard. But I was weak, too. I am only human. I could not turn away a source of comfort during such a horrid time of grief."

"Then why did you not apologize? Tell me all of it?"

She held his gaze. "You refused to see reason. You had just lost your father in more ways than one. I did my best, but you were furious. You must understand that it never occurred to me that you would think Daniel had been kept in the dark. If only I'd known…"

"Yes, well, that is all in the past now, isn't it? It does not change anything. I would never wish to be seen with Patrick Humphries. Father's memory deserves far better than for this secret to be widely known."

Mother looked less convinced. "You are a loyal man, Silas."

"I learned from the best," he said coolly. But he knew his anger would need to end soon. Mother had put him in his place, and he could see the error of his ways in holding the grudge for so many years. He would not have changed his decision to hide away even had he known all of this. But the truth was that the threat to their secret being revealed would soon be gone.

He had a lot to make up for because of his own pride, but if the mess of his mother's life taught him anything, it was that he would marry for love and nothing less.

And the woman he loved was Hattie.

CHAPTER 26

*H*attie searched her brain for a way to get Mr. Warren outside alone but was coming up empty. She needed to embrace the man, to determine if she felt the same way in his arms as she'd felt in Bentley's. The room was full, growing busier by the moment as the crowd crushed against the walls and bled into the taproom to give the dancers adequate room. Hattie's chest heaved from the exhaustion of her last set. She noted Mr. Warren looking about the room, likely for Lucy so he could return Hattie to her chaperone's side.

She needed to act fast.

Clutching Mr. Warren's sleeve, she leaned against him, making her voice weak. "I am overcome…"

He looked down at her, alarmed. "What did you say?"

The music and conversation in the room combined and mounted in volume, so she tried again, louder. "I feel faint, Mr. Warren."

His gaze sought the room again. Drat. Was he looking for Lucy once more? That would never do.

"Perhaps a bit of fresh air," she suggested, and he nodded despite his panicky expression.

Warren let her lean on him as he made his way through the crowd of mostly unfamiliar faces and through the taproom. Hattie noticed Giulia glancing about in search of someone, but she managed to slip away before they were seen.

The cool air outside was a blessed relief against the stuffy heat and cloying perfumes and odors indoors. Hattie followed Mr. Warren along the side of the building where men waited with carriages and coachmen stood idly in conversation.

They were not alone. She would need to improvise.

"Shall I fetch you something to drink?"

"No, I thank you," Hattie said breathlessly. She gulped in the fresh air, discomfort nipping at her. "The air is helping quite a lot."

"I am glad."

A man must have made a joke nearby, for the group of coachmen laughed loudly behind her and she cringed. It was not exactly the best place to test her theory, but she had no other option available to her. She needed to know if Mr. Warren had the same effect on her as Bentley had.

Sliding her hand up his arm, she felt him grow stiff underneath her touch. "I quite enjoyed dancing with you, Mr. Warren."

Though in all honesty, it had felt no different from any other dance she'd participated in. She simply enjoyed dancing.

"Quite enjoyable, yes," he agreed, though he sounded noncommittal, his eyes darting about the dark street. "Shall we return inside? We do not wish to be seen alone."

"We are not alone," she countered, snaking her hand under his arm and around his back.

But the moment she pressed herself against Mr. Warren she knew with blinding certainty that she'd been wrong in her assumption—or perhaps she had known all along that what she'd felt with Bentley was special and was merely fighting it. The overwhelming warmth and wholeness that had filled her when she was wrapped in Bentley's arms had not been simply because he was a man—it had occurred because he was Bentley.

And she loved him.

A small gasp slipped through Hattie's lips, and she stepped back at the same time that Mr. Warren moved to disentangle himself from her grip, alarm on his face.

"Forgive me," she said. "My foot slipped, and I fell. I'm so grateful you were there to catch me."

He regarded her silently, likely trying to determine how her foot slipped while they were standing still, and how it would cause her arm to slide around his back.

She swallowed and hurried to continue before he could say anything. "I'm sure we can return inside now. I wouldn't wish to be found."

"No, I should think not."

She stepped forward when he put up a hand to stop her, his jaw working as though he was considering what to say. "Miss Green, Bentley is my cousin and closest family member. I care about him a great deal."

"I am glad of it."

He narrowed his eyes. "I would never do anything to stand in the way of his happiness, and while I found myself interested in a certain young woman when I first arrived here, things have since been made known to me that would prevent me from acting upon any of my initial attractions. You can rest assured I have squashed them completely."

Hattie gaped. So she had not been wrong about his interest during the Carters' ball. But then...

"What things were made known to you?"

He leaned close, lowering his voice. "I know of the painting, the drawings...all of it. It is quite clear that my cousin loves you, for what other reason would explain why he's drawn your likeness dozens of times? When I found the note you left him in the tree yesterday, it occurred to me that his feelings must be returned."

They were returned. Undoubtedly. It was quite freeing to admit it, even if only to herself. She swallowed, her heart racing. "*You* found the note? Has Bentley not returned yet?"

"No, not yet."

"Then perhaps you oughtn't take letters that do not belong to you, sir."

He cracked a smile. "That is undoubtedly true, but I needed to know what it said. I will not stand by and allow my cousin to be hurt."

"Will you...you will not tell him of my slip, will you?" She swallowed. "I merely wanted to test a theory of mine."

"That depends entirely upon this theory."

Drat the man. He was forcing her to admit to her stupidity. "Well, you see, Bentley causes me to feel a certain way. I get a little lightheaded around him sometimes and feel as though I am falling even when I stand still. I wish to be near him, always, and his smile makes my entire heart feel warm, as though I've stood near a fire too long."

A smile flickered over Mr. Warren's lips. "You wished to see if perhaps another gentleman could make you feel the same?"

She cringed, hiding her face in her hands. When she removed them, she smiled wryly. "Yes."

"And your findings?"

"That no other gentleman makes me feel the way Bentley does."

He nodded, understanding. "That, my dear, I believe is called love."

"Perhaps. But love can be one-sided."

Mr. Warren's gaze was fixed on her, the muscle jumping in his cheek as though he was ruminating on something. "Have you seen the painting he's done of you?"

Done? As in finished? She shook her head. "No."

"Just wait. I have a feeling your anxieties are not warranted."

Hattie could not allow herself to hope, despite the surety Mr. Warren felt. Bentley was a duke. He was vulnerable. He wasn't her fox.

But what did that matter? Hattie gazed at Mr. Warren's red hair and put away the fox hunt at once. What did the white magic matter when she felt love for a real man? "How long do you think it will be until he returns to Wolfeton House?"

Mr. Warren glanced up, calculating something. "Another fortnight? It depends entirely on the welcome he receives in Kent."

Bentley's mother would undoubtedly welcome him heartily after her many attempts to convince him to visit and would likely press him to stay longer. All hope for his speedy return drifted away. "Then he is likely going to miss our dinner."

"I would count on it. The journey is long, and this weather only lengthens it. It would be near a miracle if he was to return by the end of the week."

Hattie nodded, but anticipation filled her, nonetheless. The moment he returned, she was going to tell him how she felt—foxes be hanged.

Bentley stood in the lamplit corridor outside of Patrick Humphries's door and waited for his heart to calm. Mother slipped her hand around his, and he wanted to pull away but forced himself to accept the gesture of support and kindness.

It would take work to replace the prejudice he'd built in his mind over the last seven years, but he could admit that he'd been wrong, and they had decided to work together to rebuild their relationship. He'd never been particularly close to his mother, but he was determined to make an effort.

He was only grateful that Mr. Humphries now lay in the mistress's room and had not taken over the duke's chamber. It was a respect for his father he had not anticipated but was grateful to discover.

"Take all the time you need," Mother said.

It only made him want to do the opposite. He nodded. "I am ready."

He reached forward and opened the door before stepping inside. The room was well-lit and well-aired. It did not smell of the sick, and he was glad of it. But the man lying still in the bed was unwelcome and memories assailed Bentley of the last time he'd entered a sickroom.

Mother leaned close and whispered, "The doctor doesn't believe he will last the night. I think he's been holding out for days."

Bentley swallowed. He did not inquire what Mr. Humphries was holding out for. He believed she was referring to him.

He crossed the room and sat in the seat at the head of the bed, his mother standing just behind him. Gazing at the wrinkled face so similar to his own, he was suddenly overcome. Is this how Bentley would look thirty years from now? Most likely. The similarities were striking.

Mr. Humphries shifted, murmuring incoherently, and Mother moved into action. She skirted Bentley's chair and sat on the edge of the bed, taking her husband's hand in both of hers. "He has come, Patrick. Silas is here."

The man blinked, and he murmured again. He looked about for Silas, but his sight was clearly cloudy. Mother reached for Bentley but hesitated, allowing him to make the choice. He leaned closer until Mr. Humphries's gaze stopped on him, and the man roamed his face, searching it, it seemed. A faint smile touched his lips and he reached forward, resting wrinkled, weak fingers on Bentley's cheek.

Tears gathered in Bentley's eyes and dripped down, falling over the man's hand and gathering in the creases between his fingers.

"Father," Bentley said, his hoarse voice hardly more than a whisper.

Mr. Humphries's frail hand pressed further into his cheek, and he curled his face into it.

"He cannot speak," Mother said softly. "But he can hear you, I believe."

Bentley's heart pulsed, and he swallowed hard. Emotions flickered and faded, regret, anger, sorrow, and love filling him simultaneously, and he didn't know what to say. But he could not change the past. He could only use this time wisely.

Mr. Humphries's hand fell away from Bentley's cheek, and he reached to hold it, curling his fingers around the man's aged, wrinkly skin. "I have inherited the cleft in your chin, it would seem. That certainly did not come from Mother."

"And his eyes," she added.

Bentley nodded, raking his eyes over the man whose blood ran through his veins. "I should thank you for the eyebrows, but they are a touch too large for my liking."

A faint smile flickered over Mr. Humphries's lips, and it went straight to Bentley's chest. He found his breath wavering and the fingers in his hand twitched before Mr. Humphries closed his eyes. Bentley looked to his chest, but the man was still breathing, albeit labored.

When his hand fell limp in Bentley's, he let it go. Mother's expression was misty, and she reclaimed her sleeping husband's hand.

Bentley stood. "I will leave you now," he said.

She looked up, stricken. "You are returning to Devon already?"

"No. I will remain in the house as long as you need me."

Relief washed over her face, and Bentley sent her a small smile before he quit the room, his chest bursting with too many emotions to name. But the most present, clear feeling was contentment and resolution. A burden had been lifted from his shoulders, and he felt as though his vision had cleared. He'd given his mother what she'd asked for relentlessly, and he believed they had stepped forward together on a journey of healing.

For now, he had one thing on his mind, and he wanted nothing but to return to her.

Hattie Green.

CHAPTER 27

*T*he last week had passed painfully slowly, and Hattie had a feeling the dinner party they were holding would follow suit. She stood at the top of the stairs, waiting for Lucy to reach her.

"Are you prepared to see Mr. Warren this evening?" Lucy asked brightly.

It hardly mattered what Hattie said, Lucy was convinced that Hattie and Mr. Warren had come to an agreement after learning that they had spoken outside of the assemblies for a quarter of an hour. No one had caught them, thank heavens, but Hattie explained herself to Lucy and had long since regretted telling her anything.

"I am quite prepared," Hattie said.

"Do you think the duke will attend?"

Hattie's heart jumped. "No. I think he is likely still seeing to important things at his estate."

Lucy pouted. "I rather wish I hadn't bragged about his acceptance to Caroline at the assemblies. She is expecting to see a duke. She'll never believe we are on comfortable terms with the man if he does not come."

Hattie had checked the lightning tree *twice* that day. Bentley was not yet home. Instead, the letter she'd written following the assemblies and tucked in the tree still sat untouched. She'd asked Mr. Warren to leave it be, and he had agreed not to meddle with her letters again.

The door opened below them, out of sight, and the high-pitched sound of Caroline's voice filtered up to where they stood. Lucy stiffened beside her, and Hattie immediately took her arm. "Why do you let her treat you so badly?"

"Not everyone is blessed with friends like you, Hattie."

Her heart hurt at that. Everyone *should* be blessed with friends like hers. It was certainly a universal need to be cared for, loved, and supported. "But that is my point. Why waste your time on a woman who is hot and cold to you in turns? Is it not worth it to seek out kind women with whom you can spend your time?"

"Fortunately I do not have to see this woman very often. She only comes to London for the Season. Besides, we couldn't very well attend her ball without returning the invitation. It simply isn't done."

"Perhaps next time we ought not to attend her ball in the first place. I can come down with a cold, surely. Or we can contrive to make you ill if you think that would suit our purposes better."

Lucy smiled, squeezing her arm back. "You always say the most outlandish things. Come, our guests are waiting."

Hattie refrained from correcting her sister-in-law. She had been completely serious.

Halfway down the stairs, she took Lucy's arm. "You may think I'm outlandish, but I do care for you. We may not always see eye to eye—"

"We *never* see eye to eye," Lucy corrected.

Hattie suppressed her desire to argue, especially since she

agreed with that particular point. "Yes, well, I am trying to say that I love you, Lucy. Even if I do not always agree with you."

Lucy's pale blonde eyebrows hitched together faintly, and she regarded Hattie silently for a moment. "I know that, Hattie. I love you as well."

They found the group waiting in the drawing room, Jeffrey speaking to Mr. Carter as Mrs. Carter stood beside them, boredom etched into the slight frown on her face. She looked about the room, likely measuring it against her own freshly decorated house, and Hattie felt the strong desire to turn around and march upstairs. She simply could not abide vain or prideful people.

Amelia appeared in the doorway, Giulia by her side, and Hattie knew instant relief. With the Fremonts and the Peppers, their party was decidedly balanced toward kindness. It would all work out well.

"I should have invited the vicar," Lucy whispered harshly. "At least he would have evened out our numbers. I'm bound to look so countrified."

"As if that is a bad thing," Hattie countered. "Besides, you've counted wrong. Mr. Warren evens out our numbers." She pulled Lucy alongside her to greet her friends. She was not about to leave her sister-in-law unattended before Caroline, not when the woman had hidden claws.

The company was soon gathered with the exception of Mr. Warren, and proper introductions were made.

"I quite like your house, Miss Green," Caroline said, her gaze tripping over the walls. "It is so quaint and so very charming."

"Indeed," Hattie agreed. "We are rather comfortable here." She wouldn't allow Caroline the satisfaction of disparaging her home.

"It is perfect for a reprieve in the country, to be sure." Turning to admit Lucy into their conversation, her eyebrows rose. "Now, I did hear that you were seen in a cozy situation with a certain gentleman, Miss Green. Was Lucy successful in her endeavors?"

Hattie froze. No one had seen her with Mr. Warren outside except for a handful of coachmen who likely had no idea who they were. She looked at her sister-in-law, but Lucy's cheeks were bright red, the blush bleeding down her neck, and cold fear slithered down Hattie's spine. "What endeavors do you speak of?"

"Oh, you know," Caroline said, delivering a false, grating laugh. "How your father asked Lucy to come and help you learn how to obtain a husband."

Hattie's stomach dropped, and she wished the floor would open up and swallow her whole. The group of men had gone silent, and Jeffrey turned sharply toward them, making it clear that he'd heard Caroline as well. Given the guilt splayed over his face, it was quite clear that Caroline had not been lying.

No, it would appear that Hattie was nothing but a charity case in need of fixing, and Papa had recruited *Lucy* of all people to help. Evidently, everyone in the room except Hattie's friends was already aware of this embarrassing tidbit of information. Just how desperate was Papa to be rid of her? Hurt sliced through her stomach, and her mouth went dry.

Amelia stepped between Lucy and Hattie and slipped her hand around Hattie's arm. "Did you hear that a man in Melbury lost his pocket watch during the assemblies? They later found it around a horse's neck. It's now up for debate whether the man was in his cups and did it himself, or if someone else was playing a joke."

"I should like to meet the person who can subdue a horse long enough to slip a chain around his neck," Charles said, smiling. "It nearly makes me disappointed that we were forced to miss the assemblies."

Nick laughed. "Well, it doesn't surprise me. We are well acquainted with the sort of folks who hail from Melbury."

Giulia raised her eyebrows, shooting her husband a look. He didn't seem to understand her meaning, or perhaps he was unaware that the Carters came from Melbury. Regardless, Hattie was grateful for her friends' speed in stepping in and changing the conversation.

Barking echoed from the tall ceilings in the entryway, traveling toward the drawing room. Someone needed to put Daisy and Rosie down in the kitchen if they continued to be so noisy. They quieted as though they'd heard the threat in her thoughts, and the door to the drawing room opened. Their butler stepped forward to introduce the newest guest.

"His Grace, the Duke of Bentley, and Mr. Warren."

Hattie's head whipped around so swiftly she felt a distinct twinge go down her neck. Her lips parted, and she caught Bentley's gaze across the room. He held her eyes briefly before sending a smile to her sister-in-law and stepped forward with Mr. Warren to make their bows.

"We did not know if we would have the pleasure of your company this evening, Your Grace," Lucy said, fighting a broad smile. She must feel inordinately relieved.

"I sped my travels particularly for this occasion," he replied prettily, bending over her hand. Lucy delivered a slight giggle, and her gaze immediately sought Caroline, who stood frozen, her wide eyes trained on Bentley.

Perhaps her pride could not withstand the presence of an actual duke.

Dinner was announced before Hattie could so much as step away from Amelia, and she was swept into the dining room, finding herself seated diagonally across from Bentley, at the precise angle to see him well, but not close enough for conversation.

It was excruciating. She longed to ask him about his visit

with his mother, if he had seen his stepfather, how the journey was, and if he loved her as much as she loved him. Something about seeing the man in a black coat and snowy white cravat made her knees weak, and it was a blessed thing she was sitting down or she was certain her legs would've buckled beneath her. He was so handsome, and she hoped he was hers.

Bentley's appearance made the sting of Papa's betrayal lessen, but she wished to speak to him about it, to ask his opinion and beg his advice. She caught his eye a few times over dinner, but he seemed caught up speaking to Lucy. The dinner seemed to drag on for hours, and when they were finished, Lucy stood. "Ladies, shall we?"

Bentley wiped his mouth and set his napkin on the table. "Actually, I believe the men should come, too." His gaze slid to Hattie. "There should be a surprise for Miss Green in the drawing room."

Hattie's heart raced and murmurs of the party followed her as she led them toward the drawing room, Lucy one step behind her. The woman tried to take her arm, but she was not feeling quite that charitable yet. She might love her sister-in-law, but she was still hurt. She stepped into the drawing room, and her eyes immediately fell upon Papa, sitting on his favorite chair near the fire with a tray beside him bearing an empty plate and half-filled wine glass.

"Papa," she said, hurrying toward him. She'd missed him these last weeks, and his familiar smile and scent of pipe smoke and leather made her feel at home again—regardless of the fact that she was not the one who'd left.

He stood, drawing her into his arms warmly before setting her aside and greeting the rest of the party. She had so many questions, but none she should voice at present. Namely, how had he come to be here, and how was Bentley aware of it?

"Perhaps we ought to leave so you can spend time with your family," Nick said, sliding his hand around Giulia's waist.

"Indeed," Amelia agreed, her gaze darting between Bentley and Hattie. "We shall leave you to it."

Oh, no. What if Bentley left with the rest of them? She needed more time with him. She'd yet to speak one word to the man. "You needn't go," Hattie said. "Lucy and I planned games to amuse us."

Caroline did not appear quite ready to leave, either. She eyed Bentley. "We could remain for a game or two."

Amelia reached over and pinched her husband's arm, so subtly Hattie would have missed it if she was not looking at them as she spoke. "I think it is best if we go," Charles said. "But we would love to play your games another night."

"It is getting late," added Giulia. Her friends believed they were helping, undoubtedly. But they weren't.

Bentley skirted the group and spoke quietly to Papa as the remainder of the party said their farewells, Giulia all but pushing Caroline ahead of her as she left the room. Hattie felt helpless watching the guests drain from the room. Warren slipped out after Charles and Amelia, Lucy and Jeffrey on their tail to see them to the door. It all happened so suddenly; then she was left alone in the drawing room with her father. Her shoulders sank.

Lowering her face into her hands, Hattie rubbed at her eyes, fighting an exhausted yawn. "I learned something interesting about Lucy tonight, Papa. You have some explaining to do." She turned a look of consternation on her father. Only, he was not alone. Bentley still stood beside him, and the very serious gaze he leveled on her made her bite down hard on her bottom lip.

"I believe we do," Papa said. He patted Bentley on the shoulder. Papa patted the *duke*. "But first, this young man has something he would like to say to you."

Stunned, Hattie could say nothing as Papa placed a light kiss on her cheek. She shook herself alert and took his hand. "No, wait, Papa. Why did you do it? Why did you ask Lucy to come and not tell me of your reasons?"

His familiar, kind eyes sat on her steadily. "If I had told you of my intentions, would that have made you more amenable to Lucy's help?"

Hattie said nothing. Papa knew her so well. She would have fought Lucy even harder, most assuredly, had she known. But, still. "You thought I was so desperate as to *need* help?"

"I love you, Hattie. I only want you to be happy." He glanced to Bentley before turning and leaving the room, closing the drawing room door behind himself.

She watched him go, unable to make complete sense of all that had transpired. He was doing his best, and Lucy was his best, apparently. She couldn't fault him for his efforts, even if she wished he'd have gone about it in a much better way.

Bentley looked at her, quietly standing just an arm's length away. His gray eyes pierced her.

"'This young man?'" she asked, to break the silence. "And he patted your shoulder like you were a lad. Bentley, how have you and my father grown to be on such intimate terms?"

"Since I discovered that he is a close friend of my natural father, Mr. Humphries."

Hattie had no words. They had absolutely escaped her, traveled away on the back of the Carters' elaborate carriage.

Bentley must have sensed this. He clasped his hands behind his back and took a step forward. "I made it to Kent and saw my mother. You will be happy to know that we have mended our differences—indeed, there was a misunderstanding that we've since cleared up, but I shall tell you more of that later."

Her heart warmed. "I am so glad, Bentley."

His lips formed a soft smile. "There is more. I spoke to my mother's husband briefly, but it was enough, and I was able to comfort my mother at the time of his death early the next morning. Your father was a dear friend of my stepfather's, apparently.

He was visiting his sister and learned of Patrick Humphries's illness and remained in Kent so he could be near at hand. He was there the morning Patrick died, and stayed at the house afterward to help my steward arrange the funeral satisfactorily."

"I knew his friend had taken ill, but Bentley…oh, what are the chances?"

"Yes, well, it almost feels as though fate is to blame, do you not agree?"

She swallowed. "Fate?"

"Yes. Of all the people in all of England who would happen to be in my ancestral home to support my stepfather at the time of his death, could there be no other reason than fate that it just happened to be the father of the woman I love?"

Hattie held her breath, her lips parting as Bentley took another step closer. "You *do* love me? I thought it was impossible."

He stopped approaching, puzzlement overtaking his brow. "How so?"

Stripping her long gloves, Hattie pointed to her skin. "Freckles. I'm positively *covered*, Bentley. It's absolutely revolting."

Amusement danced in his eyes. "I don't think they're revolting. I rather love your freckles."

Hattie screwed up her nose, narrowing her eyes. "I'm not sure I believe you. My father is the only person who's ever liked them. And even then, I'm nearly positive he's blind when it comes to me."

"He isn't blind, and we share the sentiment." Bentley closed the distance between them, brushing his thumb across her cheek and sliding his other hand over her smooth forearm until his bare fingers wrapped around hers. "I think you are the most beautiful creature in the world, and your heart is even lovelier. After the episode in the barn, I was quite desolate, but upon returning home, I was given reason to hope that you might return my feelings."

"Mr. Warren," she accused, warmth filling her body from his touch.

Bentley laughed. "Very well, yes. Warren told me of what happened outside of the assemblies."

"I blame Melbury for my foolishness," she murmured. "Just ask my father. It is a horrid town."

Bentley's smile grew. "I don't think you actually believe that."

His fingers caused shivers to dance up her arms, and it was sheer torture in the loveliest way. "No, I don't. But I needed to test my theory. I needed to know if what I felt was specific to you or was only a result of you being a man."

"What did you discover?" he asked, his voice low and husky.

"That no one else makes me feel the way you do."

Bentley's eyes darkened, and he released her, sliding his hands around her waist. "Marry me, Hattie. I've no claim to red hair, but I will love you deeply for the rest of eternity."

"Even when I'm sick with a child? Or cross? I do get rather cross at times."

"Even when you're sick or cross."

"Then yes, Bentley. I shall marry you, even though you aren't a fox. I've long given up on white magic anyway. I'd much rather have you."

"On the contrary," he said, pulling her tightly against him. Her heart rammed against her breastbone. "My given name is Silas Fawkes."

Hattie gasped but was quieted suddenly by Bentley's mouth covering hers. Her body erupted in a warmth that she would wager was hotter than the sun, sending tingles over every inch of her. Running her hands over his pristine coat, she found his cravat and began working at the knot.

He broke the kiss, looking down at her, chest heaving. "What are you doing?"

"I like you without the cravat."

He chuckled, exasperated. "We're in your father's home. You can't very well remove it now."

"I think it's only fair," she argued. "Consider this your recompense. You never told me you were a fox."

"F-A-W-K-E-S," he said, spelling his name. "And you will be one, too."

Hattie grinned, abandoning the cravat knot and reaching up around his neck, pulling his face toward hers. She kissed him, and Bentley deepened the kiss, his strong grip holding her flush against him. She had never before felt so contented as she did in that moment.

Breaking away, Hattie gasped for air. "You do realize that now you shall have to go out in public," she said cautiously. "I do like to see my friends."

"I will happily escort you wherever you would like to go." Bentley brushed her hair away from her face and dropped a kiss on her nose. "I've been considering taking my seat in Lords, anyway."

Hattie grinned. "Yes, you should. You have so much wisdom to bring to the people. You can do so much good."

He chuckled softly. "And you will stand by me?"

"Of course. Regardless of what happens, I will never leave your side." She frowned, considering her Papa asking Lucy to help her find a husband.

"What is it?" Bentley asked.

"Do you think Lucy will take credit for our union? Evidently, my father invited her here to help me learn how to obtain a husband."

"Ah, yes. He told me of that."

"When?"

"We shared a carriage home. We traveled quickly, changed horses often, and barely made it home in time for this dinner. I wanted to surprise you, and the trip gave us plenty of time to get to know one another. In fact, he's given our union his blessing already."

Hattie scoffed. "Well of course he has. I knew he'd love you."

"You did?" he asked, his forehead creasing.

"Of course. What's not to love?" She reached up to kiss him again.

CHAPTER 28

*B*entley stood back from the easel, appraising it with satisfaction. He'd somehow managed to get the freckles just right, and he found the portrait to be a precise replica of his lovely Hattie. He glanced up. "Are you ready to see it?" he asked.

Hattie lifted her gaze from the portrait she was drawing on her lap, her brown eyebrows knit together. "I am. But I really think you won't want to see this one."

He chuckled. "Surely it can't be worse than a pig."

"Oh, I wouldn't place any wagers on that if I were you."

Good heavens, how bad could it be? "Very well. Remain where you are, and I shall reveal my painting first."

Hattie seemed to like that idea, and she lowered her drawing, arranging herself in her chair. "I'm ready."

Lifting the easel, Bentley carefully spun it around so the painting faced Hattie. He held his breath and looked to see her response. She was frozen still, her mouth parted and her eyes widened just a bit.

"What do you think?"

She shook her head before closing her mouth. "That is how you see me?"

"Yes."

Pressing the portrait she drew—she'd refused to add paint, saying that it would only make it worse—against her chest, she rose and crossed to the window, away from him. "Oh Bentley, it's absolutely stunning. I'm at a loss for words, I just love it so much."

"Then why are you walking away?"

"Because now that I've seen that, I know you can never see this." She turned and tried to raise the window, but Bentley rushed to her side.

"What do you intend to do, throw it outside? It cannot be that bad."

"It can, and it is." She grunted, trying again to lift the old, finicky window. "Help me open this."

"No," he said, laughing. "I want to see the portrait."

Pausing, she narrowed her eyes at him. "Very well. But first, you must promise that you will still marry me next week, regardless of what you see on this canvas."

"I solemnly promise that I will marry you next week regardless of how hideous you made me look," he said, leaning down to kiss her once.

Her cheeks bloomed a delightful pink color, and she sighed. "I did warn you." Turning the canvas around, Hattie held up the most awkward looking rendition of a man with his cravat missing, and a few days' worth of shadow covering his jaw. It rather did look more like a pig than a man, but Bentley could see how that was due to the way she'd drawn his nose.

He grinned, in spite of the hideous portrait. "I love it."

"It's horrendous."

"Yes, but *you* drew it." He leaned forward to kiss her again and she squealed, dropping the picture on the floor.

"What is it?" he asked, alarmed.

Hattie tried to get the window up again. "It's your blasted chicken! And what is Romeo doing back here?"

Bentley followed her gaze toward the lawn and the chicken there, picking a fight with Hattie's cat. "What are you—Hattie! You mustn't go through the window. Go through the front door."

"Oh, of course." She turned, lifting her skirts, and fled. Bentley ran behind her, following her outside toward the animals battling on the grass. She deftly retrieved her cat while Bentley chased the chicken, managing to get the fowl under his arm, her talons tucked neatly away.

"What are we going to do with you?" Bentley asked, looking down at the chicken, her beady eyes darting around and her beak closed. She looked completely unrepentant.

"We aren't going to eat her, that is for absolute certain."

Bentley scoffed. "No, of course not. That would just be barbaric."

"Indeed." She looked up at him. "Oh, you are teasing me. You realize that we cannot eat her simply because she is mean. That wouldn't be right."

No, Bentley did not understand that line of thinking. She was a chicken. Her jobs were to lay eggs and provide meat. But he loved Hattie so much that he did not care if they didn't see eye to eye on this particular matter. He would spare the chicken's life for her sake.

"I do wonder if she is missing affection and that is why she chooses to fight every animal that comes in her path. Perhaps if we gave her a name…"

Oh, good heavens.

Hattie snapped her fingers, adjusting Romeo in her hands. "These two are enemies, but we want them to become friends. We should call her Juliet."

Bentley laughed until he realized Hattie was serious. "Very well. It looks like you have a name, Juliet."

Beaming, Hattie turned toward the house. "Now, I should really be getting home. But first, I need to burn that picture."

EPILOGUE

Ten years later

*T*he Duke and Duchess of Bentleys' monstrous house felt the warmest when it was filled with people they loved. Hattie sat snugly against her husband on the sofa, their three-year-old daughter, Faith, curled up and sleeping on her lap. Bentley's arm was over her shoulder, his other hand absently stroking Faith's dark hair, and Hattie was absolutely contented.

Their friends had arrived the day before to spend a fortnight with them in Kent, and Hattie had been near to bursting with excitement all month preparing for them to come. They managed to split their time evenly between Devonshire, Kent, and London when Bentley sat in the House of Lords, but that hadn't stopped Hattie from eagerly awaiting the arrival of their friends.

Mabel sat on a chair across from them, holding her baby, and a very pregnant Amelia was seated on the settee near her chair, Charles beside her. Nick and Mac had taken the older children down to ride the boats in the lake but should be returning shortly.

"Where has Pippa gone? I haven't seen her in hours," Giulia said from the other end of the sofa.

Mabel's mouth flattened into a thin line. "I vow, my sister is bound to be the death of me."

"Oh, dear," Amelia said, her hands resting on her rounded belly. "What's happened?"

Mabel leaned forward slightly, looking over her shoulder, likely to make certain her sister was not about to walk into the room. "We took Pippa to London for the Season, and it was an absolute disaster. She has no interest in any of it, and she's nearly nineteen."

Hattie cringed. She'd been in London, too, and had seen Pippa firsthand disregarding interested gentlemen and avoiding social situations.

Mabel shook her head, sighing. "Suitors haunted our doorstep day after day, but she just wanted to leave London. The girl isn't interested in making a match. But there aren't really any eligible young men near Camden Cove, either."

Amelia laughed. "Uninterested in making a match? That does sound familiar, Mabel. Perhaps it runs in the family."

Mabel shot Amelia a wry glance.

"Is your father concerned?" Bentley asked.

"No, and in truth, I'm not overly worried either. Pippa is so helpful with the children. They absolutely adore her. But she cannot remain in Camden Cove forever—no matter what Gram says."

"How is Gram?" Charles asked.

Mac stepped into the drawing room, Nick just behind him, and threw a sardonic smile at Charles. "Gram is full of opinions and spunky as ever. She wanted to come with us, but you know how difficult it is for her to travel."

"Of course," Hattie said. "But I miss her. I wish she could have joined us."

Mac pulled a chair closer to Mabel and sat, reaching for her hand. "She would have come if Mabel allowed her to. Sometimes I wonder who's more obstinate—the five-year-old or Gram?"

"Definitely Elinor," Mabel said, laughing. Her five-year-old, Elinor, had spent the better part of the morning directing her older brother in a game of princesses and dragons. She was quite the spitfire.

Guilia turned to Hattie. "You attended the Season as well, did you not?"

"Yes." Hattie pressed herself closer to Bentley's side. "But Mabel has already heard my opinions on this matter."

Mabel laughed, her gaze reaching the ceiling. "It should come as no surprise to anyone in this room that Hattie sympathizes with Pippa. Love shan't be forced. Don't press fate."

A wide grin spread over Amelia's mouth. "It's Midsummer's Eve just next week. Shall we find ourselves some hempseed and teach Pippa the incantation?"

"You may jest, but I did find my fox," Hattie argued, and Bentley squeezed her shoulder. "It could work for Pippa, too."

"The trouble is, Pippa is far too practical for anything of that sort," Mac said, his deep voice carrying easily across the room. "Mayhap it's worth a try, though? If anyone can convince her, it'll be you, Hattie."

"What is worth a try?" Pippa asked, stepping into the drawing room. Her long, brown hair was piled at the nape of her neck in a simple knot, and her mouth was turned down in a frown. She was a smaller version of her sister, so similar in appearance despite the years that spanned between them. "You did not seem to mind my practicality when I took to helping James with his French."

"I adore your practicality," Mac said. "Particularly when you help my son with his French. But Mabel wouldn't mind if you had a touch more romanticism."

Mabel shook her head, arranging the baby in her arms. "It was nothing. We were only speaking of your refusal to see reason when we were in London."

Pippa glided into the room and released an exasperated sigh. "Yet the reverse can also be said about you, dear sister." She looked about the room. "How many of you were married at eighteen? Well, except you, Amelia."

Giulia and Hattie shared a smile. Pippa had a valid point. Why was Mabel trying to push her sister into matrimony, anyway? Surely she recalled how little she appreciated it when her father did something similar to her.

"Very well. I will leave you alone," Mabel said. "You can wed when you are ready, and in the meantime, you are more than welcome to teach all of my children their French." Mabel lifted her sweet, sleeping babe and whispered. "Even this one."

Pippa grinned triumphantly. "Good. Now if you'll all excuse me, I think I'll walk down to the lake." She turned and flounced from the room without a backward glance.

"She reminds me so much of you, Mabel," Charles said, chuckling. "In all the best ways."

Mabel didn't grace her cousin with a response.

"Did you tell me you have a set of lawn bowls in the back?" Charles asked, directing his question to the duke and duchess.

Bentley nodded. "Indeed. Care to play?"

The men all stood, and Bentley disentangled himself from Hattie's side, causing Faith to stir in the process. She looked up at Hattie, dark brown eyes above a freckled nose blinked at her mother as she awoke from her nap.

"Shall we join the men?" Giulia asked. There was a general

murmur of assent as the remainder of the group rose and followed their husbands from the drawing room.

"I need to take Faith upstairs first, but I will see you outside shortly," Hattie said, lifting her child and resting her against her hip. Faith was growing far too big to be carried everywhere, but Hattie couldn't help it. She loved holding her dear little one. "I'm sure she'll be hungry after that long nap."

Hattie's friends left the room, and she carried Faith to the stairs and up toward the nursery. Children's voices filtered in from the front garden, and it did Hattie's heart good to hear her children playing with the children of her friends. There were a dozen between the four couples, with more on the way, and the women were all gratified that their children seemed to care for each other as much as the literary society ladies did.

Children's laughter and adult conversations drifted away the higher Hattie climbed, and by the time she reached the nursery, she could no longer hear any of her guests. "Shall I ring for tea, Faith? I am certain you must be famished."

"I am hungry," Faith said sleepily, rubbing at her eyes as her mother carried her to the table. Hattie set her daughter's feet on the floor and pulled the bell rope. She busied herself with tidying the books that had been left strewn before their shelves while she waited for the nursery maid to respond.

The door opened behind her, the familiar creak ringing through the room.

"That was quick, Fanny." She looked over her shoulder and smiled. "Oh, Mother. I was expecting the maid."

The dowager duchess shot Hattie a soft smile before crossing the room and taking a seat at the little table beside her grand-daughter. "I heard you come upstairs and thought to ask if Faith would like some company during her tea."

"Yes, please," Faith said after covering a yawn with her small palm. "I love company."

Hattie and her mother-in-law shared a smile.

"Have you enjoyed spending time with your friends, dear?"

Hattie nodded, sliding the last of the books onto the shelf before joining them at the table. "Amelia's brother Andrew and his wife, Lydia, are set to join us at the end of the week. You remember them from London last year?"

"I do. He is the doctor?"

"Yes, so he didn't feel he could come for the entire length of the house party. But we're grateful for the week we'll have with his family. Did I mention that Jeffrey and Lucy intend to join us, as well? Faith will be glad of it. She simply adores her cousin. And they're bringing Papa with them."

"No, I hadn't heard that. But I'll be glad of it, too." She sighed lightly. "I just love Lucy."

"As do I," Hattie said, reaching forward to brush a strand of dark hair from Faith's forehead. "I'm not sure anything can make me happier than this: having everyone I love under one roof."

The doorway darkened and the women glanced up to find Bentley standing there, his hand resting on the handle. "I came to find what was keeping you."

"I'm waiting for Fanny to bring Faith some tea."

"I can wait with her," Mother said. "You go on outside. We will be perfectly happy in here, will we not, Lady Faith?"

"We will," Faith said obediently, grinning up at her grandmother. She loved being called a lady, despite her tender years.

"Thank you, Mother," Bentley said, stepping forward and dropping a kiss on her cheek. "You are welcome to join us for lawn bowls when your tea is finished."

She smiled in acknowledgment before turning her attention to Faith. Reaching for Hattie's hand, Bentley wrapped it in his own and tugged her up. They left the nursery, passing Fanny with a tray in the corridor. When they reached the stairs, Bentley pulled Hattie past them and down the seldom-used corridor until they'd turned the corner out of sight.

Dropping Hattie's hand, Bentley took hold of her waist and backed her up until she was pressed against the wall.

"Bentley, our guests—"

He cut her words off with a kiss, which she readily returned. She clutched his coat, pulling him closer, kissing him as though they'd only been married for ten days instead of ten years. When he pulled back, he shot her a wicked grin. "You were saying?"

She grinned, her cheeks flushed. "I was saying that we shouldn't leave our guests waiting."

"We wouldn't want to be negligent in our hosting duties," he agreed. "But I'll have you know that I caught Giulia and Nick in a similar embrace downstairs before we all gathered for breakfast."

Hattie gasped lightly. "What did you say to them?"

"I pretended not to see and immediately went a different direction."

Hattie laughed. She took her husband by the lapels and pulled him down for another kiss, and her chest erupted with warmth. When they separated, she reached for his hand and they started toward the stairs.

"Are you quite happy with our little house party, Hattie?"

"Yes. I'll be glad when Lucy and Jeffrey arrive. I have been wanting to ask them what their plans are for Christmas."

He looked at her, his thick, dark eyebrows drawing together. "Were you thinking to invite them here for the holiday?"

She shrugged. "Either that, or we could all return to Devon for the holiday and stay with Papa. I think it would be wonderful for the children to spend time together over Christmastide, to have us all under one roof."

Bentley leaned over and dropped a kiss on her temple. "That sounds like a splendid notion."

Hattie squeezed his fingers, unable to dampen the smile curving her lips. Her heart and her home were full of love, warmth, and friendship, and she felt inordinately blessed with all that fate had chosen to give her.

"Are you quite ready?" Hattie asked just before they reached the door to the back garden.

His gray eyes trained on her. "Ready for what, exactly?"

Hattie smirked. "To lose at lawn bowls, of course."

ACKNOWLEDGMENTS

Ladies of Devon has been years in the making. From the first draft of The Jewels of Halstead Manor during NaNoWriMo years ago to now, the four women who make up the literary society (dubbed the Ugly Duckling Society in my mind) have lived in the beautiful Devonshire landscape and built lives and found love and happiness. Every woman tackles insecurity in some form or another, and the four ladies of Devon are no exception. There was a general theme in each of the stories of insecurity, whether it was physical or otherwise, and how they overcame or managed it. And of course, there was romance. Thank you, readers, for reading my stories, and I hope you were able to smile, to swoon, and to live in someone else's shoes for a short while.

Thank you Lauren for being my first beta reader, for pressing me to try NaNo all those years ago and supporting the start of this series from page one. I wish we could get See's and read all night.

Thank you to my husband for doing all the dishes, putting the kids to bed, and supplying me with Cadbury mini eggs so I could write. No one believes in me like you do, and I could not do this without your support.

Thank you to my critique partners and friends, Jess, Deborah, and Martha. I'm so lucky and grateful to have you ladies in my life, and your notes make my stories so much richer.

Thank you to my amazing editor, Jenny Proctor, who combs through my grammar mess and makes my manuscript beautiful. Thank you Shaela for creating such stunning covers. And thank you to all of the beta readers, ARC readers, and people who help support and promote my books.

It takes a village to publish a book, and I'm so grateful for mine.

ABOUT THE AUTHOR

Kasey Stockton is a staunch lover of all things romantic. She doesn't discriminate between genres and enjoys a wide variety of happily ever afters. Drawn to the Regency period at a young age when gifted a copy of *Sense and Sensibility* by her grandmother, Kasey initially began writing Regency romances. She has since written in a variety of genres, but all of her titles fall under sweet romance. A native of northern California, she now resides in Texas with her own prince charming and their three children. When not reading, writing, or binge-watching chick flicks, she enjoys running, cutting hair, and anything chocolate.

Made in the USA
Las Vegas, NV
10 June 2023

73239957R00173